After a career in public relations, advertising and marketing, **Blythe Gifford** returned to her first love: writing historical romance. Now her characters grapple with questions about love, work and the meaning of life, and always find the right answers. She strives to deliver intensely emotional, compelling stories set in a vivid, authentic world. She was a finalist in the Romance Writers of America's Golden Heart™ Award competition for her debut novel, THE KNAVE AND THE MAIDEN. She feeds her muse with music, art, history, walks and good friends. You can reach her via her website: www.BlytheGifford.com

Recent novels by the same author:

THE KNAVE AND THE MAIDEN
THE HARLOT'S DAUGHTER
INNOCENCE UNVEILED

Author Note

Sometimes history sparks ideas. Other times you get an idea and discover only later that it is documented in history. When I began work on this book I knew the premise might stretch my readers' credulity. How realistic is it to expect that a woman could live as a man undetected, particularly in the Middle Ages? There was no co-education, no trouser suit, no common ground for the two to meet.

But sometimes history calls to us in mysterious ways. As I began my research I discovered a medieval woman who had done exactly that: attended the university in Krakow, disguised as a man. And she maintained this façade for two years. So as you embark on Jane's journey, remember: it could have happened this way.

Dedication

To the boys in the locker room.
Thanks for letting me in.
You probably think this one is about you.

Acknowledgements

Phil Cushman for loaning the book;
Lindsay Longford for persisting when I looked dazed; Beverly Long and Pat White for early reads;
Anna Louise Lucia for finding the right pele tower, and Chris Hodak for the Olympic cheers
at the finish line.

O Swallow, Swallow
by Alfred, Lord Tennyson

'O tell her, Swallow, thou that knowest each,
That bright and fierce and fickle is the South,
And dark and true and tender is the North.'

Jane held out her hand and Duncan shook it. As it lay safely clasped in his, she felt a different kind of closeness.

One only a woman might feel.

Her hand trembled against his and she saw the same feeling touch his eyes. Then he leaned forward and took her lips, softly. She laced her fingers through the waves of his hair, clinging, wishing there was a way to be closer.

As he cradled her head in his hands, pressed his lips to hers, explored her with a gentle tongue, she felt the elemental, unavoidable connection of a man and a woman. It went far beyond the feeble camaraderie that she had yearned for.

He broke the kiss, but neither could break the gaze.

'We mustn't,' she whispered. Unnecessary, futile words. 'Ever.'

'I know.' But his answer did not erase the desire in his eyes, and his hands still lingered in her hair…

IN THE
MASTER'S BED

Blythe Gifford

MILLS & BOON®

First published in Great Britain 2010
Harlequin Mills & Boon Limited,
Eton House, 18-24 Paradise Road, Richmond, Surrey TW9 1SR

© Wendy B. Gifford 2009

ISBN: 978 0 263 21460 4

Harlequin Mills & Boon policy is to use papers that are natural, renewable and recyclable products and made from wood grown in sustainable forests. The logging and manufacturing process conform to the legal environmental regulations of the country of origin.

Printed and bound in Great Britain
by CPI Antony Rowe, Chippenham, Wiltshire

Chapter One

England—late summer 1388

The smell of the birthing room was smothering her.

A crackling fire kept the water boiling, adding to the August morning's heat. She pulled aside the dark curtain cloaking the castle window and grasped a breath of fresh air.

She looked with longing at the sunshine. Perhaps later, she might borrow a horse and ride.

'Jane!'

She dropped the curtain. 'Yes?' Had her mother called before?

'This pain has passed. Solay needs something to drink.'

Jane walked to the basin in the corner and scooped cool water into a cup. She should have noticed her sister's need and answered it. It was as if she lacked some inborn instinct that other women had, something that whispered to them and told them what to do.

Her sister's pet popinjay paced on his perch, green neck feathers stiff and ruffled. *'Jane! Jane!'* His screech sounded like an accusation.

She turned back to the bed where her sister lay, belly big as a mountain. The pain had come in waves all night and after each one, Solay had less time to recover. Her long, dark hair was tangled and matted, her deep violet eyes red-rimmed.

Justin, Solay's husband, pulled aside the curtain covering the door, but did not step in. 'How is she? What can I do?'

Solay opened her eyes and waved a hand she barely had the strength to lift. 'Shoo. I'm not fit to be seen.'

Her mother went to the door and gave him a push. 'Go back to the hall. Play chess with your brother.'

He didn't move. 'Is it always thus?' Jane could barely hear his whisper.

'Solay's birth was much like this,' her mother answered, not bothering to lower her voice. 'They said it was the shortest night of the year, but it was the longest I ever spent.'

Her reassurance did not wipe the fear from his face. 'It's been hours.'

'And it will be hours more. This is women's work. Go wake the midwife from her nap if you want to do something useful.' She touched his arm then, and whispered, 'And pray to the Virgin.'

Jane took a step, wanting to follow him, but he was a man and free to do as he liked. She wished she could go wake the midwife, or play chess, or rummage through Justin's legal documents as he often let her do.

She wished she were anywhere but here.

'Jane! Where's the water?'

She returned to the bed and held out the cup. Solay, too weary to hold her eyes open, reached for it, but her hand knocked Jane's and the water spilled across the bed.

Solay yelped in surprise.

'Now look!' her mother barked, her worried glance on Solay.

And Jane knew she had failed all over again.

'*Look!*' the bird screeched. '*Look!*'

'Quiet, Gower,' Jane snapped.

She grabbed some linen to mop the spill, but she bumped Solay's swollen belly and her mother whisked the cloth away. 'Lie back, Solay.' She dabbed the soaked bedclothes without jostling her daughter. 'Just rest. Everything will be well.'

'*Is* it always thus?' Jane whispered, when her mother handed her the spent cloth.

She shook her head and answered in a whisper, 'This babe is coming too soon.'

Jane squeezed the soggy linen not knowing what to do, fearing she would do something wrong, wanting only to escape. 'I'll get fresh linen.'

'Don't leave.' Solay's voice surprised her. 'Sing for me.'

With a warning glance, her mother stepped into the corridor, looking for a serving girl and clean cloths.

Jane tried the first few notes of 'Sumer is icumen in', but they caught in her throat. She gazed at Solay, helpless. 'I can't even do that right.'

'Don't worry. I just like having my little sister here.'

Solay stretched out her hand and Jane grabbed it. She looked down at their clasped fingers. Solay's were slender and white, tapering and delicate. Like the rest of her, they were everything a woman should be: beautiful, graceful, deft, accommodating.

Everything that Jane was not.

Her own hands were blunt and square. The short, stubby fingers were free of the smell of dirt and horses only because the midwife had insisted they bring clean hands into the birthing room.

Her grip on Solay's fingers tightened. 'Are you all right?'

'The pain is bearable,' she said, with a slight smile. 'But I think you'll have to greet your future husband without me.'

Husband. A stranger to whom she would have to surrender her life. She had forgotten he was to arrive within the month.

She had tried to forget.

'I don't want to marry.' A husband would expect her to be like Solay or her mother, to know all those things that were more foreign to her than Latin.

Solay squeezed her hand in sympathy. 'I know. But you're seventeen. It's time. Past time.'

Jane felt a pout hover on her mouth.

Solay reached over to pinch Jane's lower lip. 'Look at you! The popinjay could perch on that lip.' She sighed. 'At least meet the man. Justin has told him you're…'

Different. She was different.

'Does he know that I want to travel the world? And that I read Latin?'

Solay's smile wavered. 'He's a merchant and so you may be able to do things a noble's wife could not. Besides, those things may not be so important to you soon.'

'You've said that before.' As if marriage would turn her into a strange, unrecognisable creature.

'If you don't like him, we won't force you, I promise. Justin and I just want you to be as happy as we are.'

Jane pressed Solay's hand against her cheek. 'I know.' Impossible wish. She would never be anything like her beautiful sister who tried to understand her, but never really did.

Solay slipped her hand away and tugged on Jane's short, blonde hair. 'But I do wish you hadn't cut your hair. Men admire long, fair curls and you—' Her face stiffened. Eyes wide, she looked down. 'Something's coming. It's…I'm…it's all wet down there.'

Jane sat motionless for a moment. Then, she ran to the door and flung the dark curtain aside. 'Mother!'

Her mother, the yawning midwife and a servant carrying linen had just reached the top of the stairs. They ran the last few steps into the room.

The midwife put a hand on Solay's brow. 'How many pains did she have while I was gone?'

Jane looked down at the bed, ashamed to meet her eyes. Jane's job had been to count. 'I don't know.'

The midwife threw back the covers. The bed was soaked with more water than the cup could hold.

And it was red.

'Mother!' She could barely get the word out. 'Look!' It was less a word than a shriek.

'Look!' Gower squawked from the corner. *'Look!'* He flapped his wings, reaching the limit of the leg chain as he tried to fly.

'I can see, Jane.' Her eyes held a warning.

Solay's eyes widened. 'Mother? What's happening?'

'Shh. All is well.' Her mother patted Solay and kissed her forehead.

Jane backed away from the bed, helpless. How did her mother stay calm and comforting? How did she know what to do?

Any minute her sister might die while Jane, useless, could do nothing.

I can't. The shriek in her head was all she could hear. *I can't.*

And when her sister screamed, Jane started to run.

She ran, but the screams chased her.

They followed as she fled the room and ran to her own, where she wrapped her breasts, shed her dress and pulled on chausses, tunic and cloak.

The screams did not cease.

They trailed her as she ran out of the castle gate and out on to the road, cascading, one after the other, as if the baby were clawing its way out of her sister's belly.

She didn't stop running until she realised the screams still sounded only in her head.

No one had seen her leave and it wasn't until she was clear of the house, breasts bound, men's clothing in place, that she realised she had been planning to escape for a long time.

Everything had been at hand. The tunic and leg hose, the food, the walking stick, the small stash of coins were all there, but when the moment had come, she had no plan but to run.

Scooping fresh air into her lungs, she battled her guilty thoughts. Solay would not miss her. The others were there, women who knew how to do those things—her mother, her sister-in-law, the midwife—any one of them would be more help than Jane.

She didn't belong in that world of women, full of responsibilities she didn't want and expectations she could never meet. She wanted what a man had—to go where she wanted, to do what she wanted, without a woman's limits.

She squeezed her eyes against the sadness of losing her family, squared her shoulders and faced the future.

She could never pass as a fighting man, but she knew something of clerking from listening to her sister's husband. As a learned man, surely she could live among men undetected.

And as a clerk, she might find a place in the king's court. Not the place she should have had, but still one in which she could represent the king in important affairs of state in Paris or Rome.

She hoisted her sack.

Free as a man. Dependent on no one but herself.

If she had calculated correctly, Cambridge would take her three days.

Two days later, Jane woke, broke her fast on berries and headed again for the sunrise, squinting towards the horizon for a glimpse of Cambridge.

On the road heading east, the birds chirped and a placid, dappled cow turned to look, chewing her cud.

You ran away from your sister when she needed you, the cow seemed to say.

She turned her back on the accusing eyes. There was nothing she could have done that one of the others couldn't have done better.

Her stomach moaned. She should have stuffed more bread and cheese in the sack, but she was not accustomed to making plans for her own food.

Two days on the road already felt like ten.

After two nights of sleeping by the side of the road, she looked and smelled nothing like a lady. She had lost the walking stick in a tumble into a stream on the first day, walked in damp clothes for two, and then been stung by a wasp.

She itched her swollen hand, wondering how far it was to Cambridge.

Behind her, she heard a horse at a trot and turned, too tired to run. If it was a thief, he'd get little enough.

Unless he realised she was a woman. Then the threat would be much greater than losing her meagre purse.

She put on her most manly stance as the black horse and rider came closer. Good shoulders on them, both the steed and the man.

The man looked as rough as an outlaw. Perhaps in his mid-twenties, his face was all angles, the nose broken and mended, black hair and beard shaggy. The stringed gittern slung over his back was small comfort. Travelling entertainers were the personification of all vices.

He pulled up the horse and looked down at her. 'Where's t' gaan?'

She eyed him warily, puzzling over the words, run together in an unfamiliar accent. Yet his eyes, grey like clouds bearing rain, were not unkind. 'What do you say?'

He sighed and spoke more slowly as if in a foreign tongue. 'Where are you going?'

She cleared her throat. 'Cambridge.' She hoped she had pitched her voice low enough.

He smiled. 'And I. You're a student, then?'

She nodded, afraid to risk her voice again.

He studied her, running his eyes from crown to toes. She shifted, feeling something like lightning in his glance.

'Students dinna travel alone,' he said, finally.

'Neither do jongleurs.'

He laughed, a musical sound. 'I play for meself alone.'

She felt a moment's envy of his stringed instrument. To live as a man, she would have to abandon song, the only womanly thing about her.

'What's your name, boy?'

Boy. She bit back a grin. 'Ja—' She coughed. 'John. What are you called?'

'Duncan.' He held out a hand. 'Where's t' frae?'

Frae? He must mean from. She swallowed, trying to think. She had planned to say Essex, where she'd lived until spring, but she was on the wrong side of Cambridge to tell that tale. 'What does it matter?'

Looking down at her from his horse, he didn't bother to answer. It always mattered where a man was from. 'You're not Welsh, are you? The Welsh are no friends of mine.'

She shook her head.

'Nor Irish?'

'Do I look Irish?'

'You look as if you have a drop of the Norse blood in you.'

She bit her tongue and shook her head. Her fair hair came from her father, the late King, one more thing she must hide. 'Where's *your* home?' she countered.

'The Eden Valley,' he answered. The words softened his face, just for a moment. 'Where Cumberland meets Westmoreland.'

That explained his strange tongue. He had raked her with his eyes and now she returned the favour. 'You eat your meat uncooked?'

She had never seen someone from the north lands. Everyone knew the people from there were coarse, uncouth creatures and he looked the part, except for that moment his eyes had been gentle.

They looked gentle no more. 'You've heard the stories, have you?' He growled, leaning down to bare his teeth at her. 'Aye, we do. We tear into the raw flesh like wolves.'

She stumbled backwards, as if blasted by the wind, and ended up sitting in the dirt.

When he laughed, she realised she'd been played with.

She waited for him to offer his hand to help her up, then remembered she was a lad and could rise on her own. 'Well, that's what they say,' she answered, brushing the dirt from her seat as she stood.

He shook his head. 'You're a south lander, that's certain. While you spent the summer growing pretty gardens and spouting poesy, we've been keeping the Scots from cutting across England like a scythe through wheat.'

Ah, yes. She would have to learn to relish talk of war. 'And you're a long way from having to face the *French*.'

'You think so, do you? And are you so ignorant you've forgotten that the last time the French set foot on English soil it was a Scot who opened the door?' His expression was grim. 'While you stand here fluttering like a woman, the Scots have delved our borders and burned our crops.'

Like a woman. The Scots were a less immediate threat than discovery. She lifted her hands and spread her feet. 'Come down from that horse and face my fists and we'll decide who's a better man.'

His grimace turned to laughter, a wonderful sound, and he leaned over the horse's neck to clap her on the shoulder. 'Well, Little John, I see you've much to learn, but I'll spare you a brayin' today.'

She tried not to look relieved.

'Come.' He held out his hand. 'Share my horse. You'll see Cambridge afore day's end.'

Caked with the dirt of her days on the road, she slouched and shrugged as if it didn't matter. Men, in her experience, were not good at welcoming help. 'Well, if you insist. I can take care of myself, you know.'

Unlike a woman, dependent on a man for the food that filled her belly and the air that filled her lungs.

'Oh, yes, and a fine job you're doing, too,' he said, raising his eyebrows at her bedraggled state. 'Now accept a hand when it's offered.'

He swung the gittern from his back to his chest and slipped his foot from the stirrup so she could have a leg up. Then he grabbed her arm, his grip firm and safe, and hauled her up behind him. She scrambled to keep her seat as the horse trotted sideways and the stringed instrument bounced against Duncan's chest.

'Hold on, Little John. Fall and you can walk the rest of the way.'

She patted the horse as the beast started down the road, then grabbed the man around the waist, reluctant to press too close. Her breasts were bound, but would he feel a softness against his back? Her legs, splayed wide and tucked against his hips, seemed to expose her most intimate secret. Would he notice what was missing there?

Talk. Talk would distract him. And her. 'You had a skirmish with the Scots, you say?'

'Skirmish? Aye, if you want to call it that. Three thousand swooped into the valley and were halfway to Appleby before I left.'

'You left?' Astonished, she could not stop the words. Men did not shirk battle.

'I was *sent* to ask, nay, to plead for help from our illustrious King and Council.' The sentence held a sneer.

'You've seen the King?' Her mother, the old King's mistress, had fled the court at his death. Jane had been five then and re-membered little, but Solay had returned to Court last year and her sister had listened to her every tale.

'Seen him? I've spoken to him. He knows me name.' The return of his accent hinted at his pride.

She was dumbstruck. The relationship was muddled in her mind, but the new King was some sort of half-nephew of hers, although he was older than she by a few years. Yet she had never even seen him.

It seemed that even a commoner from the north had more stature than a lowly woman. 'So what did they say, the King and Council?'

'Next year.' His words were harsh. 'They said next year.'

Invaders would not wait on the Council's convenience. She wondered how far away Appleby was. 'Why not now?'

'Because they've no money, winter is a miserable season for a campaign, and a few more excuses I can't remember.'

Neither her sister nor her sister's husband held the current government in high regard, but they held their tongues. When one was the illegitimate daughter of a dead king, it was dangerous to demean a live one, even if he was devious and less than trustworthy.

'Then why go to Cambridge?' Wouldn't a man return home to fight?'

'Among other reasons, because Parliament is meeting there.' His tone implied that she was an idiot who should have got all the information she needed from that simple statement.

'Well, I can't divine your thoughts.' In her family's experience, Parliament was worse than King and Council, but it wouldn't be wise to say so. 'You sit in the Commons, then?' Minstrel? Representative? Who was this man?

'Nay, but I must speak to those who do.'

'And the King? He'll be there, too?'

'Within a fortnight,' Duncan answered.

'I hear he's fair and well favoured.'

'You must have heard that from the lasses. But he looks the part, all pomp and gilt. He makes certain you know who he is.'

She would know him if she saw him, she was certain of that. And if the King was coming to Cambridge, she would make sure she did.

As they rode in silence, there was nothing to distract her from the breadth and strength of his back. He blocked the wind, but the heat that filled her came from some place inside. She had never been so close to any man, certainly not to one from the border lands.

Questions itched her tongue. Northerners were half-beasts, or so she'd been told. Yet he looked little different from other men.

'Tell me about it,' she said, finally, 'where you're from.' She would not have another chance to ask.

He did not speak at first.

'Full a' mountains,' he said, finally. 'I'd lay a wager you've never seen a mountain.'

She shook her head, then realised he couldn't see her. 'No.'

'Well, there's fells and crags and becks—all of earth a man could ever want.'

This did not sound like the cold and gloomy Lucifer's land she expected. 'You like it, then?'

'The soil speaks to me.'

'That sounds like poesy.' She bit her lip, afraid he would take insult, but he nodded.

'The land is poem enough.' He said the words without shame.

The pleasant phrase was more than she would have expected from a bumpkin. Still, God had given man dominion over the earth so he could control its fearsome power. Only a savage would choose to live in the wilderness.

Then he shook his shoulders, as if sloughing off a thought. 'But it's not home any longer. And where's yours, lad? Answer me now. It's not a fighting question.'

She chewed her lip, trying to think.

'Is it?' He looked over his shoulder.

The truth first. The lie second. 'I'm from Essex, but I've been living near Bedford. With my uncle.' She could say it safely. This man would not know the region. 'Since my parents died.'

A family would prove inconvenient, so she orphaned herself without a qualm and braced for expressions of sympathy. She could answer with the appropriate emotion. After all, her father *was* dead.

But instead of clucking and compassion, she heard only a mumbled grunt that could have been 'sorry'.

There was another stretch of silence. It seemed a man had much less to say than a woman.

'I'm going to Cambridge to study law so I can serve the King,' she said, finally. That was sure to impress him. He could probably not even read.

'Oh, are you?' He did not sound impressed. 'And where did you school, then?' He asked as if he knew something of schooling.

Too late, she realised she might have made a dangerous boast. 'Uh, at home. With the priest.' Schools were for boys.

'And how old are you?' Something more than a northern accent lurked in his tone. 'Fifteen? You can't be much past that. You're still talking treble.'

She gulped, glad her voice had always been low for a woman. To pass as a boy, she was willing to lose a few years. 'I'll be fifteen after Candlemas.' Only half a year away.

'And this is your first time at University.'

'Yes,' she answered, before she realised it was not a question.

'How much Latin do you have?' His questions were coming thick and fast.

'Some.'

'*Ubi ius incertum, ibi ius nullum,*' he said, with nary an accent.

It was something insulting about the law, that much she recognised.

'*Varus et mutabile semper femina,*' she answered, haltingly. An insult to women was always a good rejoinder.

'*Varium*, not *varus*. "Woman is an ever fickle and *changeable* thing" not a bow-legged one.'

Her cheeks burned. The man was not the country simpleton she had thought. 'I read better than I speak.'

'I hope so. And you're set on being a man of law?' Amusement and disgust twisted in his tone.

She sighed. 'Mostly, I wanted to get away from home.'

Another laugh. She was beginning to like the sound. 'You'll be in good company. Sometimes I think more come to university for that than for learning.'

At the burr in his voice, a pleasant buzz lodged between her legs where they nestled against him. More than pleasant.

Her sister had tried to explain it once, this thing between men and women. Solay had waxed poetic about bodies and hearts and souls and lifetimes. It sounded like a sickness, or worse, madness, meant to warp a woman's mind so she would submit her life to a man's control.

Jane had never felt such a thing and didn't want to. Another way, perhaps, that she was different from other women.

But this, this was pleasant.

He shrugged, 'I've not much use for lawyers, meself, but if you're set on it, you'll find John Lyndwood's as good a master as there is.'

She mumbled something vague in reply. She didn't need a Cumberland farmer's advice about Cambridge, even if he had picked up a few Latin phrases.

She knew what to expect at University. Her sister's husband had been educated at the Inns at Court in London and he'd told her all about it. There were lovely quadrangles and courtyards. She would stroll the gardens, read interesting books and debate their meaning with fellow students.

But as the horse ambled across the bridge and through the gate, the city pressed in around her, denting her dreams.

Houses jumbled tightly together in crooked, smelly streets, punctuated with gaps, like a row of pulled teeth, with only charred timbers to show where the burned-out homes had stood.

'Where are you staying?' Duncan asked, raising his voice to be heard over two squealing pigs chasing each other around the corner. 'I'll take you there.'

The late summer air was ripe with the smell of horse droppings and raw fish. Where was the peaceful, cloistered garden Justin had described? She had come to Cambridge because it was out of the way and her family was less likely to look for her here than in London or at Oxford. A mistake? She had wanted to be on her own, responsible to no one, but poised on the brink of it even a stranger with a northern tongue looked safe.

Her arms tightened around her rescuer.

'Don't squeeze the air outta me, boy.'

She released him quickly. This was no way for a man to act.

'Let me down here.' She scrambled off the horse to escape the contradictory feelings and the shelter of his back.

He eyed her, standing in the street clutching her small sack. 'You've no place to stay, have you?'

'Not yet, but I will.' The sun was still high. She had time to find a bed. 'I'm grateful for the ride.'

He looked down at her, frowning. 'Have you friends who've come before? A master expecting you?'

She put on a cloak of bravura and shook her head. Did men feel this frightened inside when they looked so fearless? 'I'll make my own way.'

It was time to walk away, but she could not turn her back on his searching eyes.

'You've no place to live, no master to take you and no friends to help.' He leaned back in the saddle and stared her down. 'You've made no plans at all, have you?'

She shook her head, suddenly ashamed. Cambridge loomed large and frightening around her. She'd never had to find her own food and shelter, but she would not cower like a woman. Royal blood ran through her veins.

She held up her head and met his eyes. 'I can take care of myself!'

He shook his head. 'The Fair starts tomorrow, so there's nary a room to be had and Parliament's lords and squires are still to come. I can give you a pallet for the night at least.'

Pride warred with fear. For a country newcomer, he seemed to know a lot about this city, but she knew nothing of this stranger. It was a woman's way to depend on a man. She had abandoned her family in order to control her own fate, not turn it over to a bumpkin with strong arms and a lilt in his laugh. 'Thank you, but I don't need your help.'

He leaned over, put a hand on her shoulder and gave her a shake. 'You're going to need some friends, Little John. There's no shame in taking an offered hand.'

She straightened her shoulders. This man scared her, some-how, and not because he ate his meat raw. 'I would rather take care of myself.' If she said it often enough, it would be true.

'Ya would, would ya?' His country tongue had returned. 'Well, g'luck t'ya then.' He turned the horse away, ready to ride on.

She bit her lip. Now she'd angered him. 'But I thank you for your kind offer,' she called, as he started to ride away.

He shouted over his shoulder at her, 'You'll nae get another.'

Feeling unsteady on legs that had been straddling a horse, she started walking in the opposite direction, trying to look as if she knew where she was going. She forced herself not to look back.

'Hey! John!'

She turned, wondering whether he had called the name more than once before she answered. 'Yes?'

'Stay away from the butchers' district. And if you get to the alehouse near Solar Hostel, stop in. We'll lift a few together.'

She gave a jaunty wave and kept walking, wondering how she was to know where the butchers lived.

Duncan pulled up the horse and watched until the boy's fair hair was swallowed by the crowd, resisting the urge to go after him. The poor lad had clung to him so tightly he could scarcely breathe and then refused his help. Young, vulnerable, full of en-thusiasm and too proud to accept what was freely given—it had been years since he'd felt that way, but he remembered.

He should have kept his grip and dragged the boy with him. He was on better than speaking terms with pride, but the world was full of danger. It only took a moment. If the lad wandered into the wrong place, looked at someone the wrong way, met someone in the wrong mood—

Well, he would find out. Like all the rest, the boy had assumed Duncan was a Borderland bumpkin. Let him wander the streets alone, if he was so prejudiced.

Yet there was something else about him, something that

niggled at Duncan's brain and irritated him beyond reason when his help was rejected. Why was the boy so skittish?

Duncan turned his horse down the street towards Solar Hostel. He had more important things to think about than an ungrateful slip of a lad. Pickering would be here any day and there would be plans to make before Parliament convened. In the meantime, he had to be sure the hostel's kitchen was stocked and the beds ready before the rest of the scholars returned.

Yet he knew, somehow, that he'd be worrying late tonight whether the boy had found a bed.

Chapter Two

Jane's stomach growled as she watched the men come and go from the alehouse. She'd had nothing since yesterday's porridge, doled out by a kindly porter at King's Hall.

Controlling her own fate was dirtier and lonelier than she had expected. She'd seen little food and less bathwater for five days. When it was light, she went from college to college seeking a master who would take her. And when it was dark, she lay awake praying for her sister and the babe, hoping God and her mother would forgive her for running.

The college masters seemed no more sympathetic than the Almighty.

She was the right age and sex, or so people thought, but she had little money and the Latin that her family had so admired failed to impress the masters. They were not sympathetic to her excuses for her weakness in a language she must not only read, but speak in daily conversation.

Perhaps she should have let the northern man help her.

She had thought about him more than once. A woman's thoughts, not a boy's. Of the feel of his strong hand, warm on her shoulder. Of the musical laugh that spilled from his lips. Of the hardness of his chest, and the feel of him nestled between her legs.

Dangerous thoughts.

Yet this afternoon, she found herself outside the alehouse near Solar Hostel, looking for a scruffy, black-haired northerner. When she saw him, she would walk up and say hello as if surprised to see him. As if she were there by chance.

But she did not see him, and, after a time, the woman across the street was eyeing her as if ready to call the watch so Jane squared her shoulders. Perhaps he was already inside. She would just take a look.

She put her hand on the door. She had never been in an alehouse. Who knew what waited on the other side?

The open door threw light into the dark room and drew all eyes. She ducked her head, hoping no one would look closely, but when the din of conversation didn't halt, she breathed again and let her eyes adjust.

She saw him, finally, in a corner, at the same moment he saw her. A flicker of delight—did she imagine it?—crossed his face. Her breath fluttered. Only because it *was* nice to see someone smile instead of scowl at the sight of her.

He waved her to the table and when she didn't thread her way through the room fast enough, he came to her, draping his arm over her shoulders to lead her to the corner. 'Oust fettal?'

Words she couldn't understand, but in a kind tongue. She blinked back tears. 'If you're asking how I am, I've been well.'

'Good. Sit.'

She did, hoping her smell wasn't too potent. She had taken to sneaking into a stable and bedding down with the horses. She had always got on well with horses. A little pat and a crooning song and they would settle down and let her catch a few winks.

He continued to smile. She answered with her own, and for a moment too long, they simply looked at each other, speechless and happy.

The alewife interrupted. 'A cup for ya?'

'Here's Little John at last,' Duncan said, pounding her back so hard she nearly fell off the bench. 'Bring him some peeve.'

She wondered what he had ordered.

The alewife's grin was toothless. 'He's been telling us about this lad he met on the road. Glad your head and body are still attached.' She chuckled as she went for his drink.

Startled, Jane looked at Duncan, warmed to think she had been important enough for him to mention. 'And why wouldn't they be?'

He sat back and took a sip of his drink. 'Cambridge isn't always a friendly place.'

'Worse than that. People are mean.'

'Harder than you expected, is it?'

Mustn't show her weakness. She shrugged. 'It's not too bad.'

Her drink appeared and she sipped it, wrinkling her nose at the cloudy brew.

Duncan chuckled. 'That's student ale, lad. Good as daily bread.'

She nodded, grateful to have sustenance filling her empty belly. It tasted of oats and oak.

Her shoulder brushed Duncan's and the feel of sitting behind him on the horse flooded back. There, pressed to his back, she had learned the size of his chest and the strength in his muscles, but she had not had to face him.

Now, he peered at her in the dim light. She leaned into the shadow, afraid he would see too much. Most men only glanced at her, seeing what they expected. Duncan's eyes lingered.

To avoid his gaze, she looked at his hands. Large and square, strong, but gentle. Firm when they had gripped hers.

'Have you found a master, then?'

'Not exactly.' Even a cursory quizzing had revealed she was not ready for the rigours of rhetoric and grammar. She was in grave danger of ending up as a glomerel, condemned to do nothing but memorise Latin all day. 'I've talked to a lot of them.' She hoped her indifference was convincing. 'Still deciding.'

'Well, don't be too long about it. You must be registered with a master within fifteen days of yer arrival.'

She tapped her fingers against the table, counting. Ten more days. 'I'll find one by then.'

His smile was sceptical. 'If you haven't, you'll be expelled.'

'Expelled?' She groaned. How could she be expelled before a master had written her name on the *matricula* list?

'Or detained,' he answered cheerfully, with a lift of his mug, 'according to the King's pleasure.'

The King. She wanted to draw his attention for her academic prowess, not for being a student no one wanted.

But Duncan might be teasing again. Surely the King had more important things to do than worry about Cambridge schoolboys. 'You made that up.'

His smile vanished. 'No, it's true.'

She would not let him scare her again. 'How is it that you know about the University?'

'Would it surprise you if I told you I'm a master?'

Now he *was* teasing. 'You can't be.' A master would have completed seven years of study and be ready to teach his own students. He looked the right age, but scholars were sober, celibate fellows, usually seen in a flowing robe, never seen in alehouses. 'You don't look anything like a master.'

'Oh? I can see you know as much about masters as you do about the north country.'

He thought her a fool. No scholar was allowed to wear a beard. 'You don't even have a tonsure.'

He rubbed the top of his head and smiled. She noticed, uneasily, that the hair was shorter there. 'It went to seed over the summer.'

She narrowed her eyes, trying to judge him. 'If it's true, what do you teach?'

'If? Are you calling me a liar as well as an ignorant barbarian?'

She groaned. 'No.' It was wiser to placate him before he asked her to step outside and put up her fists. 'What do you study?'

'Not the law, I can tell ya.' His rough accent had returned. 'I'm teaching grammar and rhetoric and studying something that actually helps people. Medicine.'

The very word made her queasy. She shut her eyes against the memory of her sister's screams. No, she wanted nothing to do with sick bodies.

'Did ya find a place to stay, then?'

She opened her eyes, glad to see a sympathetic smile replace his moment of irritation. The ale had begun to work on her empty stomach and muddle her wits.

He wanted to help. Why didn't she let him? If she asked him to teach her, he would certainly say yes. Then, she would have a master and a bed in his hall and her troubles would be over.

But sitting beside him made her chest rise and fall. Looking at his hands made her mouth go dry. Meeting his eyes, her boyish bravado evaporated into feminine silliness.

He was the only man who had ever made her want to act like a woman.

Which made him the most dangerous man of all.

No. She could not take help from him.

'I'm staying off High Street.' She jerked her head vaguely in the direction of Trumpington Gate. 'Widow lady. Needed help in exchange for a bed. So you see, I didn't need your help after all.'

'Well, you're settled then.'

He turned away and she felt as if a cloud had stolen the sun. No, she must spend no more time with this mercurial man. She was beginning to seek his smiles and long for his laughter.

She rose, a little unsteady on her feet. 'Thanks for the ale. I'll be taking my leave.'

Duncan grabbed her arm to steady her.

His touch ricocheted through her, setting off a tingle in her breasts that even the binding couldn't squash.

'You drank that quickly. Are you kalied?' Concern touched his voice, though the word meant nothing to her. 'I can walk you to the widow's.'

She pulled away. 'No, no, you stay and finish.' Reckless, she drained the rest and wiped her mouth with her sleeve. She must leave before she confessed she was sleeping with the horses. 'I must go now. She'll be expecting me. For evening tasks.'

'Well, if you get into trouble, come to Solar Hostel and ask for me.'

She fought the girlish smile threatening her lips. 'Oh, I don't think I will.' She would not see him again. It was a promise she made to herself. 'I'll be busy. With my studies. And helping the widow.' She forced the words out. Words to push him away. If she insulted him again, an easy task, she had learned, he would let her leave.

'I won't have much time myself,' he answered, dropping her arm and sitting back. She heard the pique in his voice and longed for the laughter. 'I have better things to do than to worry about a boy who has no sense.'

Good. He was angry. So angry he did not tell her to fare well.

She was out of the door quickly, but hid in a shadow across the street, hoping to see him again. She did not have to wait long. Duncan came out and lingered, looking up and down the street, as if for her.

And as she saw him turn towards a warm, dry bed, she bit her cheek to keep the tears from slipping.

You're gonna need some friends, he had said.

Fifteen days. She had ten more. But five Colleges had refused her. If the other four did the same, she would start visiting the hostels.

The one called Solar would not be on her list.

'What word?' Duncan asked, without preamble, a few days later. He knew from the look on Pickering's face that the news was not good. He had no patience to wait while the man washed off the road dust. 'Tell me.'

Sir James Pickering slumped against the table, the lines on his face deeply shadowed by the morning sun streaming into Solar Hostel's empty gathering room. 'All the talk's of Otterburn, but it's in the west they hurt us worst. Carlisle's still standing, but Appleby—' He shook his head. 'Appleby is gone.'

Sweet, defenceless city. It would have had no hope. 'Damn the Council. I begged...' The remembrance of his entreaties, and the Council's refusal, seared his heart like the mark of a hot iron.

'They told you no?'

'They told me next year.' He had almost, almost succeeded. 'The King was ready, I vow. He told the Council he was going to mount a horse and go off riding in all directions.'

'But the Council's not his to command.'

He knew that, but it made no difference. 'I should have said something different, something else. Something that would have convinced them to send help now!'

'You swayed the King.'

'No victory at all.'

Pickering sighed. 'Well, the Council's cautious these days.' At February's Parliament—*Merciless*, they'd called that one— the King's closest advisers had been condemned to death at the Council's behest. Now, the Council's Lords Appellant themselves were wondering whether Parliament would turn on them.

'Tell that to those facing the Scots alone.'

'Winter's coming. The Scots won't be back until next year.'

'Ah, you're sure of that, are you? What if you're wrong?' *Are ya still breathin'?* 'If I'd persuaded them, if they'd ridden that day—'

'Don't punish yourself. Before you even reached the King, the Scots had crossed the border for home.' The man paused, as if holding worse news.

'What else?'

'Your father.'

Duncan gripped the rough wood of the table, then sat, feeling the world shift. 'What about him?'

'The Scots. They took him.'

The words hit him like one of his fadder's punches.

He could see the old man, scarred from countless battles, many of them waged against his own sons. All of home that he had tried to escape was tied up in the old man.

And all that he couldn't.

'Me madder? Michael?' The words of childhood were all he could speak.

'Unharmed, by God's mercy. Your brother has taken over as he was born to do. The tower held, but the village, the fields…' He shuddered. 'Burned.'

Duncan stared at the Common Room's blackened hearth, seeing charred huts and homeless serfs. There'd be nothing to harvest.

They must pray for thick wool on the flock or there'd be nothing to sell.

Nothing to eat.

You left, Little John had said. He should have stayed. Much as he hated it, he should have stayed. His strong arm would have done more good there than his useless tongue had here.

He let Pickering describe the battle and his fadder's bravery, only half-listening. He knew what the end would be.

'They're holding him for ransom,' Pickering said, finally.

'Then they'll be sore disappointed.' There was no joy in his laugh. 'We've barely a pot to piss in.' The funds it took to send him here were hard won. Now, at last, he was ready to take on students who would pay him, but it would be no knight's ransom. He rose. 'I must return.'

Pickering's hand on his shoulder was gentler than his fadder's had ever been. 'You've given your oath here, son. To teach. And what little there was at home is less now.'

Waves of The Death had rolled over the countryside every few years, over and over until it seemed the land was trying to purge itself of people. Between the Scots and The Death, the ground, once lush with oats and wheat, had turned bleak.

'I've got one mouth to feed, but two good hands.' He held them up, proud of their strength. He could swing a spade better than some of the serfs. 'I can help rebuild, replant—'

'You can help here, persuading Parliament to send money north. They're in no mood to vote more taxes.'

He shrugged off Pickering's hand and paced the room, his rage too strong to let him sit. 'They'll never listen to me.' All of them, even the boy, thinking they were cleverer and better because of where they were born and how they talked.

'If they don't, there will be no ransom money.'

He stopped in mid-stride and stared at Pickering. Helpless fury lodged in his gut. 'But my fadder, the rest, they defended the border while these southerners listened to poetry readings.'

'Between the battles in the west and the east, the Scots took more than three hundred knights, including young Hotspur and his brother.'

Duncan smacked the wall, welcoming the sting on his palm. The Percies and their knights would be redeemed long before his father. 'That's how it is, then? The lords who already have money are worth saving, but those of us who live in dirty stone towers and guard the borders year in and year out are not?'

'Parliament convenes in five days,' Pickering said. 'We'll have to entreat every single member for his vote.'

Duncan sighed, relief glossing over his guilt. The time had come to put on his southland demeanour. The accent first. Then he would shave the beard, and, finally, don the master's costume he'd earned.

Finally, he would be ready to do his work here. The work he could do instead of going home again.

'The University has two votes,' he began. 'I'll make sure they go our way.'

Chapter Three

Restless, Duncan left the hostel late that afternoon to walk the city. Plucking the gittern had not soothed him today.

At home, he would have been roaming the countryside. Harsh land, but he saw beauty in what civilised folk feared. Clear lakes. High hills. Fields, when they thrived, green enough to hurt the eyes.

Unlike this place. If he strayed too far from the city, he'd be in the fens and up to his knees in water, as if the land were sinking into the sea.

So he circled the narrow streets and it wasn't until he found himself passing St Michael's again that he realised he was looking for the boy.

At the sound of a quarrelsome voice, he slowed his steps and readied his fists. He should have given the boy more warning about the townsfolk. The last row between townsmen and students had left a bachelor's student dead.

Little John, with his cocky attitude, would be fair game for a bully. The lad was quick to wave his fists, but he wouldn't last two minutes in a serious match.

Just ahead, a large man towered over a young lad, pinning him in place with a hand on one shoulder. It was near dusk, but Duncan recognised the pale gold hair.

Little John was in trouble already.

His heart lurched. Without thinking, he stepped over and put his hand on John's other shoulder and his best Cambridge accent on his lips. 'What's going on here?'

John jumped at the touch, but his eyes—blue, Duncan noted for the first time—widened in recognition.

The man didn't let go. 'This boy was sneaking around the stable. Probably going to steal a horse.'

'I was not,' John began. 'I just wanted—'

Duncan squeezed his shoulder. He was oddly glad to see the boy, but the lad was no good at holding his tongue. 'There must be some misunderstanding.'

The man peered at him. 'Who are you?'

'I'm his master.'

John's head snapped up in surprise. Thankfully, this time, he kept his mouth shut.

The stableman wasn't ready to let go. 'You don't look like no grad.'

Duncan's strong arms and shoulders didn't fit their image of a scholar and he hadn't yet shaved his summer beard. 'Maybe not, but that's what I am and he is one of our Solar boys.' That would put his punishment in the hands of the University, not the town. 'I'll vouch for him.'

The man's grip loosened enough for Duncan to take control. He turned to John, ignoring the other man as if the matter were settled. 'Come along now. The bedchambers need sweeping and the laundry's waiting.'

The lad's grateful expression turned belligerent. 'But—'

'Not a word!' One wrong move and the stable master could still attack. 'Leave one more time without permission and you won't get another chance.' He put his hand behind the boy's neck and pulled him up High Street, out of the man's reach.

'You're a wretched lot, all of you!' he called to their backs.

Duncan heard boots crunch on gravel, then something sharp

and hard hit his back. The next rock hit John's shoulder. He grabbed the boy's arm and shoved him ahead. 'Run!'

Duncan's back took three more blows before they turned the corner, out of range.

When he was sure the man was not going to follow, Duncan stopped, gasping for breath, and shook the boy for lack of sense. He searched the lad for damage, but his blond curls seemed to halo a flawless face. 'I warned you.' The words came out in a snarl.

'You warned me about the butchers!' He tried to twist away, but was no match for Duncan's strong hands. 'That was a stable master.'

'Well, they don't like us much either.'

'Us?' Little John stopped wriggling and looked up. Not only were the lad's eyes blue, they had a disturbing tendency to linger. 'You and me?'

His palm pulsed against the boy's shoulder. 'Not exactly.' The phrase implied a connection Duncan didn't want to feel. 'I meant any University men. And you might thank me for saving your miserable hide.'

John's gaze, like Duncan's hand, refused to let go. 'I thank you, then, but I didn't ask you to rescue me.'

There was something in those eyes, some combination of bravado and vulnerability that tugged at places uncomfortably deep inside.

'If you don't want to be rescued, stop getting into trouble. What were you doing there?'

A sullen frown marred the boy's face. 'Nothing. I didn't hurt anything.'

Duncan sighed, exasperated. 'The widow turned you out?'

The boy hung his head, mercifully breaking his gaze. The words came slowly. 'There never was a widow.'

Prideful liar. What else had the lad lied about? 'You had no place to sleep, did you?'

'I did, too! I was sleeping in the stable until he threw me out!'

'You wouldna have been so lucky.' His voice rose and his Cambridge accent fell as he envisioned what had almost happened. He could have lost the boy, lost another one because he'd looked away, just for a moment. 'He was going to bray ya bloody, break yer neb, and hand ya to the sheriff, who would have thrown you in gaol with the murderers.'

Even in the fading light, he could see the boy's face turn pale. Something stirred inside him. The lad's shoulder trembled beneath his palm and he pulled it away. 'When did you eat last?'

Little John raised a thumb and then two fingers. 'Monday. They gave me a bowl of porridge at Michaelhouse.'

Duncan sighed. 'Well, I'll not leave you to be beaten like a stray dog, though I've a mind to beat some sense into you myself. If you've got no more brains than to refuse help when it's offered, you'll never earn your bachelor's.' He might not have saved Peter, he might not be able to save his fadder, but he could save one would-be scholar from starving in the streets. 'I'm taking you back to the hostel.'

'As your student?'

'I didn't say that.' He wanted to help the lad, but the idea of becoming his master made Duncan uneasy. It seemed like more than an academic commitment. 'Besides, why should I? You've turned down every offer of help I've made.'

His words were met with a pout. This lad was the most prideful piece he'd ever met. 'Oh? Does that not please you, young gentleman?' he said, with a sharp tongue. 'Then stroll over to Trinity Hall and ask for a bed.'

The lower lip quivered. 'Trinity turned me down.'

Duncan regretted his harsh words. Beset with his own demons, he forgot the lad was alone in the world and still young enough to cry.

Duncan had never been that young. 'A man doesn't meet defeat with tears.'

'But they've all turned me down. St Peter's, King's Hall, Clare Hall, Michaelhouse—' He stopped for a gulp of air. 'All of them.'

Duncan felt a twinge of sympathy. As a young student, he'd forced his way into St Benet's Hostel. He'd had to force most of what he'd got from life. The only reason he was here at all was because some self-righteous bishop thought a Cambridge education would overcome the 'waste, desolate and illiterate condition' of a young man from the north country. The man's exact words.

Duncan had memorised them.

'What did they say? Why won't they take you?'

'My Latin isn't good enough.'

'Well, I said the same, lad. Did you not believe me?'

'I don't know what to do now.'

'You go to the hostels, of course.' The colleges had permanent buildings and wealthy benefactors, but hostels like Solar, which outnumbered them, were a truer community of scholars, to Duncan's mind.

'They won't take me either.'

'How many have you been to? Five? Ten? Twenty?'

John looked down at the street again, silent. One thing about the boy. He knew when he'd been caught.

'Confess, Little John. You haven't been to Solar Hostel, I know that for a fact.'

'Five. Maybe six.'

Duncan sighed. 'Well, you've many more to try. And if you can't find a master among them, you'll go to grammar school until you're ready and try again.'

He wrinkled his nose. 'That's for the little boys.'

'Your father never took a rod to you, I can tell that.' The boy's sagging jaw confirmed it. 'You'll never make a bachelor if you give up so easily.'

'I've been trying ten days and they've all said the same. Please. Will you take me?' The boy's eyes pleaded as strongly as his lips.

Duncan wanted to say yes, but for all the wrong reasons. Peter would have been just a little older than this if...

His thoughts followed their familiar wheel ruts.

If only he had watched more carefully, if only he hadn't turned his back, if only he'd tied the boy to him.

His fadder had beat him for his sin. No harder than he beat himself.

He watched the boy's expectant, upturned face and wondered at his change of heart. He'd saved John from a beating tonight, but he wasn't sure he, or anyone, could make him a scholar. Besides, he would do the lad no favour if he threw him into rhetoric ill prepared. The other scholars would eat him before they broke fast.

'I'll have to think it over.'

'But you *said* you would help me!' Now, it seemed the lad *was* going to cry. If he didn't develop tougher sensibilities, he'd never last a year under *any* master. 'If you don't, there's nothing else I can do.'

Duncan's sympathy vanished. 'Nothing else? Are ya still breathin'?' How many times had his father asked that question?

John's head snapped up, eyes wide. He nodded, biting his trembling lip.

And every time, knowing the answer was *aye*, his father had said the same. 'Then there's more you can do.'

The boy squared his jaw and swallowed. Face calmer, he nodded, tears gone. 'Tell me and I'll do it.'

The blue eyes, defiant and pleading, didn't leave his. Drawn into the gaze, Duncan had the strange sensation of staring into a reflecting glass, in which things appeared real, but were actually backwards.

He shook off the spell. 'All right. I won't leave you to the mercy of the Master of Glomery. I'll help you with your Latin until you're ready to study with a master.' He had the feeling he would regret this, but he couldn't leave the poor helpless orphan alone in the street. 'We pay our own way. Do you have money for board and fees?'

'A few farthings.'

He sighed, having known the answer. He was stuck with a penniless orphan with rudimentary Latin who deserved to be in grammar school. 'Then you'll have to work for it.'

'I will. I promise.' John nodded, all smiles again. Then, he gave Duncan an assessing frown. 'What happens when my Latin improves? Will you take me on then?'

The lad was relentless, he'd give him that. But those eyes seemed to claim something more personal than lessons. Something he wasn't ready to give to anyone. 'When I'm through with you, you'll have your pick of masters.'

'Your Latin's that good?'

Cheeky lad. He had to admire the boy's outspoken pluck, even when it was insulting. 'My Latin received a special commendation at my inception.'

The answering grin was mischievous. 'Probably because no one could understand your English.'

He socked the boy's arm, gently. 'It's your Latin that needs work, Little John, not my English. But if you're willing to work, I'll make you fit to lecture in Latin to these flatlanders.'

'You don't like people from this part of the country, do you?' John gave him an odd glance through his eyelashes.

Odd. He'd never noticed a man's eyelashes before. 'Some days, I hate them. And they don't like me much either.'

'Do you hate me?'

The lad had twisted his feelings in all directions, save that one. 'No, I don't hate you, lad.' He put his hand on the gilt-gold hair and tussled it. A few strands wound their way around his fingers. 'You've some growing up to do, but when you're not whining or pouting, I nearly like you.'

And the blinding smile John gave him caused a strange shiver in the pit of his stomach.

* * *

Alys de Weston watched Justin squeeze Solay's hand. His wife did not respond. As the hours lengthened and the candles shortened, Alys had tried without success to shoo him out of the lying-in room. He was not swayed.

Stubborn, that man, always.

She had told neither of them that Jane was gone. As long as his wife had been in childbirth, he could think of nothing else. And in the days since, the babe was so small and frail it took all of them to keep little William alive.

William and his mother.

So she had said nothing, not wanting them to worry. But Alys? Alys was worried.

'Come,' she said, tugging his tunic. The man hadn't eaten in days and had slept less than his wife. 'Solay is sleeping and you need food.'

She forced him down the stairs into the dim, smoky kitchen. The kitchen girl had fallen asleep, waiting for her summons, so Alys served the soup herself.

'Justin,' she said, as he munched bread and cheese without savouring it. 'Jane is missing.'

She could tell from his absent gaze he had not understood her words. 'What do you mean, missing?'

A wonderful man and a good son-in-law, but sometimes, they all were dolts. 'Missing. She's run away and left her skirts behind.'

She had his attention now. 'How long?'

'Since the day the babe was born.'

'And you didn't speak til now?'

'Could you have listened?'

He shook his head. 'I'm sorry. Solay, the babe... I didn't even notice.'

She patted his arm. 'You wouldn't have noticed if the sun had fallen to earth.' Her older daughter was a fortunate woman.

'You're sure? You've searched?'

'The entire property. I knew she did not want to wed, but I had hoped…'

She had hoped marriage would turn her younger daughter into a normal girl. She'd been a pretty blonde-haired, blue-eyed child, but they had left the court when she was five and, during the years of exile, she had become a different creature. Shoulders too wide and breasts too small for beauty, only her singing voice marked her as a woman.

It was Solay who garnered Alys's attention. Beautiful Solay, who understood what it meant to be a woman and what women must do to survive. Jane, poor, strange child, never did.

So Alys had made no demands, trying to make up for losing their life at court. She let Jane play with horses and books, more boy than girl, until, too late, she realised that her daughter had become fit for nothing else.

Alys sighed. Yet another of her failures as a mother.

'I would never have forced her into marriage,' Justin said. 'Surely she knew that. But I thought if she met him, they might, she might…' He shook his head. 'Solay warned me. I should have listened.'

'The bridegroom comes next week. What shall we tell him?'

'The truth. He will recover. My worry is Jane.' Yet he glanced towards the stairs, as if he had already been away from Solay too long.

'Solay must be your concern.' She did not have to say it. For this man, there would never be a question of who was first in his life. 'Besides, where would we look? Where could she go?'

In the spring, Alys and Jane had moved into the empty dower house on Justin's family's land. Until then, the sheltered girl had known nothing but the house she had lived in with her mother after they had left court.

The house Alys's stubbornness had lost.

'She once said she wished she were a man so she could be a

lawyer and serve the King, as I did,' he answered. 'Maybe she went to the Inns at Court.'

Their eyes met. London. A naïve country girl would be swallowed whole.

He rose, all attention. 'I'll send a messenger that way. She's been gone for days. She could be in the city by now.'

Oh, Jane. She felt her lip quiver. Alys de Weston, who had stood before the condemnation of Parliament unbowed, was afraid she was going to cry.

She bit her lip. She never cried. Not when they had charged her. Not when she had fled court with her children. Not even at the death of the King. The man she loved.

Who had called another man's daughters his.

Jane woke, snug on a warm, dry pallet, and sighed with delight.

Normally, the hostel would have been full of men, every room shared, but the term's start was still days away. She had a chance at privacy she would not see again to rewrap her breasts and relieve herself without fear.

What she really wanted was a bath, but that would be quick, cold and risky.

She said her prayers for Solay and her mother and started downstairs. She would spend the day reading, she decided. The hostel had a few volumes that would afford her good Latin practice.

But at the bottom of the stairs, Duncan handed her a pile of tunics and hose. 'Wash these.'

She crossed her arms, not touching the garments in his hands. 'Laundry's no work for a man.' Nor for the child of a king.

'For a poor orphan, you've elevated expectations.' Duncan dropped the clothes on the floor at her feet. 'I told you you'd have to work for your lessons. Now do as I say.'

'I want to talk to the principal,' she said, lifting her chin. A man in power wouldn't make her do such menial tasks. 'Who's responsible for this hostel?'

Duncan raised his eyebrows and looked at her aslant. 'I am.'

She swallowed, grateful that her blunder had made him laugh instead of roar. From the first, this man had been nothing that she'd expected.

She tried not to think about how many ways she had insulted him already. 'And you don't have laundry women?'

'We don't waste money sending out the wash. And it's the gaol for any women found within these walls, laundress or lady.'

Gaol. She stooped to gather the pile, shuddering. She was at this man's mercy in a world beyond women. She'd have no one to turn to, no one to confide in and no protection if she were discovered.

'And wash your own clothes, while you're about it,' he said, leaving her to grapple with the laundry. 'You smell of the stables.'

As she grudgingly heated the water to fill the washtub, she savoured his words and allowed herself a secret smile. No women allowed, yet here she was. She had cracked their kingdom and they didn't even know.

And yet she was still doing women's work.

The thought lingered as she set up the tub in a sunny corner of the yard. She started to throw the garments into the water, but the coarse linen lingered in her hand, warm and alive with the smell of his body and his days on the road. She buried her nose in the fabric and breathed his scent until she sat behind him on the horse again, felt him nestled between her spread legs.

The memory made something within her run soft and wet.

She dropped the shirts in the hot water as quickly as she dropped the thought. What would Duncan think if he saw 'John' with his nose buried in another man's shirt?

She plunged her arms into the wash water, the damp heat taking her back to the birthing room. What had happened to Solay? The babe must have been born days ago. Something weighed heavy in her chest, reminding her of what she had lost. She would never see her family again, never even know if they were safe.

She sent up a prayer for them as she swirled, scrubbed and

pounded the clothes, then wrung out the rough linen, and stretched his shirts and braies on the grass beside hers.

The water, still warm, beckoned. Her skin ached to be clean. She had dipped her hands in the Cam River once or twice, but after she saw a dead sheep float by, she did not touch the water again.

She looked over her shoulder. She was in a secluded corner, shielded by the wall around the property and the vines that had grown up during the summer. She might not have such an opportunity again.

She skinned off her chausses and stepped into the tub, closing her eyes to savour the feel of the leftover water swirling into her hidden crevices, washing away the dust of the road and the stables.

Her tunic floated on top of the water, hiding everything below. She snuggled lower with a satisfied sigh. Just a moment. She would take just a moment's ease.

Are ya still breathing?

A harsh question Duncan had asked. And a harsh man, when his eyes carried anger's thunder.

He had offered his help, so she had expected that as soon as she asked, he would take 'John' as a student. If she had known she'd be working as a servant and relegated to studying Latin again, she might never have risked being so near him and his all-too-perceptive grey eyes.

She had told him how hard she had tried. She had explained how unfair and difficult it all was. But all he could say was *Are ya still breathing?*

He was no more understanding than the rest of the masters she had met. Well, when she was a clerk to the King, he'd be sorry he had been so rude. In fact, since the King was coming to Cambridge, she would introduce herself. The King might even—

'Little John! What are ya doing in that tub?'

Chapter Four

Her eyes flew open.

Duncan stood across the yard, hands on hips, fresh shaven, the menacing set of his jaw exposed.

Startled, she started to stand, then, just in time, crouched lower. Her tunic would cover her, but damp as it was, it would mould to her body, making it obvious she was missing what would make her a man.

'Come no closer,' she said, waving him away. 'I've finished your wash.'

'I see that. That was not my question. I asked why you're sitting in the laundry tub.'

'Well, you're the educated one.' Her heart skipped faster. From fear? Or something else?

Without the beard, she could see his mouth clearly, the top lip sculpted, the lower lip unexpectedly full. She wondered how they would feel against hers.

A dangerous idea when she was sitting half-naked in a tub of cooling water. 'Can ya not see I'm taking a bath?' She mocked the lilt of his accent.

'Do you truly think me such a miscreant that I'd have you bathe in the laundry tub?'

He was in one of his testy moods. Bathing in leftover laundry water was eminently sensible and many households did it. 'I don't see how my bath says anything about you at all.'

He blinked, then gave her a sideways smile. 'You may succeed in logic after all, Little John.' He started across the grass. 'The University's Proctor frowns on the bathhouse, but since you've been sleeping with the horses, he might make an exception. Come with me. We'll share a tub. Wash off the journey's dust.'

The thought of sitting knee to knee, naked, with Duncan in a bathhouse tub stole her breath. 'No, you go without me.' She waved him away, praying he would come no closer. 'I'm done. I don't need another bath.'

'Ah, don't be daft, John.' He took another step. 'You smell like the King's Ditch in August.'

'No!' She cursed the shrill panic in her voice. 'No closer!'

He paused, praise Mary. 'Why not?'

Why not? 'I've an injury.'

Her words released him. 'I'm studying medicine. Let me look—'

'No!' She shouted this time. 'It's an old one. I don't want... I mean it's not...'

He held up his hands and took a step back. An embarrassed red tinged his cheeks and clashed with the teasing lift of his brows. 'War injury?'

Her cheeks, and something lower, heated. 'Accident.' Sometimes, men's few words were a blessing.

Something in his face shifted and the smile disappeared. 'Take your time, then.' He turned and went inside.

She slumped lower in the tepid water, glad she had enjoyed her bath. There would not soon be another.

And next time Duncan looked her way, she would have something stuffed in the front of her breeches that looked as if it belonged to a man.

Little John was a strange one, Duncan thought, uneasy, as he took inventory of the precious bound volumes in the hostel's library. He'd had an unusual sensation, seeing the boy in that tub. Almost as if—

He slammed the door on the thought.

An injury, the boy said. Duncan had seen no limp, no deformity in the lad, but it must be something severe to make him so sensitive.

He nearly dropped Cato's *Distichs*.

Something that would make the boy less than a man.

He shuddered, glad he had not forced the lad to confess his shame. Such an injury would be rare, but if that's what troubled the lad, it would explain the pitch of his voice.

At the thought, his own manhood inconveniently stirred to life. The war, the journey, his meeting with the King, had all conspired to make him neglect his own needs these past weeks. But to live without them, if the boy truly had lost his manhood—the thought swept over him with a kind of agony.

He enjoyed the life of the mind: new ideas, arguments with colleagues. But he also loved the life of the body: to walk the hills, to swing a spade and, he was not ashamed of it, to join with a woman.

What defined a man, after all? Strong arms, sharp mind, strong drives. Deprived of any one of those, why would a man want to live?

All the better, he told himself, when guilt threatened, that his brother had died, rather than live as a cripple.

And if something *had* happened to John, he would need the protection of a University life.

No matter what the boy's wound, he'd discover it in time. The lad would lose his womanish modesty soon enough. There were few secrets when thirty men lived side by side.

Young men arrived with the morning bells and kept coming all day.

Jane stood back, watching everything they did. Loud, boisterous, they slapped each other's backs, punched each other and hugged, performing a sort of greeting ritual.

They filled every corner of the hostel, but they occupied more than physical space. Their vigour reached beyond their bodies, penetrating every nook of the house until she felt even her thoughts could not remain untouched.

She kept Duncan in sight so when he needed someone, she was close at hand, ready to bustle purposefully to fetch clean linen or inform a scholar that he would be sharing a room of three this year instead of two.

'I'm here for the principal,' she would announce, to anyone who would listen. It sounded as important as *for the King*.

And she tried hard not to look down at the rolled-up linen she had stuffed in the front of her breeches. Just in case anyone glanced below her waist.

Late in the day, she was wishing she could scratch the place between her legs where the linen roll had shifted when two scholars appeared at the door.

When he saw them, Duncan dropped his principal's demeanour. He embraced the taller man, slapping his back, then broke and put up his fists to engage the shorter, stockier man in a mock battle.

Here again, at last, was the exuberant man she had met on the road. She blinked at the transformation. These men must be special to him. She eyed them carefully, trying not to call her interest jealousy.

'Oust fettal?'

'Ahreet, marra. Owz it gan?'

'Bay gud!'

Her ear had learned to follow Duncan's tongue, but she could not understand this babble. They spoke the tongue of the north, though she thought she caught a Latin word or two.

'Come,' Duncan said, finally, 'the house is settled for the day. Let's celebrate before the term starts and the beadles start patrolling the alehouses.'

'Get your gittern,' the shorter one said.

'I'll do it,' she said, without waiting for permission, and ran up to Duncan's room.

As she came down the stairs, cradling the precious instrument, the shorter man, with reddish hair, turned. 'And who's this?'

Duncan glanced over his shoulder. 'That's Little John,'

She stuck out her chin and her hand.

He took it, seeing her as Duncan did, blind to the girl beneath the tunic. 'Henry. Of Warcop.'

The taller one had stooped shoulders, thinning hair and a narrow face. 'Geoffrey of Carlisle.' He turned back to Duncan. 'Opening a grammar school, eh?'

Duncan sighed. 'It's a story to share over a tankard.' She handed him the gittern, careful not to brush his fingers. He barely glanced at her. 'Come. I want the news from home.'

She cleared her throat, then coughed.

'Well, come along then, whelp,' Duncan said over his shoulder as they walked out of the door.

She scampered after them and kept her mouth shut as they settled around a corner table and sipped their ale.

She studied them as if they were a Latin lesson, these friends of Duncan's, sprawled around the table. Each staked a space with his elbows. She glanced below. While her knees were neatly matched, their legs were spread wide.

Opposite her, Duncan's legs were as wide as if he had mounted a horse. She let her knees fall apart a hand's breadth. The linen roll slipped lower and wedged between her legs. She snapped her knees together and glanced up, quickly, but no one was watching.

She put her elbow on the table and leaned on her forearm, carving herself a few more inches of the tabletop. It brought her within touching distance of Duncan. She tightened her fingers, but didn't pull back. She would not shrink in the corner like a girl.

Below, out of sight, she crossed her legs.

'This dry-bellied goat's betrothed,' Henry began, nodding at Geoffrey, then swatting the serving woman.

The woman assessed him with a look he didn't see, but her eyes met Jane's as she set the other tankards on the table.

Jane looked down, as if fascinated by the oat flake floating in the golden brew.

'I can scarce believe it,' Duncan said. 'I thought you'd stay here long enough to become chancellor.'

'What could a woman like Mary see in you?' Henry said.

Jane blinked, wondering where she could duck when the first blow was thrown.

Instead, Geoffrey laughed. 'You're just jealous no woman will look at you unless you pay her.'

Shocked, Jane watched Henry grin. It was a foreign tongue, this language men spoke among themselves, harder to decipher than the dialect. An insult might be cause for a fight or a smile, depending on whose lips spoke it. And how.

'You're giving the lad the wrong impression of me,' Geoffrey said.

'Because you've foolishly fallen into a woman's clutches?' Henry said.

Next to her, Duncan shook his head. 'You're the lucky one, Geoffrey. Betrothed to a woman from a good family who thinks you're the earth's master.' He lifted his mug in a toast.

He had never spoken of marriage before. Was there a note of longing in his voice? No, she thought not. He had taken an oath to teach here, in this world without women.

'And she'll wait for you?' Henry asked.

Geoffrey sighed. 'Until next spring. When the year's over, I'll have earned a master's. Then I can make my way clerking in Carlisle, eh?'

'If Carlisle is still there.' Duncan's voice was grim.

Geoffrey and Henry exchanged glances. 'Sorry,' Geoffrey said.

'About your fadder,' Henry added.

His father? He had said nothing of his father. 'What about him?' All three looked at her and she wished she had not asked.

'Scots took him,' Duncan answered, finally. 'And they want a fine ransom before they'll send him back.' Then he shook his head, which seemed to mean *don't talk about it.*

He turned back to Geoffrey and Henry. 'And yours?' he asked.

'The city's walls are strong,' Geoffrey answered.

'Spared,' Henry said. 'They turned back just north of us.'

'Pickering thinks I can persuade Parliament to supply the troops and taxes we need.' Duncan swallowed a sigh along with his ale. 'And the ransom money as well.'

Her eyes widened in awe. So the fate of his father and his homeland now rested on his shoulders. No wonder he furrowed his brow. She wished she could bring back his laugh.

'You can do it,' Geoffrey said. 'You've a nightingale's tongue, eh?'

'It shouldn't take a clever tongue,' he answered. 'The truth should be enough.'

No one answered him. Even Jane knew that truth was seldom enough.

Geoffrey turned to her. 'You're not from the north, are you, Little John?'

She shook her head. 'Bedford.' The answer came easier now.

'Second son?' Henry again.

Duncan answered for her. 'Little John's an orphan.'

'I've only a sister.' There were no first-born sons at Cambridge. The oldest brother would get the land. For the rest, the choice was war, university or the church. She must invent another tale to explain why she would not have the family land. 'The lord took back the castle.'

Duncan looked at her sharply. She had not mentioned a castle or a sister before. 'Until you're of age?' Did Duncan's question sound suspicious?

'No. It's, uh, my injury.'

She waited for questions, but no one asked. Duncan was studying her, assessing. She dropped her eyes to her lap, uncrossed her legs and stretched them out beneath the table, knees still tight together.

Perhaps she needed to tell a longer story to be convincing.

'You see,' she began, 'a horse kicked me, when I was six—'

'No, John. You don't have to—' Duncan's voice had an urgency to it. His palm covered her arm. Her blood ran faster.

She held her ground. She must explain, create an excuse, some reason that she was not like them. 'Right here, in the ribs.' She pulled her arm away to show them. 'And they never healed properly, so I cannot wield a sword...'

Her words trailed off. Geoffrey and Henry stared at their ale, but Duncan had burst into an inexplicable grin. 'Just your ribs, you say?'

'And around there. I've got to keep them wrapped and sometimes, when it's damp, they ache—'

Suddenly, Duncan yelled, 'Gurn!'

Jane jumped. Was it a warning? Danger? Should they run?

But instead, the three men started making faces. Distorted, silly, grotesque faces.

She sipped her ale, wide-eyed. Finally, all three ugly faces froze. Then, Duncan and Geoffrey pointed at Henry and they all laughed and Henry raised his hand for the alewife.

Jane felt as if she were five again, watching the fearsome beasts prowl their cages in the Tower menagerie, unable to decipher their wild behaviour. 'What was that?'

They answered in chorus, 'Gurning.'

'What's that?'

Now, they stared as if she were the odd one.

'Making faces.'

'The worse, the better.'

'Worst one buys the next round.'

'Ah.' She nodded as if what they said made sense. She had expected men to be serious, not silly.

'Although,' Geoffrey said, 'now that Duncan is principal, he's too dignified to win.'

'Or he just doesn't want to pay up,' Henry added, as he gave the returning alewife a coin.

Duncan's smile was indulgent. 'Don't they do this where you come from?'

She shook her head. In the world of women, no one made ugly faces for fun.

A girl must be pretty and nice and smile, no matter what her feelings. Feelings might be shared with other women, but in front of a man a woman was always pleasant.

Men, it seemed, had different rules.

She suspected Duncan had called the challenge to stop her from saying any more about her injury. In a man's world, it seemed, wearing ugly faces was acceptable, but sharing something painful and personal was not.

She threw down the gauntlet. 'Gurn.'

Jane sucked in her cheeks, crossed her eyes, lifted her elbows like a scarecrow, then looked to see what the others had done.

Henry and Geoffrey were pointing at her and she couldn't help but grin.

Duncan, however, was not. 'Cheat!' he said. 'He used his arms. It's face only.'

She stuck her tongue out at him, suddenly hoping she hadn't won. She had few farthings to spend on ale.

'Challenger pays!' Geoffrey called out, waving for another round.

Duncan shrugged and nodded.

She smiled. A game, she reminded herself. It was only a game. But she had played it like a man.

They did not leave until several rounds later, after a number of choruses of a drinking song Duncan seemed to know well. Jane hummed along to the refrain, a series of nonsense syllables, suitable to be sung late at night when the singers could no longer remember the words.

They stumbled back to the hostel on dark streets. Jane thought she might fly. She had been accepted in the company of men. In front of her, Henry sang loudly enough to wake the dead.

Beside her, Duncan tried to sound stern. 'Shut yer maup. You'll bring the beadles down on us with your bellowing.'

Geoffrey was trying to shush him, too, but he could no longer pronounce 'shush'.

Then, ahead of them, she saw a woman, no older, surely, than Jane herself. A girl, then.

'Here, wench,' Henry yelled. 'Do you like my song?'

She waved, but didn't stop. 'Not tonight.'

'Hey!' he shouted. 'I asked you a question.'

She kept walking.

'I'd ignore you if I were her,' Duncan said, reaching out to pull him back. 'You sound like a croaking toad.'

But Henry was not to be dissuaded. 'Answer me!' he called.

He wrenched his arm from Duncan, then ran ahead and grabbed the girl, pushing her against a wall. The others moved in, Jane with them, close enough to recognise the serving woman from the alehouse.

No decent woman would be out alone.

Jane saw both fright and anger in her stance.

The anger won. 'You all sound like toads to me.'

'Hey!' Geoffrey said, stumbling towards her. 'Don't insult my friends.'

'Kiss her, Geoffrey!' Henry said, pushing him at the girl. 'Your betrothed won't know.'

'That's enough.' Duncan said. 'If we rouse the Proctor, I'll have to explain this all to the Chancellor.'

But Henry was beyond persuasion. 'Don't worry. She's got enough kisses for all of us.'

Gittern in one hand, Duncan reached for Henry, but

Geoffrey lurched towards the girl, stumbling into her, holding her against the wall.

Jane's throat ached to scream *no*. What had turned her happy comrades into monsters who thought a woman would welcome their drunken kisses? 'Don't! Stop!'

'Don't worry, Little John.' Henry tumbled to his knees, still laughing, nearly bringing Duncan down. The gittern strings jangled. 'You'll get your turn.'

The thought churned her belly. All the ale that had lain peacefully a few moments before rose up in protest. She doubled over and spewed the contents of her stomach on to the dusty street.

A hand, Duncan's, rubbed her back, the motion steadying.

Still sitting in the dirt, Henry laughed. 'That's a good time for the lad.'

She squeezed her eyes, but that made her dizzy. Barely able to stand, she swayed closer to Duncan, but she wanted to flail them all. How could these men, scholars, treat a woman so? Even Geoffrey, near married and the gentlest of them, had joined in. Only Duncan had made a protest. Was that for fear of the watch or for care of the girl?

'Come on, you oafs.' Duncan's voice rumbled in her ear. 'I've trouble enough keeping us in the Chancellor's good graces without an affray in the street. Leave her.'

When she opened her eyes, the girl was gone. Henry, barely noticing he'd been deprived of his kiss, staggered to his feet, and resumed his song. She took one shaky step and Geoffrey came to her other side.

Duncan held him back. 'I've got him. He's too kalied to walk.'

And she felt herself lifted into his arms.

Cradled against him, she cherished the rise and fall of his chest against her cheek and caught the scent of his skin, a warm, steadying whiff of juniper.

Geoffrey's voice came from close beside her. 'I'll take him for a while if you like.'

'He weighs no more than a grown ewe,' Duncan answered, in his northern lilt. 'I'd toss him over me shoulder, but he's likely to bowk down me back.'

She stiffened, unable to relax in his arms. What if *she* had been discovered on the street when she'd been searching for a bed? What if she were discovered now?

The thought made her stomach rebel again, but she pursed her lips to quell the rumble.

Henry had quieted by the time they returned to the hall. He and Geoffrey helped each other up the stairs.

She wiggled against Duncan. 'Put me down.'

'Are you sure?'

She nodded and he swung her on to the first step. She lifted her foot and tripped.

He sighed. 'Come on, then. I'll put you to bed.'

He reached to scoop her up again and she put up her hands. 'I can do it myself.' Even to her ears, she sounded like a petulant child.

'I'm sure you can,' he answered, his voice patient and soft, 'but it will be easier if I help.'

She slapped his hand away, stumbling backwards to land hard on the step. 'No!' Would he ignore her protest, as they had ignored that girl's?

He leaned against the wall, weary. 'I'm too tired for your foolishness. Now let me put you to bed, Little John, and we can all get some sleep. I've got to open St Michael's door for prime mass tomorrow and I've no patience for this.'

He reached for her, but she kicked and slapped, not knowing where her blows landed. Fear blurred her vision. What would he do if he uncovered the woman under Little John's clothes? Would he hold *her* against a wall and demand a kiss?

Or something worse?

Her heel connected with his ribs and her elbow with his ear. 'No!' she shrieked. Loud enough to wake the house.

'Enough!' He held up his hands. 'Take yourself to bed then.

And don't whine to me tomorrow about how you bowked your guts out all night.'

She clambered to her feet, then abruptly sat again as her stomach started spinning. 'Don't need your help.' A man could do things by himself. 'I'll be better by the morning.'

He shook his head as she walked herself up the stairs on her bottom. 'Actually,' he said, 'I expect you'll be worse.'

Chapter Five

She *was* worse the next morning.

Not just in her stomach and her head, but in her heart. She felt a kinship with that unknown girl last night, one she'd never felt for a woman before. And the male camaraderie she had embraced now left her feeling alone on the other side of a high wall.

She spent the day in silence, not knowing what to say to such creatures as her men had become.

Duncan called her into the Common Room late in the afternoon. 'Let's see what kind of Latin you have, lad. *Portare.*'

She stumbled through the conjugation, simple and perfect, active and passive, not raising her eyes to meet his, no longer sure she knew him. Or wanted to.

'What's the matter, boy? Is last night's ale still talking to you?'

She glared, wanting to hit him with words for disappointing her. 'Don't you wonder what she thought?'

'Who?'

'That girl last night.' So callous he did not even remember. 'When you, when we…' *We.* She had been there, too.

'Is that still bothering you?'

She met his eyes then. 'Yes.'

His expression shifted, hard to capture as smoke. Then he looked at the unlit hearth. 'It was not a night to make us proud.'

Henry and Geoffrey entered, still showing ill effects. Duncan's shoulders relaxed and they laughed, rucfully, about their aching heads and roiling bellies.

Geoffrey spared Jane a glance. 'A rough night, eh, lad?'

She nodded.

'Little John's disturbed about the common woman,' Duncan said.

Her brows darted together. It was not a subject for a crowd.

'But women are not like us, John,' Henry said, serious as a stone.

She was just beginning to appreciate the truth of those words.

'You'll understand when you are older and have more experience with them,' Geoffrey added, with the gravitas of one soon to be wed.

Henry punched his friend's shoulder. 'No, he won't. No one understands women.'

She looked to Duncan, but he remained silent, the whisper of a frown on his brow.

'What's so hard about understanding women?' she asked. Even when she most despised her sex, she found them incredibly transparent.

'Everything!' Henry said.

Duncan shook his head. 'Not to a wise man.'

'But Henry tried to kiss that girl, even when she objected.'

Yet she looked to Duncan, expecting him to answer for all their sins.

But Henry spoke instead. 'If I *had* kissed her, she would have enjoyed it!' Henry vowed, drawing her eyes again.

And under her steady gaze, Henry's ears turned red. 'It didn't mean anything.'

'Not to you.' She knew enough of women to recognise *that* one had wanted to either box his ears or burst into tears.

Or both.

Geoffrey took up the defence in a calm, scholarly tone. 'But she's a common woman. She's been with lots of men.'

Common woman. They had called her mother that. And worse. 'But she said *no.*'

'Sometimes a woman says no when she just wants some persuasion,' Henry answered.

'How did *you* know what she was thinking?' Jane knew. That woman on the street had wanted nothing like persuasion.

'John, when you read the masters, you will understand what Henry's telling you,' Duncan began, in his pedagogical voice. 'A women is weak and deficient, but that's as nature intended. Man must rule over her because he is a rational thinker. Women don't think, you see. They feel.'

'And no one knows how a woman feels!' Henry said, setting off a round of laughing.

Jane did not laugh. Heartsick and confused, she felt too much like the woman she had never wanted to be.

She had admired men, wanted to be like them, but she was discovering their knowledge had gaps she had never imagined when she lived in the same house with her sister's husband.

Safely beyond a woman's gaze, men were totally different creatures. What happened after marriage, when the man and the woman were finally trapped in the same life together? It must be quite a revelation. The strong knight who belched at breakfast. The beautiful maiden who had a short temper during her time of the month. What a different world it would be if men and women truly knew each other.

'You'll see when you're older, Little John,' Henry said. 'Women are lustier than men.'

'Is that what you think?' She prodded Duncan when he didn't speak.

'It's not a matter of opinion,' he began as if ready for a formal disputation. 'Aquinas, Hippocrates and many other masters have written it. Women were created to be protected by men. They are a lesser creature and do not have the mind to understand intellectual things.'

She chomped on the inside of her cheek and raised her eyebrows, as if considering his words instead of choking on them. Yet the Church, the University, they all said the same, things that were not true for her. She could not truly be a woman if she was so different from all the others of her sex.

Was she?

'*Varium et mutabile semper femina,*' she said, finally.

'Exactly!' Duncan said, pleased as if she had mastered the lesson. 'Women are not designed by God for thinking and self-direction. They lack the *virile animo*, the manly spirit that you and I have.'

She'd like to see Duncan disguised as a woman. Then he'd see what a challenge a woman's life could be.

But University men battled with words and wits instead of swords and steeds. She could do the same. She could argue as a man would.

'There are, of course, exceptions,' she began. 'Queen Eleanor, for example.' The Queen had died two hundred years ago, but everyone knew she had been as powerful and strong as her husband, Henry.

'Ah, not an example to prove your case,' Duncan countered, brushing off her challenge. 'She used her body to manipulate her husband and her emotions to dominate her sons. She did nothing herself. It was the men around her.'

Henry nodded sagely. 'We are the logical ones, Little John. Women are ruled by their natural lusts.'

Jane clamped her jaw shut to stop herself from pointing out it was not the woman's lust on display last night.

'It's a mysterious power they have,' Duncan said. He leaned closer. 'Never underestimate it, Little John. This isn't just rhetoric I'm telling you now. The unlearned man is no better than a goat at the mercy of his impulses.' He looked across the table at Henry. 'As this *ribaldus* was the other night.'

Henry hung his head, for once silent.

Duncan resumed his lecture. 'Here, you'll learn how to be a man, how to conquer your own wanton nature. A woman will never be able to do that.'

'And if you allow yourself to follow those impulses, a woman can own you before you even know it,' Henry began with a repentant tone, but ended with a grin. 'Just ask Geoffrey.'

Geoffrey, smiling, seemed all too happy to be owned, but he threw a punch at Henry anyway.

Duncan nodded. 'Only when he masters himself, can a man master a woman. If he does not, she will master him.'

She stared, open mouthed.

They saw woman as a dangerous, dumb, lustful animal, incapable of controlling her body or her thoughts. She had never expected their fear of the mysterious creature they saw only as a baffling 'other.'

Just for a moment, she wanted to *be* that woman and claim that mysterious power. To stand and announce that *she* was a woman, that *she* thought as well as felt.

And that it was not so mystifying to understand that a woman longed for respect and for love.

Only unlike a man, a woman was willing to admit it.

But Jane didn't move. It was a perilous game she played. If she ever lost the support of these comrades, what would happen to her?

Without a man's protection, she would be as helpless as that poor girl on the street.

Duncan awakened before dawn, realising he had dreamt of a woman he had never seen. One with fair hair and blue eyes rimmed with darker blue.

He rolled on to his back and looked up at the ceiling, thinking about Little John's reaction to the common woman.

And his own.

As principal, he should have kept the scholars in line, not let his friends run wild in the streets. He'd not only put them at risk, he'd risked the future of the hostel he'd worked so hard to create.

But he had scant patience with the University regulations. The rules were silly, the lines murky, and many were ignored as often as they were followed. What did it matter if a scholar caroused all night, as long as he showed up for *dies legibiles* the next day?

He rolled out of bed and into his black master's robes, grabbed the church keys and set off to unlock the door for the waiting worshippers. His church duties were part of the price of a life of scholarship.

But the dream followed him across Market Square and on to High Street, reminding him of the very needs he'd lectured Little John about.

An inconvenient topic to have in his head as he headed to early morning service.

Perhaps the encounter with the woman in the street had awakened his lust. Or the conversation about women and men.

Or relief to learn that John was whole.

Well, not whole. What happened to the boy had left him damaged, if not obviously so. In a man, such an injury should have healed in months. But in a lad? It might have caused lingering pain, perhaps enough to stunt his growth and leave him too weak to handle the heft of a sword. So crippled, he would certainly be unable to hold his lord's property.

Well, tender ribs were one thing. Life without a tarse was something altogether different.

He was grateful that the lad would not have to forgo the pleasures of the flesh. Certainly Duncan had chosen not to go beyond the Minor Orders for that very reason.

But now that the idea had entered his mind, or, more troublesomely, his body, it stubbornly refused to leave. He rattled the key in the church-door lock, then watched the sleepy faithful enter, thankful that his flowing robe hid his body's clear sign that his thoughts were not on holy things.

The Chancellor and the Bishop, seemingly unable to distinguish between a university and a monastery, frowned on seeing the scholars mix with women. Perhaps they thought that if they kept women out of sight, healthy young men would conveniently forget about them.

He was living proof of the fallacy of that approach.

Perhaps it would be a good time to initiate Little John into the pleasures of female flesh. Now that he knew the boy's injury would not prevent it, Duncan could take his education in hand.

The lad certainly knew nothing about women.

It was the morning of the King's arrival and the boy was nowhere in sight.

Duncan had asked John to do one simple thing: gather his University garments and help him dress for the ceremonies. The others had already left. The morning was half-gone, the King was to arrive before midday, and neither his master's garb nor the boy were to be found.

Shirtless, he looked out of the window towards the privy at the back of the yard, then stormed out of his room, temper rising.

The lad was earnest enough, but too often over the past few days he'd be daydreaming when it was time to work, seemingly unaware that if he didn't appear in the kitchen, others had to work twice as hard or men would go hungry.

He was torn between wanting to protect the coddled boy and shake him. John didn't seem deliberately wilful or mean, but he didn't seem to feel responsible for anything.

Duncan felt responsible for everything. Maybe he envied the boy's carefree nature.

'Little John!' he bellowed. 'Where are you?'

The words echoed in an empty hostel. Everyone had left to claim a choice spot on the street to watch the King's procession.

'Up here.'

He followed the voice to the boys' dormitory on the top floor, stomping on every stair, angry that the boy had not come to him. 'Where in hell is my gown?' he called, as he approached the door.

The boy jumped, nearly dropping something. 'Oh, I forgot the time.'

'Hard to do when St Mary's rings the hours.'

John's eyes widened, fixated on Duncan's bare chest.

'What are you staring at?' He looked down, suddenly ill at ease.

'I'm not!' He raised his eyes, disturbingly blue, and hid his hands behind his back.

'And what are you hiding there?' He grabbed the boy's arm, fighting the warm feeling in his chest. Anger, no doubt.

'Nothing.'

Duncan pulled John's arm to the front and unwrapped the boy's blunt fingers to uncover an ivory-backed mirror.

Vain as a woman. He sighed.

Then, glancing at the carved, painted scene on the mirror's back, Duncan blinked. It was a remarkably detailed scene of a knight on horseback with his hands wrapped around a woman.

Or, more accurately, his hands wrapped around her breasts.

He dropped the boy's hand. No time to be thinking of women. 'Go. Fetch the gown. Quickly. And meet me in my room.'

John ran.

Duncan followed him down the stairs, struggling to keep his mind on the day's ceremony instead of John's endless surprises. The boy had claimed to be a penniless orphan, but the mirror could have gifted an earl's wife.

Or, with an image like that, his mistress.

And if he had been looking at that, the boy was certainly thinking about women.

Flushed, John appeared at the door, carrying a short black robe, slightly crumpled.

'I need the cappa clausa, not the tabard. And where's my hood?'

'How am I supposed to know what you're meant to wear?'

'Ask if you don't know. The cappa is the long black gown with a slit in the middle. And the hood is the one lined with grey fur. Now run!' The boy did. 'And don't forget the hat!'

John returned, arms full, looking askance at the soft grey fur lining the hood. 'You'll be roasting in that today.'

Duncan knew that. But he hadn't the coin to spend on a silk-lined summer hood. 'John, do as I say. I'm going before my colleagues and the King and I'm going to wear the garb that I'm entitled to.'

The boy shook his head. 'I've known women less concerned with their clothes.'

'You're the one who was preening before a mirror!' He let the roar escape. 'I've spent seven years of sweat and toil to earn this fur and, by God's nails, I'm going to wear it!' Seven years to prove them all wrong. And there were still those who didn't believe he belonged at Cambridge. He glared at the boy. 'When—no, *if* you ever make it through the *trivium* and *quadrivium*, you'll be proud to sweat in it, too.'

Eyes wide, John stepped back. He looked from Duncan to the pile of black cloth, then settled his shoulders. 'What goes on first?'

He walked the boy through the elaborate costume, uncomfortable with such ceremony, but determined to fulfil it. John's fingers patted the gown over his shoulders and smoothed the wrinkles carefully.

It was oddly intimate to be dressed. To feel the pressure of fingers on his chest when the lad smoothed the flowing gown. To feel the breath on his neck when the cap was placed on his head. To catch a whiff of the boy's scent. He no longer smelled of the stables but of something unexpected, unrecognisable, yet familiar.

He closed his eyes, but that brought back the image of the knight and his lady on the mirror.

His body had been too long deprived, if such a touch could rouse him. It was only that, he thought, disquieted. Not the boy.

'There,' John said. 'You look very distinguished.'

He opened his eyes to see pride reflected in John's blue ones.

He shifted, uncomfortable, grateful for the flowing cloak. Under such a cloak, who would know whether a man or a woman lurked? Or that his tarse had sprung inconveniently to life?

He started down the stairs, forcing his thoughts to the ceremony, ignoring the worldly urges still plaguing him.

The boy tagged along beside him as he left the hostel and headed for High Street. The crowd at the corner was three deep. He was going to have a struggle to work his way to where the faculty stood.

'Duncan, do I look worthy of meeting the King?'

He looked down at John, who was tugging on his wrinkled tunic. The boy's cheeks were flushed and strands of his pale, unruly curls floated in the breeze. There was something intense in the question that Duncan didn't have time to ponder. 'Don't worry. You won't be meeting his Majesty.'

'But I must! I need to tell him that I am studying so that I can be worthy to work in his service.'

'John, this is a town ceremony, not a court function. He's to be welcomed by the Mayor and the Chancellor and the guilds, not mingling with a glomeral student.'

Duncan pushed into the crowd. They parted, grumbling, when they saw his master's garb.

John stuck to his side. 'You know him. You can present me.'

'No. I can't.' He fought the urge to make the boy happy. 'I won't be anywhere near you.'

The smile fell. 'Why not?'

'Because the faculty stand together.' He reached the edge of the crowd. To his left, stands were set up halfway to Trumpington Gate. He waved to Pickering, standing across the street with the members of Parliament, and turned back to John. 'Now go stand over there. I'll see you later.'

Duncan turned his back on the boy, fighting vague guilt, and took his place with the faculty.

The Chancellor, clad in scarlet, frowned at him. 'You're late.'

'Oh?' He hoped his tone conveyed the proper disdain. If not, his northern accent would. 'Did I keep me Majesty waiting?'

Duncan didn't wait for an answer, but turned away, searching for John in the crowd of students.

Jane's arm ached from waving, but the King never looked at her.

She rubbed her shoulder after he passed. He looked like a blond angel, she decided. In fact, he looked more suited to study than Duncan.

He caught her eye from across the street and something like pride tickled her heart.

Duncan looked like a warrior.

Even the flowing robe couldn't disguise his broad shoulders and his rugged face. Now that she saw him amidst the flock of black-garbed masters, she understood why the robe had been so important. One man was garbed in scarlet, a few in blue. Some had hats as well as hoods. What did it all mean?

She did not look nearly so impressive. Duncan had nearly caught her adjusting the wad of linen between her legs this morning. When he had stormed in, wearing nothing but his chausses, the sight of his bare chest had made her gulp for air.

And then she had had to dress him.

She had stood close enough to smell his skin. Her fingers had burned as they brushed his chest. She had wanted to stroke his shoulder and explore the muscles of his arms, stronger than she had expected a scholar's to be. And her war against those wants had made her fingers stiff and awkward instead of graceful and soothing, as a woman's would be.

She had never had a woman's touch. And had never wanted it so much.

She forced her eyes away from Duncan and back to the King, dismounting, surrounded by members of his Council and the House of Lords. This was why she had come today. And no matter what it took, she would get close enough for him to see her.

Close enough to speak to him.

What would she feel when she met him, this royal relative? Would he recognise their bond? Would he see his fair hair in hers?

If she had been born a man instead of a poor, weak thing, she would already be at court, perhaps even riding next to King Richard. Bastard sons of kings were recognised and acknowledged. They became warriors, bishops, ambassadors.

Sometimes a king's bastard daughters might be married to cement alliances. Neither she nor her sister had been offered such a match, but then, most king's mistresses were not as hated as her mother had been.

The King climbed the stairs of the wooden platform to sit on a makeshift throne.

She searched his face for a reflection of her own.

He looked bored, she decided, but he did *not* look like her.

Oh, he was fair haired and blue eyed. She could see that even from this distance.

But it was more than the hair on his cheek that made his face different from hers. His mouth, a sweet rosebud, looked more girlish than her own lips. And his chin rounded to a soft point, while hers met the world squarely.

She sighed. It was probably better they looked no more alike. It would raise fewer connections between Jane, daughter of a dead king, and John, eager young scholar.

The King settled into his chair. Jane waited patiently through the procession of the guilds of butchers, bakers and chandlers.

The King gazed over the red, blue and green banners as if he did not see them. It must be as her mother had always told her: the King was the man above all men, with the power to do anything he wanted, grant any wish.

He had even provided Solay with a husband she loved, although there had been that misunderstanding about spying on Justin at first.

The parade ended and the pageant began. Her feet and knees

ached after standing for hours, but no one around her moved. In honour of the King, the play told the story of Solomon's wisdom, a fitting story for a town of learning. It concluded by equating King Richard and his wisdom to Solomon himself.

The King smiled for the first time.

Her family might not agree so readily about this king's wisdom, but wise or foolish, he could provide her with the opportunity to do important things and see the world.

So as the pageant ended, she stayed where she was, despite her aching feet. She must be close when he passed again.

Duncan stiffened as the King approached with the Chancellor and the Bishop. It was part of the royal duty, to review the faculty, though a king would not deign to speak to any of them.

Duncan was at the end of the line, sweat drenching his weary muscles. The King's eyes flickered over the black flock without stopping. But when he saw Duncan, he paused.

Duncan nodded, acknowledging the uncertain recognition.

The King walked past a dozen gape-mouthed masters. 'Duncan of Cliff's Tower?'

He bowed as deeply as his stiff back allowed. 'Your Majesty.' Deference to a man younger and untried was not in his nature. Even if that man were the King.

'The last time I saw you, you were a bearded barbarian. Now you are a learned master.'

The Chancellor, next to the King, smiled. Duncan could see the man's gritted teeth. 'This will be Master Duncan's first year of teaching. He has opened a hostel for men from the north counties.'

The King nodded. 'You are a surprising man, Master Duncan.'

He inclined his head, grateful when the Chancellor stepped away to talk with the Council members. 'Unfortunately, your Majesty, my surprises have not all been pleasant.' Now. He must take his chance. 'Since the Council meeting, I have discovered that my father has been taken by the Scots. He's being held for ransom.'

Fury distorted Richard's lips. 'Vile brutes.'

Sometimes, Duncan thought the King hated the Scots more than the French.

'Knowing your Majesty's interest, I wanted to offer you the honour of contributing to his release.' Parliament would have many demands, but a king who feasted on plates of gold could surely afford the ransom for a lowly knight.

The King assumed the thoughtful nod of the Solomon of the pageant, but he looked over his shoulder. His uncle, the Duke of Gloucester, and the other lords of his Council stood just out of earshot.

Even for this amount, Duncan understood, the King would need his Council's approval. His hopes crumbled.

There was a hint of contrition in the King's eyes when they met his again. 'There are many demands on the household accounts, but I'm certain the people of England think as I do. The Commons will surely agree the Borders must be secure.'

'I can only hope so, your Majesty.' Money from Parliament, money for war, but none from the King himself and nothing for a ransom. 'I will be working diligently towards that end.' What good would it do to send more men to war when you weren't willing to buy back those who already served? Reckless, he continued, 'And to make sure Parliament also sees the necessity to free the brave men who have already defended them.'

The King frowned, but before he could speak, Duncan felt a nudge against his side and looked down.

John.

What was the fool thinking, to interrupt his private conference with the King?

The King stared at the face peeking out behind Duncan's robe. Immediately, John dropped to one knee.

'Rise, youth,' the King said, with a smile. 'Have you a petition?'

'No, your Majesty.'

What was the lad up to? Balanced on one knee, head bowed, he showed a natural grace Duncan had never noticed in the boy before.

Duncan dug a toe into John's foot, hoping the King would not notice.

'You want nothing?' No wonder the King was willing to stop and listen. No one ever came to him without wanting something.

Even, he realised, chagrined, Duncan himself.

'I simply want to pay my respects to you, our glorious king, your Majesty.'

'Forgive him, your Majesty,' Duncan began.

The King raised his brows. 'You know the lad?'

'I've just taken him on as a student.' He glared at John's bowed, blond head.

'What's your name, young scholar?'

'John, your Majesty.'

'And what is he teaching you?'

'Latin, your Majesty. Until I am ready for grammar, dialectic and rhetoric.'

Duncan struggled to hold his temper. 'He has much to learn.'

'And when I do,' John said, 'I hope to offer myself as a clerk in your noble service.'

'Bright boy,' Richard said to Duncan.

'And full of surprises,' Duncan muttered. Interesting time the boy had picked to announce his ambition.

The King smiled, flattered at the request. 'Then study hard. If you advance well, Master Duncan can bring you to me before I leave the city and let me hear a piece you have learned.'

'Thank you, your Majesty.' John beamed.

Duncan did not. 'That's only a few weeks, your Majesty.'

The King's smile was sly. 'And you're a talented master, I'm sure. Besides, perhaps we'll have some words to say to each other after Parliament adjourns.'

The King moved on, and Duncan stared at his departing back.

Parliament and Michaelmas term both started tomorrow. How was he to make the lad worthy of the King in such a short time?

Well, this would be no time to introduce Little John to his first woman.

Beside him, John rose. 'See? I knew you would help me meet the King. And now I'm to see him again.'

'*If* your Latin warrants it. And despite what his Majesty said, that's up to you, not me.'

'I can do it.'

He hoped so. Through the boy, the King had offered him another opportunity to plead for his father.

If Parliament's vote did not go his way, he would need to take it.

Anger spent, he grabbed the boy's blond head in the crook of his elbow and squeezed. 'All right, whelp,' he said, and growled in fun as John flailed his fists at Duncan's ribs. 'We'll find you a pretty speech from Cato and see whether you can string together five minutes of decent Latin.'

He let the boy go, then gave him a swift swat on the backside.

Something glowed in the boy's sky-blue eyes: a grown man's determination Duncan hadn't seen before. 'I'll do it. I'll make you proud.'

He nodded, uneasy. The words, the set of the lad's lips, the fading sun's glint on the lad's fair hair—something triggered a tug of emotion he hadn't felt since his brother had died. Nor wanted to.

'Awright, then,' he said, without ruffling the boy's hair as he normally did. 'Let's go home.'

He liked the lad. Wanted to help him. That was all.

Nothing more.

Chapter Six

Jane studied the man beside Duncan at the table. They had been sitting together for hours.

Not a university man, she decided, looking at the stranger. White-haired, soft-spoken, but with a commanding air. Someone connected to Parliament, she guessed. Whoever he was, he was taking up too much of Duncan's time.

Parliament had convened the day after the King's arrival. Since then, Duncan had barely looked in her direction. He had certainly not tutored her.

She stood in front of the table and cleared her throat. 'When do we begin my studies?'

Duncan didn't look up. 'When I'm ready. I've other things to do than be with you every minute of the day.'

No smile. No greeting. Well, she would speak as a man would, demanding what he wanted. 'I came here to learn Latin, not work in the kitchen. I thought you were going to teach me.'

Now she had his gaze, and was sorry of it. 'Do you think the sun revolves around you instead of the earth?'

'But the King!' Days were slipping away. The King would leave as soon as Parliament was over. 'I must show him how good my Latin is.'

The older man raised his eyebrows, tactfully silent.

Duncan sighed. 'This important young scholar is Little John, an orphan whose manners are even worse than his Latin.'

Her ears felt red. I'll make you proud, she had promised. She was, it seemed, no more able to do that as a man than as a woman. 'Pardon, please, Master Duncan.' She nodded to the other man. 'And yours, too, sir. I was overeager.'

'John, you should be honoured to meet this man. He is Sir James Pickering, member of Parliament.'

She started to bob for a courtesy, then remembered to bow. He had forgiving eyes, at least.

'How many Parliaments will this be for you?' Duncan asked. 'Ten?'

'At least.'

'That's more than the King himself. And elected Speaker for how many of those?'

The man chuckled. 'A few. They're tired of hearing me talk. That's why I need you.'

Ten Parliaments. Had this man been one of those who had stripped her mother of her property and nearly exiled them? Perhaps his kind eyes were deceptive.

'What is it you need him to do?' she asked.

The man's smile was kindly, too. 'To persuade the members to vote for the taxes needed to fight the Scots.' Pickering tapped a list of names spread on the table. 'And to ransom the brave men who have already defended our borders.'

'Your father,' she whispered, turning to Duncan, ashamed to have forgotten. Something cracked around her heart. Full of her own woes, she'd been heedless of the fact that he, too, woke each morning wondering whether a dear family member lived or died.

She reached over the table, her fingers trailing the back of his hand.

He started, pulling it away, and looked up.

The grey eyes were tinged with blue today. And with ques-

tions. She knew she should look away, but she had fallen too far
into his gaze.

'Yes.' He crossed his arms, putting his hands safely beyond
reach. 'Me fadder.' There was gravel in his words. 'Now go up
to the library, pull the Cato off the shelf and read aloud until I
have time for you. You're the one who has to learn it, Little John.
I can't do that for you.'

She shifted from one foot to the other. 'Is there something I
could do for you? I'd like to help.'

Surprise touched his eyes this time, followed by resistance.
This man gave help. He didn't take it.

His momentary struggle gave her a glimpse of the other side
and she saw the anger for what it was: a wall. Anyone who could
see beyond it would know that, without the anger, he had no
defence at all.

It was Pickering who answered. 'That's a kind offer, young
John. When we have finished with this list, I'm sure Master
Duncan would be glad of your help to write a copy for me.'

She nodded and backed away, waiting for a word from
Duncan. She didn't hear it until she was on the third step.

'Nicholas from Essex.' He had regained control of his voice.
'Has he committed his vote or do I need to speak to him?'

She mumbled aloud over the volume as she tried to follow
the words. She hoped the King would be impressed with Cato.
He would no doubt approve of the lines about giving way to
your superior.

As the afternoon waned, she had to light a candle, but the
small, wavering flame made the words difficult to see and her
eyelids drooped.

'Who gave you permission to light a candle?'

She lifted her head at Duncan's voice, realising she had dozed
on top of Cato. 'I didn't know I needed permission.'

'Fees, which you are not paying, buy our food, our firewood

and our candles. When you light a candle, you're using some-thing that belongs to everyone. If you arc going to use one, be certain you're not the only one who needs the light.'

'But there's no one else here.'

'That doesn't mean you can squander a candle others will need by the solstice.'

It was the anger talking again. He had repaired the wall. 'Whose permission do I need?'

'Mine.'

She envied the word, so strong, so singular. 'May I light a candle, Master Duncan?'

He leaned over and blew it out. 'No.'

The sudden gloom felt intimate, but also safe. She could hide from the rest of them. They barely glanced at her. A dirty face, a gravelly voice, a casual slouch were enough to fool them. But Duncan looked too closely. Who knew how much he could see?

'How am I to learn if I cannot see to read?'

'You'll be speaking to the King, not reading. You've read the precepts. Put the book down and translate: 'Respect your teacher.''

'*Magistrum metue.*'

'Study literature.'

'*Littera disce.*'

'*Litter*as *disce*. Again.'

So he drilled her and she recited the words back as the darkness deepened and they worked beyond time for the evening soup and bread.

There was nothing personal in his words, but she loved the timbre of his voice. It seemed to shimmer in the air.

'Keep company with good people.'

'*Cum bonis ambula,*' she answered, without hesitation. It was the tenth time through fifty-seven precepts. Tired now, she decided to turn the tables. 'Don't laugh at anybody.'

He did laugh then, and slapped her knee in congratulations. '*Neminem riseris.*'

She laughed, too, leaning towards him, her face, her lips suddenly too close to his, her breath, his, too short. She wobbled. Her lips brushed his cheek, rough with the evening's stubble.

He jerked away.

A silence. Awkward.

He stood. 'Enough for the night.'

She could still feel his palm print on her knee, his breath on her cheek, the rough edge of his beard on her lips. She didn't want to let him go. Not now. 'You haven't played your gittern since that first night at the alehouse. I'd like to hear it.'

He was quiet and she cursed her weakness in asking. It was the woman in her wanting to keep him close. Did he sense that?

'Wait here.' He left her alone in the dark.

When he returned with the instrument, he plucked a few mindless notes and then launched into a rousing melody she recognised from the alehouse.

As brothers we wander
Eat, drink, love and squander,
As the Pope bade us do
Live as friends ever true.

'Sing with me,' he said, fingers holding the pick plucking notes at a furious pace.

She bit her tongue and shook her head. 'I'm not much of a singer. I'll just hum.' She clamped her lips shut to prevent herself from opening her throat to the melody.

'Still missing your man's voice?'

He must be suspicious. She had been too close. Shown too much. Her touch had been too quick, her breath too fast, her lips too soft.

'Yes. That's it.' When did a boy's voice become a man's? 'I still sound too much like a girl.' The disgust in her voice was not feigned.

'Well, hum, then.' A question lingered in his voice, unanswered. So she hummed so hard her lips shook.

The song went on and on, full of laughter and camaraderie, and *tara, tantara, teino* for when you forgot the words.

She hummed for the pleasure of feeling the notes vibrate in her bones, for the naughty delight of singing about things no lady was supposed to know, and for the sheer joy of entwining her melody with his wonderful voice in the dark.

He spun out verses, creating new words until they reached a final *tara, tantara, teino* and, with a triumphant strum of the strings, he lifted his hands in victory.

'You're as good as a minstrel,' she said, out of breath.

Unable to keep his hands from the instrument, he went back to the strings, plucking them idly with the small quill pick. 'Winter's long. Travelling players don't pass our way. We make our own music.'

'Your family must sing every night.'

The gentle notes dissolved into discord. Abruptly, he put the instrument aside. 'It was not your place to speak to the King.'

She blinked. All she had done was mention his family and he had become a chiding stranger. Answering annoyance fluttered through her. If he only knew who she was, he'd know she had more right to speak to the King than he did.

'I caused no harm.' She wondered, for a moment, whether discovering her blood would anger him more than knowing her sex.

'Oh, you don't think so, do you? What happens if I can't get you ready to recite for the King? What will he think of me then?'

His father. He needed the King's help to free his father. And she might jeopardise that.

'I didn't think of you when I asked,' she mumbled. She thought herself so much a man, yet she kept acting on feelings.

'You never do think of anyone but yourself, do you?'

Hot shame spread from her cheeks, lower. He made it sound selfish, the independence she craved. Yet he was a man and he had sought and carried responsibility for the hostel, his father, even the defence of England.

And what had she done for any other person? She had not even helped her sister.

She straightened her shoulders. It was too dark to see his eyes clearly, so she reached to shake his hand, still rough and warm from the strings. 'I said I'd make you proud. And I will. I promise.'

He gripped her fingers, hard and fast, and her heartbeat quickened. It surged through her hand, caught in her throat, teased her bound breasts, and threatened to expose her secret without her saying a word.

She tugged at her hand, but he would not release the handshake. 'Friends ever true, eh?' His rough voice touched her in the dark.

'I swear it,' she answered, as if the words alone would keep her at his side, close as blood kin, for all their lives.

'Dinna give yer word lightly, lad.'

She swallowed, feeling her fingers throb against his palm. 'I swear by Heaven. With God as my witness.' She did not know what she promised, but she knew that she would be bound by these words to do things she could never imagine now. 'I shall be faithful to you as a brother,' she answered.

His hand shook at the word and dropped hers. 'Off t'bed with ya,' he said.

As she paced out her place on the floor of the boys' dormitory, her thoughts were of the oath that had trembled between them.

She had never sworn an oath. Never made a promise so deep. Yet she had made it so she could stay close to him, like a squire might serve his knight.

Brother. The very word had shaken him. With a brother, no oath was necessary. They shared an oath of birth.

As she had shared with her sister.

And broken.

What made her think she could keep the oath she made to him?

And it wasn't until she unrolled her pallet and felt the tears slowly trickle into the straw that she realised he had promised her nothing at all.

Chapter Seven

Jane was startled the next day to see the woman they had tormented shopping at the Market Square, picking over the onions.

Their eyes met and the woman's narrowed with wary recognition before she turned her back and hurried across the square.

Jane followed, running, and caught up quickly, grabbing her sleeve. The woman turned, a ferocious snarl scarring her face.

'So did you enjoy their games? Are you looking for more fun?'

Jane snatched her hand away, bludgeoned by the words. 'I'm sorry.' Sorrier that she had not been able to stop them. 'They are not bad men, usually.'

The woman tilted her head, her brow furrowed.

Her face might have been pleasant if not hardened by a rough life. But her brown eyes were lined, not merry, her shoulders stooped instead of square, and her walk a shuffle, not a stride.

Shocked, Jane realised she couldn't have been much more than twenty summers. What kind of life had this woman had, while Jane had played at home? This was what happened to a woman at the mercy of men, without control of her own fate.

'I hope they pay you well,' the woman said, finally. 'For dressing up as a boy and being their private plaything.'

Jane's face flamed and then froze.

She knows.

This woman had seen right through the rough speech, the swagger and the bound breasts, not fooled for a moment.

But worse, she thought Jane was a whore. The worst kind of whore. Worse, even, than her mother. Her words suggested things Jane could not even imagine.

She clutched the woman's arm and pulled her into an alley. 'They do not know,' she whispered fiercely. 'They think I'm a boy.'

'They don't know?' The shock on her face dissolved. Then, she grabbed her belly and threw back her head, laughing so loud Jane looked over her shoulder and then forced a laugh of her own so people passing by would think they shared a joke.

Finally, the woman leaned against the wall, gasping for breath, and shook her head. Their eyes met and for a moment, they were both women.

'So you live like this?' she asked, eyes wide with curiousity. 'All the time?'

Jane nodded. 'They call me Little John.'

The woman looked her up and down. Jane stood straighter, hoping the stance did not throw her breasts into relief. How did she look to one who knew what she was seeing?

Interest, even envy, sparked her eyes. 'Your clothes, they're good protection, then? Against them?'

Them. As if her friends were an invading enemy. How could she explain she dressed so not to be *against*, but to be *with* them?

Except when they had drunk too much and assaulted a woman in the streets.

'They think I am one of them.'

'But how do you, ah…' the woman looked her up and down '…piss and all?'

'I told them I've an injury and I'm shy.' So they let her escape to the small, dark hut in the back of the yard alone. They had teased her without mercy and if Duncan had not protected her, the teasing might have become more. 'They expect me to grow out of it.'

The woman raised a sceptical brow. 'And how long has it been since ya bathed?'

Too long. 'I do the wash while they are in class. Quickly.' So the water would still be warm when she hopped in. 'No one has guessed.'

'Men.' Her companion shook her head. 'They see only what they expect, don't they?'

'I hope so.' She looked at this woman, whose very life was all she wanted to avoid. 'I am living as a man so I can be free.'

The woman leaned closer to whisper. 'What's it like?'

So she and Hawys from the alehouse stood in the shadow of the alley all that late afternoon while Jane whispered about her life on the other side of the wall.

She had been so truly alone, it was a relief to confess. And as she told the story, she heard herself admit, for the first time, that it wasn't all wonderful. Voices were loud. Fabric was coarse. There was little soft or gentle to ease the rough edges of life.

The men had made fun of her when she had wiped off a table or plumped the straw in a pallet on the bed, so she did it when they were not watching, trying to bring some beauty, order, comfort to daily life.

She could tell that to another woman, even one so different from herself.

A woman would understand.

She did *not* tell her that the independence she had run away to find remained elusive.

Maybe only a king could do as he pleased all the time.

'Have you no family?' Hawys asked, when she had heard it all.

'I ran away,' she said, ashamed all over again.

'Were they cruel? Is that why you left?'

Jane shook her head. Were there families who hurt their own? She had felt only the sting of her mother's disappointment.

'My sister was having a baby. I'm not good at womanly things, you see. I don't know what to do and when I try it's wrong and…' The helpless fear of the dark, smothering birthing room washed over her again. Tears burned and she was grateful, for once, that she did not have to hide them. 'And I don't know how she is or what happened to the babe.'

As Hawys patted her on the shoulder and gave her a 'cluck cluck' of sympathy, Jane felt a comfort she hadn't felt in weeks. Women don't think, they feel, Duncan had said. Well, she *was* a woman and she *did* feel. After weeks of stifling her feelings, the bite of that emotion, its *trueness*, vibrated inside her like a well-plucked gittern string. She had spent weeks living in her head instead of her body or her heart and it felt good to cry and talk of sad truths.

Perhaps she was more of a woman than she had thought.

She scrubbed her eyes with her sleeve. 'I wish I knew if Solay and the babe are well, but if I send word, they'll know where to find me.'

'I could send my brother.'

'You would do that?' She felt a lightness in her chest she hadn't felt in weeks. 'Could he really find out?'

She nodded. 'He's sly and quick. He'll get the answer.'

Sly and quick. He would need to be for a life on the street. 'But they would know where to find me if he went.'

Hawys thought for a moment. 'He can tell them he saw you with some pilgrims at the Fair. And he can't remember which shrine you were going to.'

'Oh, thank you, thank you.' This stranger was making a great sacrifice for her. She had travelled the road. It would not be easy. 'How could I repay you? And him?'

'Your family will reward him for news of you, I'll wager.' Hawys's smile held a wealth of experience.

Jane wanted to ask whether she were a common woman, but she didn't know how without insulting her.

Hawys looked her up and down, still taking it all in. 'So what will you do when they find out?'

'They won't. They mustn't. Ever.' Acting like a woman again had been a momentary comfort. She couldn't live like that again. Not now. 'I'm going to earn my bachelor's and clerk for the King so I can travel the world.'

Although without Duncan, the glow of the life she'd envisioned seemed tarnished. What would her promise mean then?

'Oh, are you now?' She did not look impressed. 'Well, you make a passable "Little" John, but soon they'll be looking for a beard and strong shoulders.'

'Something will work out.' The words wobbled. Clerking for the King, living as a man. Said aloud, her plan was ill conceived at best.

'Won't you want to go back? To being a woman?'

Helpless and at their mercy, like you? How could she even ask? 'No.'

Yet even as she said it, she knew there were moments with Duncan when she wanted something more, something only a woman could know.

'But what about your family?'

She shook her head. Her sister. Her mother. To go back would mean looking in their eyes and facing her failure. 'I miss them.' She had learned, after these weeks, to speak over the lump in her throat. 'But I can't go back.'

For if a man's life was not as easy as she had imagined, a woman's life, when she was not sheltered from the world as Jane had been, was harder still.

And now that she had crossed the line, she could not return to the other side, where you were prey to any man who might want to kiss you on the street.

Chapter Eight

Jane sat alone in the dim Common Room, refusing to light a candle, and muttered her Latin aloud. It was still early in the term and the men of Solar Hostel had decided the Stourbridge Fair was more enticing than their studies.

Feeling deprived but virtuous, she had stayed behind.

You're the one who has to learn it, Little John, Duncan had said. *I can't do that for you.*

She had seen little of him this week. Up before dawn, he would unlock St Michael's, give his cursory lecture, teach two paying students, then meet with a medical fellow for his own lessons. In the afternoon, he was at Barnwell Priory, standing in the hallway, trying to speak to each member of the Commons who might pass.

There were two hundred and forty-eight of them. She had copied each name. Duncan carried her list.

Her Latin had improved. The mumbled lines had become rote and she no longer needed to look at the page to say each one. Pray to God. *Itaque deo supplica.* Love your parents. *Parentes ama.* Fear your teacher. *Magistrum metue.*

'Flee the prostitute.'

Duncan's voice touched her and her tongue answered for her. *'Meretricem fuge.'* She looked up at him, joy at the unexpected sight of him mixed with irritation at his absence. 'We didn't flee that woman that other night.'

He sighed, and sat on the bench opposite her. 'Don't start with that again, Little John. I've no patience for it tonight.' Too weary to hold his back straight, he leaned his head against the wall and closed his eyes.

And she wasn't sure whether she stifled her irritation or whether it just disappeared. 'Have you eaten?'

He shook his head. 'I was plying the members with food and drink. I had to keep a clear head and a lucid tongue.'

So she rose, rummaged in the kitchen and returned with leavings from the evening meal.

And his gittern.

He took a generous swig of ale, and munched on the bread and pickled fish.

'What happened today?' she asked, finally.

He lifted the half-empty tankard in toast. 'Ten more to the "yes" column and at least a week before the vote. Parliament's all in an uproar about the livery badges now.'

'I've memorised all the distichs. Geoffrey and Henry helped.' She paused, but he didn't ask her to recite. '*Duo supplica.* Pray to God. *Magistratum metue.* Repect the magistrate. *Quod satis est, dormi.* You need to pay attention to that one. It means "sleep enough".'

He spoke as if he had not been listening. 'So how do you like the girls, then?'

She ducked her head, sure that if she looked at him her girlish blush would give her away.

Or he'd see the longing in her eyes.

What *would* a youth think of girls? 'I, uh, don't know much about them,' she mumbled.

'Haven't stolen a kiss from a merry maid in the barn?' Ten votes had put a shine in his voice.

She swallowed. 'Not many maids in our house.'

'It happens to a few like that. The north country's an empty place. I've heard of men so desperate, they'd do it with sheep.'

Her head snapped up and her jaw dropped. 'You jape me.'

'By God's foot I do not!' But he laughed, so she was not sure.

'So you're familiar with sheep, are ya?' Amazing, how his accent, and the insult, came so easily to her lips now.

Anger flickered across his face before the laughter broke. 'Not me! I've always known what my *botellus* was for. And so have the ladies who enjoyed it.'

She forced a laugh, too loud. His boast touched her body and she tingled, imagining his *botellus* between her legs, slipping inside her.

She closed her eyes to hide her thoughts. What would he do if she announced she was a woman? Would he laugh and think it a rare jape, that she had tricked him?

No. When he masters himself, a man can master his woman, he had boasted. Yet in her disguise, she had mastered them all.

'And you?' He was studying her too closely.

'Me, what?'

The silence was awkward.

'You haven't… You're still a—'

She didn't let him finish the question. 'No. Yes.'

Virgin. It could apply to a man, but the word echoed with a resonance she'd never felt before. *Virgin.* Untouched.

And yet she looked at his hands and wanted to be touched. Felt herself open, aching, for something with him, from him. Something more than friendship.

'What about you?' she asked. 'When did you…?'

She cleared her throat, unable to complete the question. Dangerous, to envision him naked, joining with a woman.

'I was about your age and had just come to Cambridge.'

'You picked someone off the street?' Until the other night, she had never conceived of such a thing. 'Like that girl the other night?' *Like Hawys.*

He frowned, she was glad to see. 'She was much friendlier. She liked it.'

'Oh? How do you know?'

'I'm a man who knows his women. She liked it.'

'And did *you* like it?'

'What do you think?' There was a wicked edge to his grin.

What she thought was that making love with a stranger sounded like the loneliest thing in the world. 'Wouldn't it be more pleasurable to, uh, be with someone you had feelings for?' *Someone you loved.*

The teasing light left his eyes. He looked another gulp of ale.

'Life is like that, Little John.' His voice held a forced bravado. 'Grab the pleasure you can. Don't worry about what you can't have.'

'But wouldn't you? If you could?' Her words spilled out, an impossible hope. '*Coniugem ama.* Love thy wife. Wouldn't you wish for a woman you wanted to be with in bed and out?'

He studied her face before he spoke. Grateful for the dusk, she struggled to keep her gaze steady, to stop her lips from falling open to him.

His eyes had turned the deep colour of smoke.

'You and I are of a kind, laddie,' he answered, finally, 'but you mustn't admit to thoughts like that. They'll think you womanish.'

'I'm no woman!' She'd said too much. Trod too close. Risked too much.

'I know that, lad. But if the others suspect you've weak feelings, they'll eat you while yer still raw.'

She blinked. Was this a man's life, then? Not to *have* what you want, but to *hide* it?

Duncan leaned across the table. 'I'm speakin' to ya. Ya must listen now.'

He was acting as an earnest older brother again and it was easier for her to feel like John instead of Jane. Except that the dark hair on his arms was so close that if she lifted a finger, she would brush against it. 'I'm listening.'

'We don't fight with swords here. We use words and wits and

a mind to keep them sharp and strong. "No plague is more harmful to the studious than a woman." Remember that. If you succumb, you're nae better than a wild goat.'

'But you…' She didn't know how to ask the question. 'That woman on the street. You were going to, uh, succumb.' Her breast bindings were too tight. She couldn't catch a full breath.

He sat back and stretched his legs under the table. 'Oh, that's just satisfying a man's natural needs. Women's lust arouses us, it's true. You satisfy it, but ya don't wallow in a pit of feelings.'

She choked on a rebuttal. Could she possibly have understood what he said? 'So to be a man, I can lie with a woman as long as I don't have any feelings for her?'

'That's about the lot of it.'

'What about Geoffrey and Mary? He has feelings for her.'

Duncan picked up the gittern and ran his fingers over the smooth wood of the body. The instrument swelled to a curve that put her in mind of a woman's hip.

Hers.

'Geoffrey's a lucky one. Most of us…' He shrugged, letting the thought hang as he picked a tune she didn't recognise. 'Most men live alone, I've found, even when they marry.'

'So you won't? Marry, I mean?' All the hopes she didn't dare think floated in her question.

What did she wish for in those few breaths before he answered? That he would say no? That Little John might live as his companion for the rest of their lives?

'Well, I'm not going to take the Major Orders, if that's what you're asking. But, no, I don't think on marriage much.' There was a finality in his voice.

'What would you do,' she asked, 'if God would grant you any prayer?'

'First I would go to Paris to study,' he said quickly. 'Or even Bologna.'

She nodded, envisioning a trip together to distant lands. She, too, wanted to see Paris. 'And then what?'

He tilted his head, as if the question of what came after was new. 'I'd take that learning back to the hills. But to a land at peace, where I could roam the fells and the tars, swing a spade instead of a sword.' His smile was rueful. 'I might even pen a verse or two.'

If he had said that to another man, his friend would have laughed and punched him in the arm and called him womanly. Yet she couldn't say *I understand. I know just what you mean. Wait till I tell you...*

Yet despite his contempt for the south, here he was. 'Why did you come here, then, if you hate it so much?'

He studied her face so closely she was afraid he would see, even in the dark, the cheek too smooth to grow a beard. 'Have you ever wanted to be something, someone it was impossible for you to be?'

His question shot through her like an arrow. Her mouth was too dry to speak. And if she had spoken, she would have said too much.

She would have told him everything.

She shrugged and nodded, a man's response, leaving him to interpret the gesture.

His fingers kept moving over the strings and he seemed to understand there was no answer. 'Well, that's how it is. It's my home, it's who I am, it calls to me. But there are things I can't abide about it, as well. And there's also a part of me that wants...'

She held her breath. *Wants what?* What can I give you?

But he did not finish the thought. 'The first year I was here, I hated it so much I left at Yuletide. Didn't intend to return.'

'Why did you?'

'There were things I wanted to leave behind.' His smile, a sad thing. 'And things I wanted...' He shrugged. 'Now, I don't belong in either place.'

She nodded, knowing exactly what he meant. She had thought

to live as a man, but now it felt as if she had just donned another disguise. And neither the man's nor the woman's disguise fitted.

'Hell of a thing sometimes, life,' she said.

He smiled then, as if knowing he'd been understood, and the moment of confession was over. 'But it's a grand one, too, for a man who knows how to enjoy it.' He picked a flurry of saucy notes and smiled. 'You've too much ahead of you to worry about marriage, lad.'

She shook her head, hard enough to convince him. 'I'm in no hurry. Not at all.'

'Don't rush into it, but learn to love the ladies and grab all the joy your body will give you. Saint Thomas called it a sin, but he only condemned fornication after he was too old to enjoy what he'd spent his youth doing.' His wicked smile returned. 'You've no fadder, so I guess it will be for me to teach you.'

And she wanted to learn, but not the way he thought.

She wanted to learn how a man and a woman could be together. She wanted to learn *him*. The yearning she had never understood before washed over her.

But if he tried to teach her *that*, tried to teach her what a man should know— 'Well, I'd better concentrate on my Latin until I speak to the King.'

His hand, warm and solid, cupped the back of her neck and he shook it. 'So you're serious about your studies at last. Well, I'm still hungry. Let's see if there's any cheese left.'

They spoke no more of serious things, but her poor body, bound and betrayed, reacted to every lift of Duncan's eyebrow, every wiggle of his finger.

This is who I am, her body yelled. *You cannot ignore me for ever, for I will betray you in the end.*

After that, she looked for reasons to laugh. Talking to Duncan about love and marriage and home had opened a wound she could not mend. And she had no woman she could share it with.

Yet another lesson she could learn from men. Pretend there was no pain. Master those foolish feelings.

A few nights later, she sat with them in the hall, humming along to raucous songs about women that her mother would frown to know she'd heard.

Men, she had discovered, spent a lot of time thinking about physical relations with women.

'Little John looks wide-eyed tonight!' Duncan said. Tune over, his hands kept moving over the strings, restless. 'It's high time you were initiated into the joys of the flesh.'

Such talk was difficult enough when they were alone. With an audience, she feared someone would see her reaction and notice something amiss.

She squirmed. 'You're just feeling your own lack,' she called back. 'Don't go thinking I need what you can't get.'

'Stop it, both of you,' Geoffrey said. 'Don't you know any songs a troubadour might sing?'

A shadow passed over Duncan's face. 'I'll take a good border ballad over a pompous courtly poem.'

Henry laughed. 'Geoffrey's just besotted. All he can think of is love.' He batted his eyes and went into a crude copy of a woman's swoon.

Geoffrey punched his arm and he fell over, laughing. 'I'm a fortunate bastard to have a woman that good who puts up with me at all. The rest of you goats should be so lucky.'

'Better you than me,' Duncan called out, then Jane's eye caught his, and he glanced away, as if wanting to forget the confession he had shared.

And she remembered how she used to make Solay laugh when she imitated the women at court. Mince and curtsy, twitter and cling. She could create a far funnier sketch than Henry could ever draw.

'Good for one thing and not always so good at that!' she called back as she rose and swished across the room.

Swinging her hips, puckering her lips and batting her eyes, she was a cruel parody of the worst a woman could be.

They all howled.

Relishing their laughter, she paraded back before them, but this time, while the others screamed with glee, Duncan's smile fell. A cloud crossed his face and when her eyes met his again, there was something new in them.

Almost as if he saw her as she was.

She dropped her arms and sat, quickly, reaching for the mug, taking a gulp, and then wiping her mouth with her sleeve. She stretched out her legs, taking as much space as she could, then forced the most masculine burp she could muster.

Stupid, stupid to risk being seen as a woman, even in fun. What if he had seen too much?

Duncan forced another laugh between clenched teeth, fisting his hand against—what? The lad's silliness had sparked, well, he must name it. Desire. No wonder for a lad to dress as a girl was forbidden. It had certainly been too long since he'd had a woman if the sight of a boy imitating a maid could ignite such feelings.

Well, he knew what he must do now. He had put it off far too long.

Chapter Nine

A few days later, Jane saw him leave the hall before sunrise, without a word. Hours passed. The bells tolled the day. Dusk settled.

He did not return.

She haunted the window, searching the street, hoping her worry wasn't noticeable. Duncan was a grown man with two good hands. He needed no nursemaid.

Yet he'd warned her against the townsmen. Parliament's session was over long ago. The Fair had ended yesterday. Where could he be?

Then she heard the steps.

She stood so close to the door that he bumped into her as he walked in. 'What th—?'

She did not wait for him to finish. 'Where were you?'

'Get out of my way.' He pushed her aside.

As he climbed the stairs, each step jerky, alternately stiff and loose, she wondered how much ale he'd drunk.

She followed him to his room, where he sat on the bed and picked at the laces of his short leather boots, his back to her.

'Are you all right? Where were you?'

'Go to bed,' he said.

It was not an answer.

'There's some dried herring left. Are you hungry?'

'No.' He never turned his head.

'I was worried.' She bit her tongue. She sounded like a woman, small and weak.

Now he rose, whirling to face her, and wavered on his feet. 'I'm not your responsibility!'

But without her wanting it, he had become so. 'It was after curfew, you weren't home, you had warned me about the town—'

'I was with a woman.'

'Oh.' She swallowed. She shut her eyes, but she could see him clearly. Duncan. The woman. He had kissed her, touched her breasts, joined with her. Jane struggled to breathe, the room suddenly stifling. 'A woman?'

A woman. Jane hated her.

Who was she? Where had he met her? Had he talked to her of home, told her of his longings, or only bedded her, with silent urgent need? Don't wallow, he had said. No feelings.

But he had been gone a long time.

'That's what I said. A woman. Short, curvy creature.' He sculpted a shape in the air. 'Big breasts.'

She swallowed her jealousy. She had no right to it. She had forfeited that right when she had bound her breasts.

'Well, then ya were havin' a good time of it.' His accent no longer fitted her tongue. It made her sound his colleague, a fellow conspirator against the women of the world.

'Yes, I was.' Yet nothing in his voice or his body reflected the joy of a man who had risen, satisfied, from a woman's bed. 'Now get out.'

He flopped on to his bed, covered his eyes with one arm and waved her away with the other.

She lifted her chin to nod, but couldn't complete the gesture of approval. 'G'night, then.'

He was snoring before she left the room.

* * *

'Wake up, lad. I've got something for you.'

Even before she opened her eyes, Jane knew he was drunk again. Kaylied. And she hoped his head and stomach would pay for it.

She struggled to waken and sit up. 'What is it?'

They were the first civil words she had spoken to him since last night. And she had gone to her pallet trying to stop the dreams of him with a woman.

Of him with *her*.

'Shhhhh,' he said, looking at the other boys in the dormitory room, sleeping on their pallets. 'Come on.'

She slept in her clothes, so there was little to do but rise and follow him down the stairs to his room. He shoved her in ahead of him.

'Wait here,' he said and closed the door.

She'd never been alone in his room before. It smelled of him, a mixture of wood and berry and something wild. She trailed her fingers across his bed linen and she wondered what it would feel to lie there—

The door opened. 'Here, boy. Here's one for you.'

When she turned, she saw a woman with anxious eyes standing in the doorway.

Hawys.

They exchanged a silent glance before Hawys stumbled into the room and fell to her knees beside the bed. Pushed.

'It's time you grew up, Little John.' He leaned on the door jam, one knee bent, weaving slightly. 'Yer too old to be a virgin.'

She tried not to meet Hawys's eyes, but it was all Jane could do to hold back sick, unending laughter. A small, barking cough dissolved into a hiccup.

Duncan heard it. 'What's so funny? Aren't you man enough?'

She cleared her throat and stuck out her chest, and propped her foot on the bed, turning her body so he couldn't see that her linen *botellus* was limp. 'Of course I am, but I don't need an audience.'

Duncan hung his head, as if suddenly aware of what he was doing. 'I paid her, but don't be all night about it.' He backed out of the room and slammed the door.

She and Hawys stared at each other. Then Jane shoved the pillow at her and smothered her own scream of laughter in the pallet.

And after the laughter had worked its way out, she dissolved into sobs.

Hawys sat beside her on the bed, arm around her shoulder. 'Poor dear. This wasn't what you thought would happen when you started this, was it?'

Jane shook her head. 'He's a beastly boor sometimes.'

'And you love him.'

She shook her head in protest, but the tears welled up anyway. No, not love. She must not love him. 'He's not worth it.'

Hawys shook her head. 'Few of them are. He's not a bad one, like ya said, but he's got some demons in 'im. And some of them have to do with you.'

Jane sniffed, rubbing her nose with her sleeve. 'Me?'

'He feels something for you and it's driving him mad. He came to me muttering something about being no sodomite.'

Jane shuddered. Wrapped in her own pain, she had never thought he might doubt himself because he cared for the boy John more than he should. 'So it was you he was with. Last night?' The thought made her queasy.

'Well, not so much *with*, if you know my meaning. He came to me, drunk, and fell asleep. Never touched me.' She grinned. 'I told him he'd been a stallion. I tell them all that.'

The tightness in her chest eased. 'Thank goodness it was you, Hawys. Has your brother gone yet?' Her family seemed impossibly far away and infinitely precious.

Hawys shook her head. 'He was working odd jobs at the Fair. He'll likely leave on the morrow.'

'Thank you.' She looked around the room and tried to think. What would a young boy do, the night of his initiation? 'Hawys. I still need your help. What details will convince him that my life changed tonight in his bed?'

'You're going through with this?'

'What else am I to do? If he were to find out now…' She couldn't imagine the consequences.

Hawys sighed. 'I see what you mean. Well, it's not the strangest request I've had. I don't think he will ask too many questions. But you have t'be sure I get outta here.' The anxious look was back in her eyes.

'I will.' She wouldn't have her friend taken to gaol because Duncan was questioning his manhood.

'But you can't keep it up, this disguise.'

'Yes. I can.' As long as she was John, she could stay close to him.

Hawys shook her head. Then, she stood up, ripped the top linen off the bed and threw it on the floor. 'When I scream with delight, you moan, panting like.'

Jane grinned. 'Loud enough for him to hear.'

It was not until John shook his shoulder and Duncan opened his eyes to daylight that he realised he had slept through prime services.

The soft yellow light of morning filled the Common Room, where he had put his head down on the table and never risen. The men must have tiptoed past on their way to class.

Damn them for letting him sleep.

He tried to sit up, but his head was at war with his belly and he closed his eyes again, groaning as it all came back to him. How he had tried to drown his fears in the woman. How he had brought her back and thrown her at John.

Cautiously, he opened his eyes again and squinted at the lad. Little John did not look as if he had been pleasured by a woman all night.

In fact, he looked no different at all.

Duncan leaned on his elbows, not yet able to sit upright. 'Well, lad. How was your first time?'

He thought he saw a faint blush on the boy's cheeks. 'Good. I think she enjoyed it.'

He grunted. '*You* were supposed to enjoy it. Did you?'

He squirmed. 'I'm sure I'll get better.'

'Better?' He cringed. The shout was too loud for his pounding head. He lowered his voice. 'This isn't something you work at like Latin, lad. Your body knows exactly what to do. And it's a damn sight better to do it with a woman than to take yourself in hand.'

He blinked, trying to see whether his lecture had registered, but John refused to look at him.

'She's a lovely girl.'

'Lovely girl? She's every man's woman.' His pounding head only reinforced his guilt. He had known it was all a mistake last night and chosen to ignore it. 'You swive her and be done with it. Like I told you. She's not a woman for marrying.'

The lad looked thoughtful. Not at all the way a man should look after he'd just enjoyed his first woman. 'Who is a woman for marrying?'

'What kinda question is that?'

John's blue eyes, relentless, refused to look away. 'What kind of woman will you marry?'

'Don't start with that. I'm not good for it this morning.' Where did the lad get these notions? 'I'm not thinking about marrying anyone this morning. I am thinking about how I'm going to explain to the priest that the church was locked when they arrived for mass.'

'It wasn't. I took the key and unlocked it for you when I smuggled the woman out before anyone could see her.'

Duncan shook the cobwebs from his head, blinking. John was showing more responsibility than he was this morning. If a Proctor had seen the woman leave, the hostel would be paying a fine until Michaelmas next.

At least the last two nights had answered one question. The boy looked like a boy again. Except…

He peered at Little John, his aching eyes taking in the boy from crown to toe.

A boy with a lumpy ball between his legs where his tarse should be.

Chapter Ten

He stared at the strange shape between the boy's legs and then back at Little John's face.

The boy's eyes followed his, then he backed away, his expression stiff with panic. 'You'll be wanting some food.' He turned his back. 'I'll get something for you.'

Duncan grabbed his arm and jerked the boy back to him.

The motion brought them chest to chest. As he breathed, Duncan could feel the bump, the wrappings on the boy's chest. It was not on his ribs, but higher.

He studied the boy, really looked at the features he had come to take for granted. The fair, wispy hair. The precise lips that popped into a pout just a little too often. As he stared down, John's face magically transformed and Duncan saw clearly what he should have seen all along.

The sight was a blow to his gut, strong as a fist.

The cheeks where the beard had not yet grown—it would never grow. The eyes that had met his so squarely, suddenly, full of timid glances. Chest and shoulders too narrow, hips just a bit too broad for a proper man.

'My God,' he breathed. 'You're a woman.' The thought, awkward, like writing with his left hand.

She shook her head, though she could no longer deny it.

Shook her head so hard and so fast against the truth that she flung womanish tears at his chest.

If anyone saw, if anyone knew—his addled brain could hardly begin to ponder consequences. He grabbed her hand, fire in his palm. 'Come. Quickly.'

The stairs were blessedly empty.

When they reached his room, he shut the door and flung her away, nearly hurling her against the wall, frightened by how much he wanted to kiss, nay, devour her. How much he had wanted it all along. How every day of these last weeks there had been a monster inside him, wanting things from this boy no man should want from another.

Because she was not another. She was The Other.

Something drove him to her. He had to know. Had to put his hands on the final proof. He grabbed her wrists together and held them. How easy to capture a woman. It took only one hand.

She kicked, growled, muttered 'let me go', but she could not cry aloud. It would only spread her secret further.

He forced his right hand down the front of her chausses, searching for it. His fingers burned against bare skin, brushed against soft curls.

And grasped a wad of linen.

He clenched it in his fist and tore his hand away from her. To be so close had been a temptation.

A violation.

He shook the poor, limp roll at her.

'Ya tricked me!' She had made him an oaf. A simpleton. The biggest country bumpkin of all, not even able to tell a tup from an ewe.

But he had not been alone. She had fooled all of them.

Or had she?

'Who knows? Geoffrey? Henry? Anyone?'

She hung her head, refusing to meet his eyes. 'Only Hawys.'

'Hawys? Who's that?'

She lifted her head and he saw a flash of anger that matched his own. 'You bedded her and you don't even know her name?'

For a man, that was not a sin. 'Who is she?'

'She's the woman you threw at my bed.' Her tone was bitter.

And a dull red roar travelled from his ears down his throat. He had heard—what *had* he heard?

Jane answered the confusion on his face. 'We made noises so you would not suspect!'

Relief washed through him. 'No one else knows?'

'No one! And no one must know. Please, Duncan. You must help me.'

His jaw fell in surprise, then closed in anger. He didn't want to help. He wanted to lift his fists and pummel the betrayer until he had rid himself of all rage roaring through him.

But he couldn't hit a woman.

Not even one who had deceived him so basely.

'Help you? Help you do what?' he choked out, finally. 'What can you possibly want?'

'The same thing you want! I want to live, to study, to walk freely without fear of assault or worse. I want to be seen and heard before you look at the size of my pommels.'

God help him, his eyes slid to her chest.

She nodded. 'Yes, I have them. Wrapped safe and tight.'

'The horse, the injury…?' He did not finish the question. All lies. She had played them like a gittern, made fools of them all.

And yet, he wanted to take her in his arms.

He fought the urge. 'It's unnatural, what you've done.'

'I have done nothing I could not admit in confession,' she answered. 'You're the one who made light of sheep.'

He winced, unable to laugh.

Sheep had never tempted him.

She was pacing now. Her imitation of his own teaching style would have amused him under different circumstances.

'What's unnatural about wanting to learn and study and travel without someone saying you can't do this, you can't go there, you can't do that because of an accident of birth?'

'Your birth is no accident. God made you a woman. You're intended for different things.' And right now, all he could think of was that she was intended to lie beneath him.

The narrow bed, largest furniture in the room, yawned in invitation.

'Different things? Do you mean walking the streets, at the mercy of drunken students who might force a kiss, or worse?'

His cheeks burned with the memory. No wonder her stomach had rebelled when they had approached that woman. 'If anyone accosts you, I will kill them with my own hands.'

Her expression softened. 'Thank you,' she said.

She had never looked so much a woman.

He struggled to breathe, to clear his throbbing head, to think of what must be done. He had brought Little John here. The lad, no, the *lassie*, was his responsibility. If discovered, not only would she be at risk, he would lose every ounce of respect he had earned over seven years. The hostel, his master's privileges, it would all be gone.

She must leave. Immediately. He stifled a pang of regret.

'You said you had no family. Was that a lie, too?'

She hesitated. 'I told you I had a sister.'

Good. There was somewhere he could take her to. 'And you're not fifteen, are ya?'

She shook her head. 'Seventeen.'

'Was naught ya told me true?' Anguish gripped his throat. John, who he had treated like a brother. John, who he had told things he had never told another man.

And would never tell a woman.

'That I wanted to study.' She met his eyes then. 'That I would be your faithful friend.'

Friend. Such a petty word for what bound them. *Dinna give your word lightly,* he had warned her. 'I told ya things, things no one ought to know, man or woman. And you told me lies.'

'Only who I was. Not the rest of it.'

'"Only?" Who a man is *is* everything. But yer not a man, are ya? Ya wouldn't know that.'

He paced now, trying to stay out of touching range. What would make a woman act so? Was she possessed? 'Your sister. Your family. Did they beat you?' That might excuse her. He would not return her to people who would hurt her.

He had taken enough beatings of his own.

'No! Never!' The thought seemed to surprise her. 'But they wanted, expected me to be like other women and I'm not. Every day, I failed.'

He recognised the flash of anguish in her eyes. He knew that feeling of trying to fit into a world that wasn't yours.

Have you ever wanted to be someone it was impossible for you to be? he had asked her.

Yes, she had answered.

He gripped her shoulders, wanting to shake some sense into her. 'Ya think a man has no fears? Ya think a man doesn't have to worry about someone bigger and stronger?'

'Not just because he's a man.'

'Then you've learned nothing of a man's heart. Listen to me, John, or whoever you are. If ya've learned anything from living among us, ya should have learned that men live with expectations, too.'

She bit her lip and looked away.

He did shake her, then. 'Haven't ya?'

She looked back at him, the fire still in her eyes, and nodded.

His palms, still gripping her, felt on fire. 'And one of the things a man must never, never do is be attracted to another man!'

He snatched his hands back and stood, unable to look at her. Or at himself.

'But you weren't!' There was the Little John he knew. Expecting all to be forgiven. As she had been forgiven, he suspected now, her whole life. No, they hadn't abused her, this family. They had crippled her with kindness. 'That's over. You…we… I am a woman.'

'Over? You thought I was such an idiot that I wouldn't notice!' And he hadn't. But now that he knew, lust rose in his body, wiping his mind clean of logical thought. 'How long did you think you could live like this?'

'For ever!' Two words. A scream.

He stared, stunned, in the silence that followed.

And then, she started to cry, big, gulping sobs, doubling her over with grief. 'I thought…' each word hard won '…I could go on for ever.'

And his heart cracked.

She had shaken his world, yes, but his pain was secret. His life was still his own. His days would unfold as before, despite the battle raging in his soul.

But with her secret told, the life she had built would be lost. Everything that John knew and loved, wanted and hoped for, would vanish.

He stepped towards her.

She raised her head, stark terror in her eyes.

He paused, suddenly understanding. She was afraid of him now, even though she had lived beside him for so long. But she had lived beside him as John.

'I won't hurt you.' Did he have to say it?

'How can you be sure? You could hurt me and not even know it.'

Her tear-blurred eyes refused to release him. They battled without words, without touch. He waved his hands to ward off her gaze, but her eyes were steadfast.

Gradually, he stopped resisting. Truth, irrevocable, became a ballast, steadying his careening emotions, bringing him to centre, calming the anger.

The lust would not be calmed.

Wordless, he gestured to the bed, the only place to sit. She sat at the foot, and he, cross-legged, safely out of touching range, facing her.

And they studied each other, silent, for a long time.

Now that he knew she was a woman, that was all he could see. Her fair hair, curling in wisps around her face. How beautiful it would be if it were long. Her eyes, circled in blue, open and vulnerable. Her jaw, square, but still feminine. Her lips, not lush, but inviting. All so perfectly a woman's, now that his eyes were open.

Memories drifted before him, all the clues he had missed before, her neat writing, the way she carefully laid the food at the table, a thousand things that now, through the eyes of knowledge, looked different.

John was a woman and Duncan did not know how to treat her.

He had temporarily calmed the war in his soul, but his tarse and his mind were in a shouting match. Just beneath that tunic, her breasts beckoned. She sat cross-legged and all he could think of was that his fingers had been so close, could have slipped inside—

He closed his eyes and stifled a groan, bringing his brain back into control. He was a master of arts, not a randy goat. 'Tell me what happened. Why did you leave?'

'My sister was having a baby. I didn't…I couldn't…they…' She gasped for breath and her words trailed to silence.

He waited for more. She didn't look up.

'They wanted me to marry. A stranger. A man I didn't even know. To share his bed, to service his…'

Something squeezed his heart. He fought it. 'So you must return to marry the man.' Hard to speak the words.

She gave him a glance that a village idiot would have cringed to receive. 'There can be no marriage now.'

She was right. No one would have a woman who had lived among men as she had. The man, her family—they all would assume she had been shared as freely as Hawys and shun her.

Her sister might not even take her in.

'And you want to be married?' She had talked about it so often.

She shook her head, a master impatient with a slow scholar. 'Never. No husband would let me live like this.' She waved her hand, a gesture that included the hostel, the University, rhetoric, grammar and even Latin.

The front door slammed. Scholars back from morning classes, the risk of discovery upon them.

Suddenly, the ramifications, for her, for all of them, became clear.

Duncan had brought her in. Duncan had championed her. If she were discovered, even Geoffrey and Henry would assume Duncan had known all along and that he and she—

His career would be over. But for her, the consequences could be even worse. 'Do you understand what will happen if they find you here?'

'I'll be thrown out.'

'That would be your kindest fate.'

Understanding drained the colour from her cheeks. 'You mean—?'

'I'd never hurt ya, lass. But there's some that would.'

Once they knew she was a woman, the men, betrayed and lusty, might choose a crueller punishment. They would assume she had been Duncan's woman all the time and was now available to all.

Only his strong arms would stop them.

She smiled softly. 'Then I must not be discovered.' He noticed a satisfied quirk on her lips and realised he had been the slow student.

She meant to stay.

St Mary's chimed midday. He should have met Pickering at the Priory long ago. Someone was certain to pound on the door soon, to tell him the parchment was running low or the firewood needed replenishing. 'We will continue as we are for now.' He told himself he'd made the logical choice, not simply the one that would keep her near. 'Until I can sort this out.'

She leaned over to kiss his hand. He snatched it back, afraid of her touch. 'You can't fool them for ever.'

'I'll be more careful.'

He shook his head. Judgement was only postponed. Surely everyone wasn't so blind.

Yet he had been.

'Nothing must change. Keep to your studies. And stay close to me.'

She smiled.

He realised then how close they had been. Duncan and John. John and Duncan. Already like brothers. Or more.

He patted her shoulder awkwardly. Dangerous tears glittered on her eyelashes. She softened beneath his hand and threw her arms around his chest.

Instinctively, his arms enfolded her and he knew, he had known all along without knowing. She was a woman. And he would protect her to the death.

He broke the hug and set her, carefully, away from him, putting a finger under her chin and lifting her head, wanting to drown in her eyes again. 'What shall I call you?'

A trembling smile. 'Jane. My name is Jane.'

But he could not call her Jane. He could not call her any name at all.

Chapter Eleven

'Jane's alive, then,' Solay said. 'God be praised.'

'*Praise God,*' the popinjay squawked.

Justin laughed with his wife. She hugged their baby son. The child wiggled, but was not deterred from her breast.

Though her month of lying in was over, she was still weak and they had insisted she stay abed a while longer. Justin had joined her in their solar at the day's end.

'She was alive last month.' The young boy had brought a note from her yesterday, the only news they'd had in nearly two months. He said he had been given it on the day of the Feast of St Denis.

That was weeks ago. Justin wondered why the boy had waited so long.

Yet he, too, relaxed at hearing the news. It released some of his guilty burden. 'I should never have tried to arrange her marriage.'

'You would never have forced her.' She reached for his hand. Solay knew the reasons why. Reasons no one else would ever know. 'You told her the choice would be hers after she met him.'

But the girl hadn't waited. The merchant had arrived to find his bride-to-be missing, but went home content after a hearty meal and a cask of Gascon wine for his trouble.

Dislodged from his dinner, little William Edward squalled. Solay settled him at her other breast, where he happily sucked again.

The sight of his healthy son erased Justin's pain. He had almost lost them both. His babe and Solay. 'Surely she knew I would take care of her, even if she refused him.'

Solay shook her head. 'Jane had little faith in men to provide.'

It was not surprising. Few men in her life had bothered to take care of her. Neither the King she thought was her father, nor the man who really was.

'Perhaps we should have told Jane the truth,' he said. 'Your mother thought royal blood was a gift to you both, just as you and Jane were her gift to the King, but how can it matter now?'

Solay shook her head. 'The secret is Mother's. Only she can choose to tell it.'

In the quiet, their thoughts mingled in the air.

Solay sighed, coming back to the present puzzle. 'So Jane was in Cambridge last month and on pilgrimage. I did see a journey in her chart, but I did not think it was a long one. And there was something more I didn't understand.' Once she was recovered enough from childbirth to be told that Jane was gone, Solay had turned to her astrology charts, searching for clues. 'But who would go on pilgrimage at this time of year? Tell me again what the note says.'

So Justin did, no longer needing to look at the words in order to remember them.

Forgive me. I hope Solay and the babe are well. I pray for them every day. I am happy. Do not look for me. Familiam cura.

Solay rocked the babe, creasing her brow in thought. 'And the lad said no more?' she asked.

Every time she asked, his answer was the same. 'The only time he opened his mouth was to eat,' Justin said, trying to make her smile.

The boy who had brought it told them little. Someone gave him the message. No, not a blonde girl. He couldn't remember who. Or when. The person had been travelling somewhere on pilgrimage, he thought. No, he didn't know where.

'The Norwich shrine is closer, but she would also have passed that way going to Durham. You told him, though,' she asked, again, 'that she could have been dressed as a lad?'

He nodded. 'She doesn't want us to find her. She just wants us to know she is safe.'

'It was more than that,' she said, stroking the babe's soft brown hair. 'She wanted to know that *we* were safe. She wanted to know about the babe.'

Justin nodded. The only time the lad had spoken voluntarily was to ask about Solay and the child. Suddenly, the pieces fitted. 'That means he will take the tidings back to her.'

Solay sat straighter, dislodging William, who wailed again. 'So he knows where she is.'

'Or at least he knows how to get word to her.'

Solay comforted William. Satiated, the child settled into sleep and Solay's eyelids drooped. 'Go with the boy,' she said. Her voice was still weak, her violet-blue eyes weary. 'Have him show you where he was given the note. There might be a trail there.'

Justin nodded, letting her drift to sleep. He would tell her the truth later. He had planned to take the boy home, wherever that was, but he had slipped away near dawn and left no trail.

Familiam cura, Jane had written. *Care for your family.* She had never read Cato before she left home.

The men they had sent to Oxford and London had failed to find her. Perhaps she had chosen the backwater of Cambridge instead.

He looked at Solay, asleep already, her head and the babe's nodding close together.

No, he could not leave her. Not yet. He would send a man to Cambridge instead. Perhaps he might find something.

A few days later, as Duncan carried the keys to unlock St Michael's for morning serices, his mind was still overflowing.

He should have been asking himself questions: how had she managed to fool them? How long could he hide her? Where was her family? And how could he find her somewhere safe to live?

Instead, as the monks and students filed past him and into

the sanctuary, he was thinking about something else altogether.

How to kiss her.

More than that.

How to take her.

She stood a few rows ahead and to his right, so he could see the edge of her face, watch her mouth move along with the priest's. But he was not thinking of the words of morning mass.

He was thinking of her lips, moving over the Latin words. Thin, yes, but when parted, pressed against his, they would taste sweet on his tongue. Her kiss would tease, as her words did, alternately bold and secretive, reluctant to be claimed.

And when he kissed her, his hands would roam, exploring what lay beneath the rumpled tunic. Square shoulders, yes, but when he lifted her in his arms, he had sensed the balance of her, so different from a man's. Now that he knew, he could see the soft curve of her hip, nudging against the chausses.

She had donned a cloak against the morning chill, but he could picture the awkward bump where the binding struggled to hide her breasts. What would they be like? Small? Pert? Was her nipple as pink as he imagined?

He had dreamed of unwrapping her breasts, shaking to think of his first sight of them. They would be a perfect fit for his hand, a perfect match for his mouth. He would tarry over them, coaxing her to moan and gasp for breath beneath him.

And finally, he would part her legs.

The violence of his vision shook him. It was not anger. He would never hurt her. It was the intensity of his need. Now that his eyes were open, it was as if she stood naked before him, temptation so strong he could barely restrain himself.

He had never felt so strongly about a woman.

The pompous words he had said to her chided him. Satisfy your need. Don't wallow.

But no one else would satisfy him. And he would not, could not take her.

* * *

He spent the rest of the day at Parliament. The session was nearing its end and the final vote tally was still uncertain.

The day passed and he did not see her again.

Yet she stayed lodged in his mind. And he realised that Little John had already been constantly in his thoughts. He had always felt a tug of loss when he parted from the lad, but he had never put a name to that feeling. Now, he realised he had thought of the boy several times a day, worrying whether he was safe, wondering whether he'd done his chores, questioning how well he'd studied his conjugations, and looking forward to their private evening time.

He looked forward to it no longer. Each evening's lesson had become extended torture. But he dare not absent himself now. The master and Little John had become a familiar sight in the hostel. A change in their habits would be remarked upon.

But now, he saw Jane recite vocabulary, not John. He had clapped the lad on the shoulder, ruffled his hair, thrown his arm around him. Now, he could do none of those things without thinking that her breast was within reach of his hand, her mouth within reach of his lips, and between her legs—

He turned, resolute, to review the day's progress with Pickering before he went back to Solar Hostel.

Just to look at her with eyes that *knew* felt like exposing her secret to the world.

Jane sat farther away from him than usual that night, trying to pretend nothing had changed.

The Common Room was empty, so she could recite aloud. The heat from the banked fire was welcome, warming her back against the chill of the autumn evening.

Her voice echoed, sounding as if she spoke in a higher pitch. Was it? Or did it just sound different because he *knew*?

She garbled every line, distracted by the feeling that his eyes could see through her clothes and touch what lay beneath.

The sun set earlier now, casting the room into shadow. She strained to see his lips correct her pronunciation, then stumbled over a word, thinking of them pressing against her.

He shook his head. 'You'll have to do better than that if you are going to speak before the King,' he said.

'Perhaps I've practised overmuch.' She snatched an excuse to avoid the truth. Next to him, she could no longer keep her mind on Latin. 'Let me try a disputation instead.'

She stood and squared her shoulders, proud that she had taken the initiative to go beyond school-boy memorisation. 'A master may ask me to debate this question: Is "Every man is of necessity an animal" true if no man exists? I will respond first with the affirmative argument. Aristotle writes in *Posterior Analytics*—'

He looked at her as if she had two heads. 'You can't talk about that.'

'Why not?'

He looked towards the door, to be sure no one was coming, then whispered, 'Because you're a woman.'

She heard a rushing sound in her ears. Here was her real disputation. *Is a woman equal to a man if a man does not know she is a woman? First affirmative argument.* 'I was a woman last week when we talked about it.'

'But I didn't know it then!'

'Look at me,' she said, grabbing his arm, desperate to make him see her as she was, whole. 'Your argument is illogical.'

'It's all different now.'

As she had known it would be.

She had insisted that nothing would change once he knew her secret, but, of course, everything had.

She dropped his arm, but his eyes did not release hers.

And she could no longer focus on anything other than *amas* and *amat*.

She sighed and pulled away from him. 'If that is your position, then I must find a new master.' Perhaps she could, now that her

Latin had improved. Besides, she might be safer away from his knowing eyes.

His head snapped up. 'You'll do no such thing!'

'A student is always free to choose another master.'

'And what happens when your next master discovers what I know?'

The fire no longer warmed her and she made a fist to stop her hand from shaking. 'All would be lost,' she whispered.

'We cannot talk here,' he said, his voice low and trembling. 'Someone could walk in at any moment.'

He stood without looking back and she followed, reluctant, up the stairs and into his room.

He slammed the door behind them and glowered at her.

Angry. He had been nothing but angry since he had discovered her secret, as if he blamed her for exposing him as a gullible fool.

She felt a flash of sympathy. How would she feel, if after her womanish confidences to Hawys, she discovered the woman's dress hid a *botellus*?

They didn't sit. The bed was too inviting.

'Please.' Calm. Logic. That's what was needed. But she felt the edge of panic in her plea. 'You can't force me to be one of *them*. I don't know how.'

'You had a mother once. She must have taught you something.'

'Oh, yes. She taught me.' Taught her that no matter who you were, being a woman was never enough for anything except to be married to a man. Nothing was yours. Everything was his. And it could all disappear in an instant. 'I just didn't like the lesson.'

'I think it's time,' he said, slowly, after a few moments, 'that you told me about your family.' He leaned against the wall near the window and folded his arms, waiting.

She sighed. She must tell him something without telling him all. 'My mother's...husband died.'

That much was true. William de Weston was her mother's husband and he *had* died, but it was the death of her father the King that had hurled them from the heights of power to poverty's edge.

She continued, watching his eyes to see if she raised questions unanswered. 'And we lived in a little house in the countryside.' He would assume her father had been a merchant, a lawyer or a knight of the lowest level. Few of nobility's sons wanted University training. 'They let me play as I liked, so I learned little of feminine airs and graces.'

'We've little use for those at home, either.' His smile was soft, but his eyes still burned.

She wondered what kind of a woman his mother was. 'When my sister married her lawyer, we—I mean, I moved to the dower house on her husband's family's property.'

'Sticks in the craw, it does, bein' beholdin'.' He nodded, mercifully still assuming her mother was dead, too. 'Your sister, though. She doesn't mind being a woman?'

'Oh, no. She's very good at it.' Beautiful Solay, who drew every man's eye and exuded femininity with every breath. No, Solay had always embraced womanhood and what it could do for her. 'But I don't want that.'

Lightning flickered in eyes that had lost their sympathy. 'You don't *want*? Do you think we can pick and choose what we want in life, as if it's a vegetable market? It's God's world, not ours, and God put you in a woman's body for His purposes, not for your personal enjoyment.'

Her cheeks burned. 'Then He cheated both of us. I tried, but I'm no good at the sewing and dancing and taking care of people.' That was, she had observed, what occupied most of a woman's time. The smothering air of the sickroom seemed to fill her lungs again. She forced a bigger breath and plunged ahead. It all must be said now, before he could interrupt. 'Yes, I'm still breathing, and with every breath I take I want something else. Something more. Some other life.'

As her voice rose, he seemed to become calmer. He stretched out his hand. A few days ago, he would have cuffed her arm or given her a mock blow. Now, he brushed her cheek, tenderness in his fingers, in his eyes. 'So what do you want, Little Jane? What is this other life you're burning for?'

She opened her mouth, but nothing came out. She had thought it was the King and the Court and to see the world, but that wasn't what haunted her now. 'I want to be free,' she said, finally.

'But you are! Fair and free, of gentle birth and breeding. Even I can tell that.'

'You think I'm free because I'm not a serf, but a woman's life is full of nothing but duties and responsibilities, prescribed and expected. I want the kind of freedom a man has!'

Sadness shaded the tenderness in his eyes. 'Ah, my fowty Little Jane. After all the time you've spent among us, haven't you learned the fullness of a duty a man bears?'

'That's different,' she replied sharply, no longer certain that it was. 'Just look at us. You know me better than anyone.' A surprising truth. One she didn't care to ponder. 'But now that you know I'm a woman you won't discuss philosophy with me. You think things are different.'

'They are different. *You're* different!'

She took a deep breath. The more agitated she became, the more feminine she would seem. She tried to keep her voice in John's range. 'It's only the eye in your mind that sees me differently. Do you remember when we first met?'

The memory of the boy by the side of the road made them both smile. She thought there was a special wistfulness in his. He would never have picked her up if he had known.

'You ended up on your buttocks in the dirt as I recall.'

'And you were angry because I thought you were ignorant.'

'You thought so because of where I was from and how I talked.'

'And now you're doing the same. Judging me on your expec-

tations of what a woman should be instead of what you know
Little John to be. And it's no more true than was my judgement
of you.'

He gave her a lopsided smile and the light in his eyes said she
had bested him. 'You've got more mind on you than most
women, I'll give you that.'

She smiled. 'So I can practise my disputation?'

He sighed. '*If* you'll concede that a man's not free either.'

She wrinkled her nose. 'More free than a woman!'

'Free in different ways.'

She filled her eyes with his serious, smiling face. Duncan,
bowed by invisible burdens, was certainly less free than her. The
hostel's future, Parliament's deliberations, even his father's captivity pressed on his shoulders. Life had offered him each responsibility and he accepted every one, never imagining he
could refuse and still be what a man should be.

It was not the expectations of others that ruled Duncan's life.
It was his own.

'Agreed,' she whispered, wondering whether she could ever
be the man he was.

She held out her hand and he shook it. As her hand lay safely
clasped in his, she felt a different kind of closeness.

One only a woman might feel.

Her hand trembled against his and she saw the same feeling
touch his eyes.

Then, he leaned forwards and took her lips, softly. She laced
her fingers through the waves of his hair, clinging, wishing there
was a way to be closer.

As he cradled her head in his hands, pressed his lips to hers,
explored her with a gentle tongue, she felt the elemental,
unavoidable connection of a man and a woman. It went far
beyond the feeble camaraderie that Little John had yearned for.

He broke the kiss, but neither could break the gaze.

'We mustn't,' she whispered. Unnecessary, futile words. 'Ever.'

'I know.' But his answer did not erase the desire in his eyes and his hands still lingered in her hair.

She pulled away, putting a respectable distance between them, still connected to his eyes. 'What if someone should see?'

He jerked his head towards the door, his spine pressed against the wall as if it would hold him back from reaching for her. 'Away with ya, then.'

At the door, she loitered, not lifting the latch. She struggled to slow her breath as the blood pounded through her bound breasts, trying to beat its way to a new kind of freedom.

'T'morrow, then.' She searched his eyes, hoping to see the same longing.

'G'night.'

She opened the door and ran, afraid if she walked she would not be able to break the spell of his gaze.

There was more to being a woman than she had thought. Wonderful feelings that leapt between her and Duncan, tying them together in a marvellous new way. But she did not know how to discover more without losing everything.

Chapter Twelve

Jane sneaked out to meet Hawys the next day, not wanting Duncan to know she had contacted her family.

They stood near each other at the fruit seller's stand, talking as if exchanging opinions about the apples.

'My brother has returned,' Hawys began. 'He said your sister and the babe are weak.'

The news, a blow, reminded her of the duty she had shirked. She wondered what her mother had said of her but was afraid to ask. 'Weak tells me little.' She shook her friend's arm. 'Does "weak" mean tired or near death?'

'I'm not sure.'

'Didn't he ask?' What if Solay were truly ill? What if the babe did not live? 'I must talk to him.'

The fruit seller eyed them strangely and they moved out of earshot.

'No.' Hawys's steady eyes calmed her. 'You were the one who set the rule. It was safer the boy never saw you. He's too young to keep a secret.' She paused. 'Unless you've decided to go home.'

She shook her head. 'Did he see Solay? Or the babe?'

'He just heard talk. She had a rough time, a fever, he thought. And the babe was small. She's still abed most of the time, but she's mending and the babe's gaining weight.'

Guilt weighed on her chest. Abed two months. Her hands would have been welcome. 'Boy or girl?'

'Boy.'

He could write his own fate, then. 'What's his name?'

'William, I think.'

Odd. She had expected Edward, after their father.

'He said they miss you.'

Her eyes burned with unexpected tears. She missed them, too. More than she realised she would.

'They wanted to come back with him, so he left while everyone was still abed. He said he let nothing slip, but I can't be sure. They may come looking.'

'They won't find me.' As long as she was a boy, she would be safe. Wouldn't she?

Hawys studied her. 'Something's happened. You look different.'

'Duncan knows.'

Hawys went pale. 'Only him? No one else?'

Jane shook her head. 'No one.'

'Are you sure?'

Was she? Now that Duncan saw a woman when he looked at her, she felt an extra sway in her hips. In time, in an unguarded moment, anyone might see what he saw. 'For now.'

'You must leave. If anyone finds out, you won't be safe.'

'They won't. We're careful.' Words more prayer than fact.

Hawys raised her brows. 'Ya better be right. Alone in that place with nothing but men. I wouldn't want to be in your shoes.'

'They wouldn't harm me. Duncan wouldn't stand for it.' He hadn't even let the cook thrash the youngest kitchen boy when he had spilled the entire evening meal into the ashes.

'You trust him with your life?'

Brothers. And now her safety was one more burden piled on his shoulders. 'Yes.'

Hawys's weary eyes searched hers. 'You've a fine home and

they want you back, my brother says. He got a heavy pouch of thanks for word of you.'

She swallowed tears. It was strange and belated comfort to realise that it was her family's loving acceptance and tolerance of her wayward behaviour that had turned her into such a misfit. Long ago, even her mother had stopped trying to change her and just let her be as she wanted until she no longer even tried to be anything else.

She felt fresh shame. Not only had she abandoned her sister in her hour of need, she had embarrassed Justin, who had only wanted to help her.

She remembered, too late, how Solay had promised she would not have to marry if she disliked the man. Remembered Justin explaining that a merchant's wife would not have the same strictures as the wife of a noble. What could she say to them now? 'It is better that they forget me.'

'But why?' Hawys's voice brimmed with envy. 'You can have the life you had before.'

'But that's not what I want.' After a tearful, happy reunion, what would be left? Only to tend her mother, the horses and the garden once again. Now she had seen a larger world and could not bear to be trapped in a life no larger than the dower-house walls.

'But you have a choice.' Wonder tinged the woman's words and shamed Jane anew.

Hawys would have thanked God on her knees every day for the life Jane threw away. Under different circumstances, they would never have met, these two women.

'And I choose to stay here.'

'Don't you want to marry?'

Hawys envied her life, but she could not truly understand it. 'I've lived in a house full of men. No man would take such a woman as a wife. Used goods.' Jane's bitter laugh overflowed with hard-won wisdom.

Cruel words. Ones that Hawys knew well.

Strange, finally, to know she could never marry now. At least she had accomplished that. But instead of the relief she had expected, she felt a strange emptiness, like a question for which she had no answer.

So what do ya want, Little Jane?

It seemed as if she had been running *from* something, without knowing what she was running *to*. A man's life had always looked easy. Go where you want, do what you want, tell everyone else what to do. Women could do none of that.

But it was harder than she had ever imagined. Did she want a hard and lonely lifetime hiding among men?

If it could include Duncan, yes.

Pickering arranged for Duncan to attend the last session of Parliament.

He stood to the side of the Priory's echoing hall, clinging to every word of the debate. The proposal was for a small subsidy, a tenth, with the stipulation that it must be spent on defence, including the protection of the border with Scotland.

He looked at Jane's neatly written list before him. If the tally was right, the proposal would pass by a slight margin.

Some who spoke were angry, disgusted with the insistence of the Lords Appellant that the defence of the north should come out of the northlanders' pockets. Others were in no mood to grant an additional tax. What had happened to the last one? It was to be spent on the invasion of France and they'd seen it squandered.

Pickering rose, finally. 'There are those of you who think defending the borders is the job of those who live along them. But we have sacrificed our homes, our cattle, our crops, even our lives so you did not have to. Now, we need your help. We have given all we have in your defence. We only ask for your hand so that we can continue to defend you still.'

There were no further speakers. The vote began.

The subsidy passed.

The ransom would be a separate vote.

Surprised, Duncan saw the King bustle into the hall with an energy he had never seen the man display and rise to address the body.

Rarely did the king stake his power on an issue. If he argued for the ransom of all the men, it was sure to sway the votes they needed.

So when he started speaking about brave men held for ransom, Duncan smiled.

Until he realised that the King did not speak of men. He spoke of one man. Hotspur.

Young Hotspur, who had lost the Battle of Otterburn.

Impassioned, the King challenged the chamber. He would give one thousand pounds towards Lord Percy's ransom if Parliament would give two thousand.

And Parliament voted *aye*.

First, Duncan staggered with disbelief, leaning against the stone columns as if his bones would no longer hold him upright.

Then rage filled him with a fury so strong that only Pickering's calm hands on his shoulders prevented him from strangling the King with his own two hands.

They staggered out together, and it wasn't until they were in the alehouse and Duncan was halfway through his first tankard before he could summon speech again.

'Three thousand pounds,' Duncan said, staring at the flecks in his golden ale.

'For one man,' Pickering echoed.

It was an amount too huge to be grasped.

And nothing left for the rest, the unimportant people like his fadder.

The ale did not soothe the ache in his throat. 'The laird who took him will have enough money to build a bloody castle and Hotspur will celebrate Easter at home with his family.'

No one would be building castles with the pence he and his family could raise for his father.

Duncan slapped his hand against the rough wooden table, which rattled on its legs. 'Can't we at least force them to tell us something? How he's doing?'

'He's not likely to be ill treated,' Pickering reminded him. The business of ransom had become, for many, more lucrative than the war itself. They would capture a rich man, take him home, and swap stories around the fire until the money came through. Next time, the captor might be captive. 'They've got to keep him alive in order to collect.'

'If they knew how little we had, they'd probably kill him. He'll eat more than they'll get.' His father would not take captivity well. As long as he was breathing, he'd be looking for a way home. And if his father tried to escape, they might kill him anyway.

Well, it was King Richard's power that had defeated his eloquence. That meant the King must make it right. 'When does the court leave Cambridge?'

'A day. Maybe more.'

'Then me Majesty is about to listen to a Latin recitation.'

The grey-stone Priory where Duncan had spent so many hours was drained of members of Parliament. Most had started home as soon as the last 'aye' was spoken. The King's household, spread between the Barnwell and King's Hall, took longer to move.

At his side, Jane looked pale, determined and excited. And, he hoped, sufficiently like a lad. He couldn't disguise her with dirt on her nose to meet the King. 'Remember what I told you.'

She nodded. 'The recitation. Other than that, I keep me maup shut.'

It had been a risk to bring her here, but she was the excuse for the visit and she swore she would behave. Besides, she had wanted to meet the King from the first. She would do her best in order to increase her chances of an eventual place in his court.

He had come unannounced, calculating that in the chaos of a household packing to move, he could get close to the King. He strode confidently through the passages, cloaked in his black gown and fur-lined hood, as if he had been summoned.

Jane, taking two steps to his one, stayed close.

No one stopped them as they approached an open door. Beyond, the King, surrounded by his chamberlain and servants packing trunks and stools, had a slight frown on his face.

Duncan cleared his throat, stifling the rage. No good would come of annoying the King now. 'Your Majesty?'

Richard looked up, distracted. But a flash of shame flickered over his blue eyes when he recognised Duncan. Followed by fear. Then, he looked around the room, as if expecting to see a guard.

'You asked, your Majesty, to see the boy again.'

Jane stepped forwards and bowed.

The King's face sagged slightly and then he smiled.

Good. He would make the King comfortable before he asked him about the ransom.

The King walked into the hall and they followed him into the cloister lining the courtyard. The autumn sun shone at a lower angle now, casting cool shadows.

'So how is the boy doing, Master Duncan?' His eyes shifted, as if impatient to be done.

'Quite well.' Better than Duncan had expected. But no doubt the King's Latin wasn't good enough for him to spot any problems.

The King smiled at Jane. 'Fit for a King's service yet?'

She looked to Duncan for permission.

He nodded.

'Not yet, your Majesty, but with diligent effort, I pray I shall some day be able to do you honour.'

Duncan struggled against surprise. In front of the King, the flippant scholar he knew had transformed into a fawning courtier with just the right edge of arrogance that demanded attention. Where had this slip of a girl learned that? 'Recite your piece for his Majesty.'

She launched into a speech from the Latin comedy of Pamphilus, the young man who loved an impossible lady.

She did not 'recite'. She gave an impassioned performance of the hero's lines as he speaks of the woman he loves, forbidden to him by the expectations of society and family. The dialogue had such verve and expression he thought even a passing peasant would understand her meaning.

She ended with a heated flourish and met his eyes.

He forgot the King.

He knew, now, why she had chosen this piece. In the story, Pamphilus got the woman of his dreams. He worked hard for his reward, but in the end, he decided his own fate.

What fate had she chosen?

The King's voice startled him. 'You've done well with him. Tell the clerk to give you ten pence. And one for the boy. Keep up with your studies, young John.'

Ten pence. A gallon of wine. He might just drink it all himself.

The King turned to leave.

'Your Majesty, there's something more.'

The King's smile flattened as he turned back. 'Yes?'

Duncan summoned all his persuasive powers. 'Parliament approved a subsidy. It remains only for your Majesty to give the word for troops to march to the defence of the north.'

In reality, Duncan knew it would take more than the King's word. Money had been allocated, but it remained to be collected and dispersed. If more troops hurried north, however, that would not be Duncan's concern.

'And I shall,' the King said, with a smile. 'When the Council meets in January, I shall insist upon it.'

Duncan stifled a groan. More months would slip by before help arrived. But he bowed his head anyway. 'My thanks, your gracious Majesty. There is one other thing I would ask. About my father.'

The King's eyes showed no recognition. 'I do not know your father.'

He felt a slight tug on his robe. Jane's eyes flickered from his to the cloister's stone floor. Emphatically.

His body stiffened. He had never been a man who bowed easily. 'My father, your Majesty.' And then, he forced his knees to bend and he dropped into submission, wondering what the old man would think if he saw him now. 'He is one of those taken hostage by the Scots while fighting valiantly to protect the King's interests along the Border.'

The King's stare continued to be blank. Did he mean to make a man beg?

Beside him, Jane dropped effortlessly on to one knee. She seemed to be able to supplicate without ever demeaning herself.

'Your gracious and generous Majesty had suggested Master Duncan request your help to aid his release, should Parliament not see fit do to so.'

Regret and shame returned to Richard's blue eyes. They met Duncan's, just for a moment, as another man's. 'Your generous Majesty is, at the moment, prevented by Parliament and by a tight-fisted Council from being free to act as a monarch should.' The King paused. 'What have they asked?'

Resisting the urge to shout that the King had just spent a huge sum on one man, Duncan told him the amount.

The man's eyes widened in surprise. 'So little?' It was a pittance, compared to what they'd spent on Hotspur's release.

'To your gracious Majesty, yes,' he began, burying his anger. 'But we have only a tower, some sheep and a few fields burned to stubble. It will take us years to raise such a sum. You have been wise, and acted when it was needful, as when you so bravely led the invasion that drove the French from Scotland. We need you to act now, so that we may continue to defend your borders.'

His Majesty sighed. 'Come and put your case before the Council in January. We should be able to loosen such a sum without calling Parliament back into session.'

'Your Majesty,' he said, dipping low, without genuine gratitude.

As they walked back to Cambridge, the late-day sun slanting into his eyes, he did not know whether to celebrate the second chance or mourn his failure.

'Can your neighbours not help ya, then?' Jane had taken to echoing his accent whenever they spoke of personal things.

'Those who have some coin will need it to buy back their own men.' Those men, one by one, who might be home by Yuletide. By Candlemas. By Easter.

While Stephen of Cliff's Tower wasted away in a lowland Scottish cell.

They passed by the convent of St Radegund, then the road climbed over the rank-smelling King's Ditch and back into town. Wisps of smoke curled from chimneys on every street, the melancholy smell of burning wood making him long for home.

'Did I make you proud?' Trouble touched her eyes.

Silently, he chastised himself. She had spoken to a King today. And well, too. 'Just as you promised. You'll be the King's chief counsel before you're thirty.' The thought did not bring him joy.

'That wasn't what I meant.' Jane looked up with sombre eyes. 'I was trying to help your father.'

And any words he might have spoken lodged, unmoving, in his throat. How long had it been since someone had truly wanted to help him?

If he still walked beside John, he would have swept the boy into a gruff hug that would pass for thanks. But he walked with John no longer. And the perilous temptation of Jane's body suddenly seemed a small threat compared to the lure of Jane's heart.

'Thank you, Jane.'

He could not remember the last time he'd said the words.

Chapter Thirteen

'First person present, not first person perfect! How many times must I tell you?' Duncan snapped. 'Again.'

So she tried again.

She had insisted they go on with the lesson tonight, though she longed to celebrate her victory. But with the King's refusal to grant the ransom, Duncan was in no mood for merriment.

And she wanted an excuse to stay near him.

How could a King be at the mercy of Parliament and his Council for such a paltry sum?

The light, and the few remaining scholars, left the room.

Darkness had always protected her before. In the dark, no one could make out a man or a woman.

But the gloom touched her differently tonight, wrapping them together in the empty room with their shared secret.

She finished the conjugation and he did not give her another. He had become invisible, silent and gloomy in the shadowy room.

'That's enough for tonight,' he said, finally.

She sensed him rise and stretched out a hand, groping in the darkness. Her fingers faltered when they touched his chest. Immediately, he grabbed her hand and pulled it away, but she laced her fingers with his so what began as holding her away turned into holding her tightly.

His chest rose and fell and she gasped for a breath that didn't drown her in the scent of him.

Then his hands were on her shoulders and her back was against the wall. His lips, his tongue, claimed her mouth. She melted into the sensation, no longer man or woman but only feeling, flowing with him like a raging stream joining a river, with no separation between the ending of one and the beginning of the other. She was truly *with* him, as she had longed to be, day after day.

Then something shifted.

His kiss, once urgent and eager, became demanding and cruel. With a woman's instinct, she knew she had lost him, lost the moment of joining. No longer a reward for being a woman, his kiss punished her for not being a man.

She turned her head, ripping her lips from his, gasping for air. His tattered breath throbbed against her ear.

Then his head fell. Defeated, he dropped his arms and turned his back on her.

She reached for his shoulder.

He whirled to face her, so close she could see the raw frustration in his face.

'No more games, John, or Jane, or whoever you are. I can't play at kissing while you frolic in a boy's garb.'

'This is no game.' She kept her voice low and urgent. No one must discover them.

'Then decide. Woman or boy. Which are ya?'

'You're the one who plays now. You know what I am.' She was a woman. She could fight it, but not deny it. Not when she was in his arms.

'Then *be* a woman, Jane.'

'Don't call me that! And stop looking at me that way.' The plea in her voice matched the urgency in his eyes. Looking into them, she was ready to throw it all away, just to be in his arms again.

'Ya canna keep this up. I canna stand it.'

Her breath caught in her throat. She knew what an admission that was for him. She couldn't stand it either.

'Choose. Man or woman. Ya can't be both.'

But she was. Living among them, she was both and neither, a creature trapped in purgatory without hope for salvation. 'I can't be just one.' And certainly not just a woman, trapped in a cage of thou-shalt-nots immovable as iron bars.

'What's the matter with being what you are? A woman's life has advantages.'

'Advantages?' Her anger matched his now, burning through the darkness, not as a woman's pique but as a man's righteous wrath. 'All I see is privileges denied. Privileges that a man has only to stretch out his hand and take.'

'It looks so easy t'ya, does it?'

'Looks?' Her fury gained strength. 'I can't even open a book without permission!'

'What does a woman need a book for? You already know more than I'll ever learn from any book!'

Her jaw dropped, but no words escaped.

'Men are just dumb animals, struggling on earth under a yoke of responsibility.' He lifted his hands and she could almost see the weight of manacles on his wrists. 'You can create beauty and order and softness—hell, even life. There's no book that will teach me that.'

She remembered the conversations, then. *Mysterious. Feelings. Mutable.*

If he does not master himself, she will master him.

All unexpressed fears of some mystical power, some secret knowledge locked inside a woman's body. Knowledge just as mysterious and unattainable to her as to them.

'I have no secret knowledge.' She had searched for it all her life, this *thing* that came so naturally to other women.

'You have it and you don't even know.' He shook his head. 'I should have seen you were a woman from the beginning. You bring in leaves to grace the plain wooden table. You fluff the pillow and choose a blanket for its pleasing colour, rather than its warmth. Who taught you to do those things?'

She squirmed. 'My mother?' She remembered only thinking she had failed the lessons.

'No one. You're a woman, just like all the rest.' A tinge of disgust mingled with the amazement in his voice. 'There'll be no more lessons. I made you presentable for the King. Now stay away from me. Study on your own. I can't bear to look at ya.'

'But what of my vow?' she said, hating her womanhood anew. 'We're companions. Close as brothers.'

He shook his head. 'Ya canna be m'brother, lassie.' The rough edge of his voice threatened to break.

He turned his back on her and started up the stairs.

'But I gave you my word,' she called to him. 'Would you have me break it?'

His step never paused. 'It was broken when ya gave it.'

As natural as it had been for them to be together, it was now as natural to stay apart.

Duncan asked Geoffrey to take over her Latin drills, pleading the excuse of catching up with his own neglected studies. Geoffrey's lessons must have concluded more quickly than Duncan's had, and he seldom saw Jane, or John—he must try to think of her that way still—reciting aloud in the Common Room.

It was mid-November before he heard her again. He came down to take heat from the common fire as she finished a reading. 'You've made good progress, John,' he said, with a moment's regret. He had wanted to be the one to guide her as she grew into a scholar ready to take on grammar, logic and rhetoric.

She bobbed her head and muttered thanks and something about helping cook with the evening meal, then left the room.

As she walked away, Duncan saw her hips move with a woman's unmistakable sway. Was he the only one who could see that *he* was a *she*? Or had she turned more woman, now that he knew the truth?

Duncan glanced at Geoffrey's face in fear as she disappeared. A frown creased his friend's narrow forehead.

'Duncan,' he said, in a whisper, so the two senior men in the corner could not hear, 'John walks like a woman.' A stunned look of horror blossomed across his face. 'Could it be the lad is a girl?'

Duncan let the silence stretch. He should have expected this. He should have had a ready answer.

Instead, he burst into laughter.

'You laugh at everything,' Geoffrey grumbled, 'but I'm serious. Do you know what this means? All this time—'

Duncan kept laughing, forcing his howls to rumble through his throat, desperate for time to think. Finally, nearly choking, he found his voice. 'A woman, eh? Then she's got the biggest tarse I've ever seen on a woman.'

He grinned, his cheeks aching with the effort.

Shock and relief mingled on Geoffrey's face. 'You've seen it? When? The lad's always been too shy to show his elbow.'

When? His laughter faded. 'He had to take a piss one night on the way back from the alehouse.'

Geoffrey's eyebrows lifted, as if not convinced.

'I swear.' Duncan prayed God would forgive the lie. 'You must really miss Mary if you're seeing a woman in every school boy's backside.'

Geoffrey's fist was headed for Duncan's face before he noticed the grin. Sheepishly, he let it fall. 'A little more than a month until Yuletide break. I'd better keep my thoughts under control, eh?'

Duncan laughed again, as if the subject were closed, but it was just beginning. He couldn't even look at John now without seeing, worse, *wanting* Jane. How long would it take until the next person saw, and suspected, what Geoffrey had?

She had become good at avoiding Duncan. Very good.

So when it was time to celebrate Henry's successful disputation, she went along to the alehouse. Henry would be incepted as a master in the spring. That was cause for celebration. But she sat at the end of the table, as far away from Duncan as she could, and finished the evening without exchanging more than a word or two.

She ignored him, too, when he motioned her over as they walked home. Geoffrey and Henry walked ahead, leaving them together, and Duncan took her arm to help her around a puddle.

She tugged it away. 'Stop treating me like a girl,' she whispered. 'You'll give it all away.'

'Geoffrey already suspects,' he hissed. 'Conjugate *amo*.'

She glared at him. Love was not a word she cared to parse. 'Strange choice.'

'Just do it,' he said, nodding his head towards the two in front of them. 'Loud. So they can hear.'

'*Amo, amas, amat*,' she called out, then lowered her voice. 'Why do you think Geoffrey suspects?'

'He watched you walk out of the room the other night and said you walked like a woman.'

She glanced ahead. As she tried to stay away from Duncan, she had spent more time with Geoffrey. She had more chances to make a mistake. 'It's your fault. You've been looking at me strangely.'

'I have not. I just saved your scraggy hide.' He called out loud. 'Now the plural.'

'How? *Amamus, amatis, amant*.' She shouted the Latin.

'Good. Now the imperfect.' He waved at Geoffrey and Henry, ahead of them, then dropped his voice to whisper at her. 'What could I do? I laughed.'

'Laughed?' She matched the rise and fall of her voice to his to hide their conversation. '*Amabam, amabas, amabat, amabamus, amabatis, amabat.* It's nothing to laugh at.' She'd been lulled into a false sense of security. Gaol, or worse, was as close as one wrong move.

'*Amabant*, not *amabat*. I needed time to think.'

'*Amabant*. So what did you say?'

'I told him I'd seen you piss and you were certainly a man.'

Then *she* laughed, relief and the sense of belonging flowing through her once more.

'Lower your voice,' he said. 'You laugh like a girl.'

'What's so funny back there?' Geoffrey called back.

'The story's too long to tell,' Duncan called back, setting her into another gale of laughter. 'It's about a proctor and a beadle and the subjunctive, passive, imperfect tense.'

'Oh, I know that one!' Henry yelled. 'It's dirty.'

'*Amarer, amareris, amaretur!*' Jane called, with glee. The laughter faded and she bit her lip, serious again. 'Are you sure he believed you?'

Something flickered across his face. 'I think I made sure of it. I insulted his manhood. Now, what about the plural?'

A moment's regret touched her. Now Geoffrey, who had been the kindest, sweetest of them all, was being made to suffer for her sin. '*Amaremur, amaremini, amarentar.*'

'*Tur. Amarentur.*'

She flashed him a sideways smile. 'So you told him you'd seen my *botellus*, eh? It's not exactly a lie. You had it in your hand.'

She saw a flush of red on his cheeks and around his ears. 'It was all I could think of.'

She grinned and held her hands a generous foot apart. 'Did ya tell him it was this long?'

He grinned back. 'With feet as small as yours? Not even half that size.'

And he didn't seem to mind when she wrestled him down into the mud of the frosty street. For a moment, at least, she was one of them again.

Chapter Fourteen

A few days later, Jane went to the alehouse after the morning meal to order the hostel's weekly supply.

She didn't look carefully at the stranger at first. After these three months, Jane knew who belonged and who didn't. She could distinguish a bachelor from a master, a doctor from a merchant and an innkeeper from an apothecary by dress and demeanour.

This man, average height, with overlarge ears, was none of these.

He was, she realised in horror, a footman in her family's service.

She stepped into the alewife's shadow, averting her face. Had Hawys's brother said too much? Did they know she was in Cambridge?

'Can I help you?' the alewife asked him.

'I'm looking for a fugitive girl.'

Jane ducked her head lower, torn between fear of being found and desire to ask for news. Her pounding heart nearly leapt from her chest.

'No new girls that I've seen,' the alewife answered. 'What's her crime?'

'Oh, nothing like that. She ran away from her family and they are looking for her.' He took off his cloak and sat. 'I'll take one. It's a cold road to travel in November.'

Jane edged closer as the woman poured a brew and chatted

about the evils of travel. Would he recognise her? Could she fool him? She must if she were to have any more news of home.

'What's the girl look like?' she asked, in her lowest tones. She slouched against the table and kept her hand over her nose and mouth, as if stroking her cheeks and thinking.

'About seventeen. Fair haired, blue eyed, not very round.' He laughed, not barely looking in Jane's direction.

She hunched her shoulders against the insult. 'Why did she leave?' She was curious. What would this man say? What had her family told them about her?

'Now that's the mystery of it. Why would she leave home? She had a wonderful life, a loving family and a bridegroom on the way.'

She swallowed the lump in her throat, unable to speak. The life she'd seen as a prison looked like a palace to him.

The alewife shook her head. 'A silly young girl from a fine family run away? I've never heard of such a thing.'

'Fine family indeed.' He leaned forwards to whisper and the alewife leaned in to hear. 'Her mother is Alys de Weston.'

The alewife gasped. 'Then her father was the King!'

He nodded. 'Royal blood in her veins. That's for certain.'

She felt herself standing taller, as she always did at the mention of her father.

'A sad story,' the alewife said, shaking her head. 'A woman alone can come to no good, especially one who's young and untried. I've seen my share come here, that I can tell you. But not this one. She probably had no better sense than to fall into the clutches of the first outlaw she met and was probably dead in a trice.'

If Duncan had been a different man, that might have been her fate.

'That's what I told them.' He shrugged. 'They've had me traipsing from London to Oxford and every burg in between. I think it's like going from Pilate to Herod, myself, but I do what I'm told. Now they think she might be here.'

The alewife clucked over his hard lot and put the tankard on his table.

He took a generous swig, wiped his mouth on his sleeve and sighed with satisfaction. 'And you know what else? Her family thinks she might be dressed as a man.'

Jane slumped lower, her arms wrapped over her chest to hide the binding that seemed suddenly conspicuous.

He didn't wait for comment, glad to have an audience. 'But I say that's foolish talk. She used to dress like that around the grounds, but no woman could do that. Not out in the world.'

Satisfied that this oaf, like all of them, would never see what was in front of his nose, Jane lifted her head and raised her voice. 'Do they think she's in Cambridge?'

'They had word she'd been seen. Some lad brought a message.'

'I might have seen her,' Jane began, heart still pounding. Would he recognise her? 'What was her name?'

He sipped his brew, giving her barely a glance. 'Jane. Jane de Weston.'

A stranger's name, now. No longer her own. 'Fair haired, you said?'

He nodded. 'Might have been a pretty one if she'd ever taken care of herself, but she lived like a ruffian. They never made her do anything, I'll tell you. She was as spoiled as rotten fruit. Good riddance, I say.'

Her cheeks burned and she swallowed hard to clear the lump in her throat. Had all the servants seen her thus? 'Well, I met someone like that on the road last autumn, but I think she *was* dressed as a man.'

The man shook his head. 'There you go. You knew right away, didn't you? Poor girl. Might have been spoiled, but she didn't deserve such a fate. Probably dead by now.'

She had wanted to reassure her family, not frighten them. 'Oh, I don't think so. She was with a group of pilgrims, so she seemed well protected.'

'That's what the boy said, but autumn's no time for a pilgrimage.'

'Perhaps her need was urgent. An illness? Private penance?' She felt the need for penance now, in a way she never had before.

He sighed. 'When I tell her family that, they'll send me chasing after shadows again. Well, what else, lad? Where were they going?'

'To Godric's shrine.' Finchale was a long way north from Cambridge. Too far for them to follow, she hoped.

'I thank you. It's not much, but it's something. Her family'll be glad to hear something. Well, I'd best be on my way.'

She gripped the table. He mustn't go. Not before she could ask about Solay.

She raised her voice to stop him, as he was halfway to the door. 'The boy I met, he mentioned a sister who was with child.'

'That would be her, then.' He paused, as if surprised.

'What happened to the sister? And the babe?'

'Ah, they had a rough time, the Lady Solay and little William.' He shook his head and continued towards the door. 'But they seem better now. Well enough to travel with Lord Justin soon.'

She wanted to stop him, to find out where they were going and why, but to him, she was a strange young man who would have no reason to care about these two.

'That must have been her, then,' she called out. 'She was worried about her sister, the one I saw. You can tell her family that.'

He waved at her without looking back.

Please tell them that.

By December, Duncan had to break the ice on the bucket before he could splash frigid water on his face.

Yuletide approached and the hostel started to empty. There was a month's break before the Lent term, but many sneaked away early to get a head start on a long journey. Winter travel was uncertain and they were eager to return to their own fires and families.

Henry and Geoffrey were the last to leave.

'You won't come with us?' Henry asked Duncan.

'I don't want to risk missing the Council meeting.' An excuse, but true. He must be at Westminster on January 20.

Duncan went home as seldom as possible. Now, he could not face his father's empty, accusing chair.

Besides, he had never, for a moment, considered leaving Jane here alone.

'We'll try to bring news of your fadder, eh?' Geoffrey said.

Duncan nodded his thanks.

'And don't get into too much trouble.' Henry waved as they rode away.

'How can I?' he called back. 'I'll be playing nursemaid to the lad.'

Jane had steadfastly refused to tell him anything more of her family, or to consider dropping her disguise. Now, alone in the hostel, he would finally have time to consider what to do next and to persuade her to agree.

He wished the idea did not excite him so much.

She would avoid him, Jane decided, creeping up to the empty boys' dormitory before the sun set. She piled three pallets on the floor, and dragged three more on top of her blanket, then lay there, shivering, her toes stiff with cold.

When she heard him coming up the stairs, she buried her head beneath the pallets, hoping he would think her asleep.

She breathed evenly, carefully, as his steps approached. A moment's quiet. He would decide she slept then go away.

Instead, he ripped away her covers.

She curled tighter against the cold and squeezed her eyes shut.

'I know you're not asleep.'

She opened one eye to see him squatting beside her. 'I was before you froze me to death.'

'Get up. You're coming to my room.'

She gritted her teeth to keep them from chattering. 'I'd rather stay here.' To share his room would be too tempting. She would want to share his warmth, as well.

'It's freezing in here and we canna pay for firewood to heat two rooms.' He raised his eyebrows, a challenge. 'I'd say the same if you were a man, so get up and stop fighting logic.'

His smile was lopsided, but she could not read his eyes in the dark.

'I'll not be layin' a hand on you, if that's that you're thinkin'.'

It was. And she didn't want him to know it.

Grumbling, she rose and followed him down the stairs, dragging her blanket behind her.

Glorious heat surrounded her as she crossed the threshold of his room. Her muscles, tightened against the cold, became slack.

She would never take it for granted again, the unimaginable luxury of a fireplace in a sleeping chamber. The wood, precious as candles, crackled with dancing flames. In his small room, unlike the Common Room, the warmth reached every corner.

'Take my bed.'

In the firelight, she could study his eyes. Grey, like moving clouds, with a mix of belligerence and tenderness. 'I will *not* sleep with you,' she began, ready to fight.

'For yourself. I'll sleep…' He looked at the empty space before the fire. 'On the floor.'

'Now you're treating me like a woman.'

'Well, you are and we both know it.'

She opened her mouth to point out that he had just switched sides and made a contradictory argument and had therefore lost the disputation, but he didn't give her time.

'Be quiet and get into bed. I won't have you catching cold.'

She should have made her argument, but the bed beckoned and she felt warm for the first time all day and she decided they could discuss it in the morning.

He stood in the doorway as she pulled back the covers and

snuggled into bed, still armoured in her clothes. She turned on her side, away from him, and tugged the blanket over her shoulder.

The heat of his gaze warmed her as much as the fire's flames. She had slept with a room full of boys for the entire term without feeling exposed, but the boys hadn't spared an extra glance for 'John'.

But Duncan knew who she was.

'Sleep well.'

'Where are you going?'

'I'll be back. After you're asleep.'

She heard the door close and he was gone before she could turn her head.

She must have dozed before the fire's flames faded and a chill crept over the room. Awake and alone, she lay still.

Waiting.

Lying snug in his bed because he had given it up for her comfort. He had taken care of her as well as her family had and she had not even thanked him.

A few soft notes from the gittern floated up the stairs as if trying not to be heard.

She turned on her back to listen with both ears.

He only played two kinds of songs. The first tunes were the rollicking songs that made the men clap their hands and bang their tankards and join their voices in a raucous bond. The others were melancholy ballads in a minor key, eerie and wild songs of loss and loneliness and longing for home. These were the ones he played alone, when he thought no one would hear.

This was neither.

She did not recognise the tentative notes. He plucked a phrase, first one way and then another, changing it a little each time, as if creating something new.

There was longing in this melody, too, but with a lilt of hope. A hint of optimism.

It was a question.

It was a plea.

Was it a new way of calling out to his beloved hills?

Or did the notes call to her?

He must have waited to play until he thought she slept, not meaning for her to hear, but the melody spoke of a longing that matched her own.

The longing of a man for a woman.

She rose, oblivious to the cold. One by one, she removed her chausses, braies and tunic, baring her skin, so the tune could touch her most private places. The melody seemed more certain now, as if he had settled on the notes he would use. Notes that played over her skin like fingers.

His.

She folded each piece of her clothing carefully and laid it aside. Finally, the only thing that covered her was the linen binding her breasts.

And she sat, cross-legged on his bed, grasped the end and started to unwind.

He climbed the stairs slowly, no more ready for bed than when he'd left, but hoping he had stayed away long enough that she slept.

But he had not really been away from her. She had been in every note that flowed through his fingers and into the cold, clear night air.

He had contained his longing when the house was full of people. But now they were alone. And he fought to remember that he must not have her.

He opened the door, slowly.

She sat in the middle of his bed, wrapped in a russet blanket, not slumped in near sleep, but erect, as if she had been waiting for him. She had lit a profligate candle and set it near the dying fire.

He gritted his teeth and set the gittern down. 'What's the matter? Are you ill?'

Silent, she stepped off the bed, opened the blanket and stood before him naked, proud at last, it seemed, of what she was: unmistakably, gloriously, female.

Chapter Fifteen

All words, all thought, all logic deserted him. And every ounce of power in his body rushed to his tarse and reached for her.

She tried to hold his gaze, but he glanced first at her breasts, finally free, small and pert, soft, pale as the moon, and as beckoning as he had seen them in dreams.

Her skin was fair, never touched by the sun, always protected from the wind. Surely God had never given any woman such fair skin. All the times he had joked with Little John, there had been this beautiful, delicate, hidden land beyond his view.

His eyes followed the curve of her waist, impossibly small, now that he could see it, and watched it swell into a hip that would never, never fall straight as a man's. He devoured each vision and moved greedily to the next, knowing her eyes were steady, waiting for his to meet them again.

Between her legs—Blessed Mother of God, he mustn't look, but his eyes were no longer within his control. A pale tangle of hair hid her woman's secret.

She dropped the blanket and stepped towards him.

He tried to talk, tried to swallow, tried to say her nay. A man's mind was stronger than a woman's feelings. Only the unlettered let their lust run free. All the sages said so. He struggled to resist. Once they had lain together, nothing could be as it was. She could never be John again. He understood it if she did not.

None of his thoughts would form into speech.

She did not wait for words. Satisfied he had seen his fill, she reached for the tabard he had donned to ward off the cold, pushed it off his shoulders and slid it down his arms. She did not fling it on to the floor or toss it across the room as he would have done. Instead, she folded it with reverent fingers and inhaled the scent of his skin that lingered on the cloth before she placed it on top of the small pile of clothes on the trunk at the foot of the bed.

Stripped of his first protective layer, he should have felt the cold. Instead, heat crackled through him, ignited by her touch.

His tunic was next. She grasped the hem and pulled the rough, green wool over his head. Averting her eyes, she turned it right side out again, shook and folded it, so it joined the tabard on top of the trunk.

He was fascinated by her fingers, short and deft, her feather's touch more arousing than if she had grappled him into bed as soon as he entered the room.

Forced to wait, his passion deepened, urgent need clashing with deliberate ritual.

How could she move so calmly when it was all he could do to keep from throwing her onto the bed? Did she feel none of the pounding desire he did?

Her eyes were averted now, but her lips parted slightly. Her breasts rose and fell. Yes, she was fighting desire, too, taking step by inevitable step, without rushing to the end.

He forced himself to stillness. If he released the river of passion raging in him, it would drown them both.

He must not take her that way. Not her first time.

Restraint took all his strength. He stood, rooted like an oak, while she pulled off his linen chemise. She held her arms away from him, tried to keep her fingers from his skin. Still, something brushed his chest. Was it her fingers, the whisper of the fabric as it left him, or the night air?

When she knelt, he looked down at her shoulders, broad for a woman. He understood, now, with the small corner of his brain that still functioned, how she had carried a tunic broadly enough to skim over her flattened breasts.

She untied his chausses and braies together and pulled them down, releasing his tarse to sway free, strong and proud. He closed his eyes and groaned.

She laughed.

He opened his eyes.

She looked up, a smile tugging the corner of her mouth, her hands held a foot's length apart.

'Well, now. There's a man with feet full grown,' she said, adopting her border-country lilt.

He laughed, grateful for the chance to breathe. 'Honey, now that I've seen you, I'll be growin' still.'

She rose, so close that her nearness touched and he trembled with everything she offered and he wanted.

She grabbed his arms, then, tightly, the softness gone.

'I want you,' she said. Her eyes, blue, fierce, met his and he saw something new in them.

A sound fought its way up his throat, as much a moan as a word. 'Jane.'

And then, it was too late for words.

He took her lips, filling her mouth with his tongue. She tasted of almonds and sweetness and beauty and hope.

Her body pressed against his, breasts, hips, thighs. He stroked every bit of her skin he could reach, tangled his hands in her hair, wild in his fingers.

He breathed heavily, as if he had already run a mile.

Slow. It must be slow.

He held her at arm's length, not because he wanted to part from her, but to fill his eyes again with Jane, sweet Jane, who had already filled his days and nights and thoughts.

She held up her chin, her smile, shy.

'How could I have not known?' he murmured.

'I think you did,' she answered, 'all along.'

He must have. She had tugged at him from the first moment. His need to help her, his irritation when she refused, somehow, even then, he knew.

She ran her hand down his arm, her skin impossibly fair next to his. 'You see? You also know things that are not in books.'

What he knew had no words, only a feeling, a humming in his veins like the melody of a song searching for its harmony. 'I know that we are going to make love. And I am going to fill ya until y've nae room for anything but me.'

'I think,' she said, eyes never wavering, 'you already have.'

And as he took her lips again, he knew she was right.

He kicked the discarded blanket out of the way, lifted her on to the bed and lay beside her, never letting his hands leave her skin.

She did not lie placid, like some women, a passive receptacle for his lust. Her kisses were eager and deep, her hands bold and daring. Her palms cupped his shoulders, then skimmed his chest, her fingers threading through his hair.

'You are so different,' she murmured, as her finger circled the nipple on his chest, a pale imitation of her own.

He pulled her hands away. His breath had quickened at her touch and he must not get too far ahead of her. 'You are the one who is different.' He kissed her nipples, reverently, marvelling at the softness of her breast against his lips, the hardness of her nipple against his tongue.

She arched against him. A moan caught in her throat.

Her hands slid down his stomach, then her fingers wrapped around him, stiff already. At her touch, his tarse jumped, throbbing against her hand.

'You're hard and you're soft.' Wonder touched her words. 'How could I have thought I could imitate this wonderful thing?'

'Why would you want to?' he gasped.

Matching her eagerness, he tangled his fingers in the soft

curls between her legs. She opened without hesitation, trying to pull him inside with trembling fingers.

'Shh. Don't hurry, love,' he said. He spoke to himself as well as to her.

He had never made love to a virgin.

The women before, common women, the occasional randy widow, already knew what lovemaking was about. They had one of two patterns: either lie silent and still or bleat like a sheep on shearing day to express excitement. Their moulds had been set long ago by other men.

They expected nothing from him. He was a man. That was enough.

But he would be all she knew of lovemaking. What he did now, this minute, would create her expectations for the rest of her life. His touch would be her song, and in any man who came after, she would look for someone who could sing the same tune.

The one that made her glad to be a woman instead of a man.

So he gritted his teeth and held himself back and tried to remember what he knew of a woman's body.

I know what to do with it. She had heard him boast of his prowess with women. But what he knew, he now realised, was *his* body, not hers. Lips, breasts, sheath. He knew where they were, but did he know how to touch them so that her pleasure would match his?

He slipped a finger inside her. Then two. She closed her eyes and rolled her head. She was slick, that was good, but she was so slim, so tight, that he feared he would split her.

I want you, she'd said.

She would know *want* before the night was over. By the time he was done, she would never want to be a man again.

He turned his lips to her breasts.

Everywhere he touched her, she caught fire. Wrists, breasts, lips, neck, even her hair seemed to burn. The only coherent thought she had was joining, so that there would no longer be two separate beings.

Where his fingers lingered, she was no longer certain which skin was hers, which his. At his touch, they groaned in tandem. When he jumped in her hand, iron sheathed in velvet, she felt an answering quiver deep inside, as if he had already entered her.

Clothes no longer separated them, but even skin seemed too thick a barrier. She wanted to shed that, too, to tear aside everything that kept them apart so they could dissolve into one.

He pushed back. 'Wait, you're not ready.'

But she was. Ready as if she had waited all her life for the man who could make her want to be a woman.

What had they said of lovemaking, all those silly women she had ignored? What had she neglected to learn about his body?

And her own?

Her palm met the rough stubble on his cheek as she turned his face so that her eyes could drink of his. The precious candle sputtered, but his eyes, darkest grey, were fully, deeply hers.

'Fill me,' she whispered.

And she opened to him.

He touched her there and the quivering came faster, not all over, as before, but concentrated in that one spot.

His touch tantalised her and she reached down, amazed at the wonders of her own body. Their fingers stumbled over each other at first, but then she joined him, awkward as they tried two rhythms, then she found hers and he matched it, vibrating in harmony, creating a chord that neither could sing alone.

And then everything in her seemed to rush to that spot where their fingers flew together. She expanded, opened, ached for him to enter, to join, to fill her.

And he must have sensed it, because he did.

In the joining there was, finally, no man, no woman. All the distinctions fell away and there were no longer separate beings, male and female, but one spirit living at once in bodies that were no longer two, but one.

Was this the secret of men and women, then?

And just before he filled her in truth, he ripped himself away, spilling his seed safely outside her womb. She held him as he shook, then quieted. As she pressed her lips into his damp temple and played with the black curls at his neck, she was torn between loving his care for her and hating its result. For without true joining, the two could never form one.

The candle burned out. She held him as he slept. The wondrous feeling of being one faded.

She was Jane again, and her old fear returned in a new disguise. Now, truly, she was dependent on this man.

Because if she did not have him, nothing else in her life would ever be enough.

Chapter Sixteen

She wasn't sure which bell finally woke them. The dull mid-winter sky made it hard to separate dawn and dusk, prime from terce. They must have slept through mass, she thought, uncertain of the time. But the college was quiet and many of the students gone, so the priests expected to open the church themselves.

But she did not have to open her eyes to know where she was. And with whom.

All night, he had touched her, not snuggling against her back so she could not move, but holding her hand. And every time she had wakened, he was awake, looking at her.

Now, finally, he slept.

She lay next to him in perfect contentment, her body feeling like a new set of clothes with a perfect fit.

Her chest rose and fell, echoing his own breathing as she heard a wood-seller calling out his wares. His voice was clear in the crisp air, his footsteps muffled. She rolled over to listen and caught the damp crunch of boots on frozen ground.

She leapt out of Duncan's bed, ran to the window and flung open the shutters.

A white blanket skimmed the ground and flecked the trees. Snow. First of the season.

Cold air swirled around the floor as she pulled her clothes from the bottom of the pile and threw them on. 'Duncan, get up.'

'What?' He sprang off the bed and stood, alert and balanced on both feet, as if expecting to find a sword in his hand. 'Who's coming?'

She smiled. The sword at attention was the one connected to his body.

'No one. But look!' She waved her arm at the window. 'Snow!'

He rubbed his eyes with both hands and glanced outside. 'That's nae snaw.' He closed the shutters against the cold and flopped back on the bed. 'Won't even wet yer boot. At home, snaw means the fell's covered so deep the sheep canna climb it.'

'Then I shall like your home very much,' she called over her shoulder as she ran towards the stairs, not thinking until the words had escaped that she had assumed he would take her there some day.

In the small yard, she stood quietly, looking at the crisp white trim on the tree branches and breathing the damp, snow-washed air. The world was new, the past covered over.

She heard his steps, reluctant, on the stairs. Then suddenly, he wrapped his arms around her waist, lifted and whirled her around, both of them giddy. Dizzy, she shrieked like a child, delighted to be frightened while held in familiar arms.

He let her down and they both staggered, rumpling the clean sheet of snow. She reached for a handful, packed it into a ball and hurled it in his direction, hitting him squarely in the chest.

Then, she ran.

He caught her and they both rolled on to the ground, she with snow in her ear, in her hair, in her mouth. He pinned her arms and she laughed up at him.

Then she met his eyes, hot with desire.

A touch, a glance, it would take nothing more to spark the fire until the snow-covered grass at her back would feel like nothing more than scorched earth as they joined again.

She tried to shrug him off, but he held her fast. 'Don't look at me that way,' she said.

'What way?'

'As if I were a honey wafer you were ready to devour. That will give me away before the lack of fuzz on my cheeks.'

Abruptly, he rolled off her. 'With those things flapping before you, no one will notice my eyes *or* your cheeks.' He reached for her chest and she realised she had not wrapped her breasts.

'Don't.' She stood, shivering as the wind met her wet clothes, and hunched her shoulders forwards to hide the unfamiliar bounce against her chest.

'Can ah nae touch you now?'

She nodded towards the house behind them. The yard was sheltered, but anyone who looked out of the window could see all.

He crossed his arms into a knot, all the ease of an arm draped around John's shoulder gone. 'You know less about being a woman than about being a man.'

And even now, when she thought she might have found herself. She walked ahead of him to the shelter of the hostel. 'Isn't that what I told you?'

But it was Yuletide and the empty hostel was theirs and in the days to come, she treated it like their private palace, and let the snow erase the world outside.

He was never farther than a touch away.

She could unwrap her breasts now, and let the night air caress them. Small, insignificant things. She had not thought she'd miss them. But they had ached at the abuse of being bound, squashed, ignored and she relished setting them free.

He delighted in putting an arm around her and capturing her breast, then taking what was left of her breath with a kiss.

They did not mark the day of Christmas, for every day was a gift. They ate with legs entwined, not bothering with two cups when they could share from one, and fed one another until food was forgotten and they fed on each other.

And they sang.

She trilled the wicked bits with relish, understanding the lyrics on lovemaking as she could not have last week. Finally set free, her voice soared. And when they harmonised, their voices touched and teased each other's notes, an echo of their bodies.

One night, leaning against him as he plucked the strings idly, she ran her fingers over the gittern's polished body, round and smooth as a woman's pregnant belly.

'It's a beautiful instrument.'

His smile was proud. 'I made it with me own hands.'

'Would you teach me to play?'

He handed it to her without hesitation, this precious possession, and she balanced it awkwardly on her lap. She had watched him pick the strings with the quill plectrum countless times, but watching was not doing. Where his fingers flew, hers stumbled across strings that jangled instead of sang at her touch.

His arms enfolded her, and he placed her fingers on the strings at the neck of the instrument. 'Just strum a little first.'

So she learned three chords and used them with enthusiasm, musical enough to enjoy the song, frustrated that it didn't come as easily to her fingers as to her voice.

She handed it back to him. 'It's harder than Latin.'

He laughed. 'Maybe, but you've more talent for the music.'

She punched his shoulder in mock battle, then sighed. 'I've missed it, that's true.'

'You have a beautiful voice.'

'My mother said it was the only womanly thing about me.'

He gave her a wicked, lopsided smile. 'I would differ with your madder.'

Smiling back, she tucked her toes under his legs, savouring all her womanly joys, and listened to him pluck a melody, unable to make out the tune.

'Yer madder,' he said. 'Tell me about her.'

Her mouth went dry.

Her mother.

In the days of bliss, she had forgotten she kept more secrets. He knew she was *a* woman. He did not know *what* woman. Which secret would he resent more?

She was not ready to find out.

'What do you want to know?' she asked, as if it were of no consequence.

'What was she like? Do you favour her?'

Was. He still thought her parents dead. She did not correct him. 'She was a strong woman,' she began.

'Then you *do* favour her.'

Jane had never thought so. Her mother had amassed lands that would have given a man a seat in the House of Lords, yet every bit of her power had died with her protector, the King. Parliament had handed everything she owned to a long-lost, long-forgotten husband. To a man.

Who had spent it all and died.

Without a man, even her mother's strength had been dust. In that way, Jane never wanted to be like her.

'But she was not…liked for being strong.' Until she said the words, she had not known the truth of them.

''Tis the world's way,' he said, the quill still plucking notes from the strings. She recognised the tune now. It was the one he had played the night they made love for the first time. 'For a woman or a man. Was she fair like you?'

She shook her head. 'Her eyes and hair were dark.' Solay had her hair, but neither girl had brown eyes.

'You favour your father, then?'

'Yes.' She smiled. The late King had been a large, golden lion of a man. It had comforted her, as a child, to bear the royal looks. When there was little else to cling to, she would pretend she had been born a prince and could simply stretch out her hand and make anything she wanted appear.

But there would be time to talk of her father later. 'What is that song?'

'It's not a song. Yet.'

His own, then. 'Does it have words?'

'A few.' He started over and sang.

To see you fills my eyes.
To touch you fills my hand.
To taste you fills my mouth.
To love you fills my heart.

Let us lay down together
Let me fill you for ever
Let us love one another

His fingers kept moving over the strings, but his voice trailed away. 'I don't know the ending yet.'

She held her breath.

She had searched his eyes so many times, trying to read his feelings between their light and shadow, but this was where they lived, unmistakable. They flowed through his fingers and poured through his throat, transformed into music and words that hadn't existed before.

And she had recognised the truth the first time she had heard the tune.

Now, every word, every note filled her heart as fully as he had filled her body until her very heartbeat matched the quivering strings.

The song ended, the last note lingering in the air before it faded. What was left was trembling hope, holding its breath within her, waiting for what came next.

She raised her gaze to meet his dear, grey, hopeful eyes.

He put down the gittern and they wrapped their arms around each other. His hand stroked her hair as she closed her eyes and snuggled close enough to hear his heart beat, allowing herself to rest in his arms and feel, finally, herself.

'Yes,' she whispered, in answer to the song's question. 'For ever yes.'

But secrets and decisions stood between now and for ever. What kind of life could for ever mean?

The question haunted her as she lay in his arms that night.

All her life, she had witnessed the power of men over women, and vowed not to live at their mercy.

When she had roamed Windsor Castle as the daughter of a King, there had been food, clothing, shelter. Fires lit and blankets delivered by servants unseen and uncounted.

Then, it had all vanished. Stolen twice over. Once by Parliament, once by a husband.

So for the next ten years, she had lived with her mother and Solay in a small country house. Every stick of firewood was counted. Every loaf of bread measured.

When her sister married, food, clothing and shelter appeared again, not as lavish as during the days at court, but ample for their needs.

It was clear that men had the power to create the stuff of life, but without a man in the house, she had only the vaguest understanding of how that happened. It seemed to be nothing but an accident of birth, an outgrowth of demeanour, a result of striding through life and demanding what was yours.

Now, living among them, she saw a man's life was not as simple as she had thought.

Food and drink did not materialise out of thin air. They were wrestled from an unforgiving earth. Everything a man called his own was moulded, shaped or created by his hands, his sweat, his will and his mind.

She had been ignorant of men, it was true. Being a man let you in the door. After that, you must prove yourself by your work and your wits.

But if she'd been woefully ignorant of men, she knew all too much about women. And if being a man only let you in the door, being a woman kept you out of the room altogether.

Nothing she had learned had changed that. Yet it had changed everything else.

She had never expected the madness to take her. Never expected to want a man as she wanted Duncan, to delight in the joy of joining, in the differences between his body and hers that still fitted perfectly as one. She wanted that, now.

For ever.

But if she became Jane instead of John *for ever*, there would be no more Latin. No more running through the streets in chausses. No more studying with scholars or singing in alehouses. No trips to Paris or Rome.

And no way to protect herself if something ever happened to Duncan.

Yes, she wanted Duncan, but not at the price of being trapped and helpless. There must be some different way.

Duncan loved her. He would understand that.

Chapter Seventeen

'Tell me of your family.' She had realised, finally, that he had spoken even less of his family than she of hers. So she had waited to ask until they were naked together, her head resting on his chest, his breathing relaxed. 'You said Michael was older. Are there just the two of you?'

His arm stiffened slightly around her shoulder. 'Now.'

Only the one word.

Held to his chest, she could not see his eyes. She wrapped the curly hair of his chest around her finger, waiting.

'Now?' she prompted, finally.

'I had a younger brother.'

Had. 'What was his name?'

'Peter.'

She could tell that the story would be difficult. His right hand lay within reach and she threaded her fingers with his.

'He died before he was six.'

'Fever?'

'No. Not fever.'

The silence stretched.

There were so many ways a child could die. Falling into the pond. Leaning too close to the fire. Crushed by a cart. She prayed again for baby William.

Duncan spoke, finally. 'We were bringing the sheep down from the fells. Walking on the edge of a corrie. The path was narrow. I was in front. He was behind. I heard him cry out just before he fell.' His breath quickened, as if he saw it all again. 'It took hours to get down to him and bring him up. I carried him home, all the way down the mountain, but his legs, all the bones...' a shudder '...mangled.'

'But he lived?'

'Days.'

'I'm sorry.' She squeezed his hand, but he pulled away.

'It was better that he died,' he said. He sat straighter in the bed, letting go of her, as if trying to shake off the memory. 'The world's no place for a cripple.'

Pitiless, she thought, that empty, harsh, windswept land where he'd lived. Beautiful and cruel. No place in that wildness for a boy who would never grow up to feed himself.

'I should have tied him to me,' he muttered to himself, gazing toward the fire. An old refrain.

She glimpsed it now, the beast that rode his back and drove him to take responsibility for everything. *If only I had been more careful. I could have saved him.*

She felt the echo in her own heart. *I should have been there for my sister.*

Something else, then, that bound them. 'How old were you?'

'Ten.'

'Ten?' She rose on her elbow. 'You were only a babe! And they sent two infants to bring in a herd of sheep?'

He looked at her, brow cocked in that way he had that said *southlander.* 'Did you have a nurse, then, to look after your every childish need?'

Heat rose in her cheeks. She had had a nurse. Two. At Peter's age, her life had been full of fruits and sweets, jesters and pets, meat and drink aplenty. Soft clothes to wear and soft music to fall asleep by.

'Yes.' She said it, hoping he would not ask more. At the age his brother had been herding sheep, she was being carried through Windsor Palace.

The troubled look hovered in his eyes. 'It would not be like that. A life with me.'

'I know.' She snuggled against him, relieved he had asked no more. 'I don't expect that. It's not what I want.' But what did she want? Never to leave his arms. 'Pull up the covers and hold me. The fire's gone out.'

And they said no more of past or future.

A few days after Twelfth Night, she woke beside him. Her hips still ached from opening for him, the bed still damp with the seed he had spilled.

Even that first, mindless night, he had been careful. Wise, of course, but she wanted to be filled, wanted the two to become one, inseparable ever after.

Still asleep, he held an arm across her waist, his head pillowed between her breasts as she lay on her back, her gaze roaming the dear, small room that had been their world.

Ovid's *The Art of Love* lay open on top of the trunk, brought down from the library so they could read in bed. It had proven a particularly delightful way to study Latin. Her clothes and his mixed in the same pile. The hostel's napkins and spoons sat beside the book. She would have to wash them before the scholars returned.

She swung her legs over the side of the bed. Her weeks of womanhood had ended.

She must be John again.

Dislodged, he sat up and scrubbed his eyes with his fists. She smiled. It was the only childish thing she'd ever seen him do. But then, he had probably never truly been a child.

She reached for the binding linen: washed, dried and ready to imprison her again. As she shook it out, he stroked the underside of her breast with the back of his fingers, reverently, in farewell. She groaned, ready again, and kissed him.

Another church bell rang before she tried to dress again.

'You make me mad as a goat,' he said, his lips moving against her shoulder. 'Me hands won't stay at me sides.'

She drew away, silent. The days of unguarded words, looks and touches were over. How would they ever go back to the way they were before?

He sighed as she finished the wrapping, shook out her tunic and slipped it over her head. The bindings chafed.

'Put some dirt on your neb or something.' He tweaked her nose. 'You look as if you have just risen from bedding a lover.'

She smiled and kissed him in answer. Her lips clung a little longer than usual, then she leafed through the clothes, looking for her chausses.

'How did you deceive us all this time? Anyone with eyes can see you're a lass.'

'Most people don't have eyes.' It was amazing, really, how simple it had been. 'They see what they expect to see. Like a stripling lad with little talent for Latin.'

'Or a northland guff, eh?' He laughed.

She ran her fingers down his side, caressing his ribs. 'It will be harder now.' A wrong look, a wrong glance would ruin him as well as her. And now, that seemed even more important.

'Not for long.'

'What do you mean?'

He rose, still naked, and started pacing. 'I'll go to the draper today. They'll be able to make you a dress. Then, I'll find you a place to stay. A nice family who needs a woman's help. Or a convent. When I do, "John" can leave the hostel. You can tell them the lord of the castle called you back. When you're settled, I can visit you. Maybe not every day…'

He was babbling nonsense, planning a life for her worse than the one she'd run from.

She grabbed his arm, jerking him to a stop. 'I'm not going anywhere!'

'You don't think to continue this disguising!'

'I can't stay here without it.'

He grabbed her shoulders. 'And what do you think will happen when someone finds out?'

'No one will.' Her words were bravado.

'Geoffrey already suspects. How long do you think it will be before Henry, or someone less sympathetic, discovers you? What happened to your Hawys will be bairn's play.'

'I don't want to leave my studies.' She wrapped her arms around him. 'I don't want to leave *you*. This way, we'll at least be close. We could have our nights.' In the unforgiving light of midday, she couldn't imagine how that would work. Once the men were back, all privacy would disappear. 'Once in a while.'

'And you think that will be enough?' The question, bleak.

She bit her lip and shook her head. 'But if I leave, we'll have nothing at all.'

'When I go to Westminster I can't leave you here alone.'

'Don't.' For a few days, she had forgotten everything, even that he must go to the Council's meeting to plead for his father's ransom. 'Take me with you. No one will know me there and no one will look twice at a young scholar.'

She lifted her chin, waiting for him to realise it was the perfect solution. Dresses, places to stay, it would all take time.

He was wavering. She could tell. 'We cannot be alone there either. You know that.'

'But we can be together.'

It would have been reason enough for her to make the trip, but she had another.

She was still searching for a way to have the life she wanted and Duncan, too. A life they both could live. The King could wave his hand and command what he wanted. And if he wanted to bring a young, eager clerk and a learned man of medicine to his court...

'Besides,' she said, putting John's best smile on her face and Duncan's best accent on her lips, 'you dinna know an honest woman in Cambridge who would be a fit companion.'

He smiled, mocking her in return. 'I thought you knew a respectable widow who needed help with her tasks.'

She smiled. 'She left town.'

'All right.' He sighed. 'You can come with me. But only because I've no time to arrange anything else. But I am going to tell Geoffrey and Henry about you.'

'No! Why?' If he did that, there would be no going back.

His implacable expression left no room for argument. 'I can't be with you every minute. I must be sure someone else is there to protect you.'

If only. If only I had done more. And now, his fears were for her.

'But if they know, they might say something, might give me away.'

'You'll not cajole me out of this, so stop your pouting.'

'At least don't tell them before we leave.' Every day borrowed was a day of freedom.

'As soon as they get back. And that's an end to it, Jane.'

'My name,' she said, eyes never leaving his, 'is John. See that you remember it.'

His eyes darkened. 'Your name is Jane. See that you don't forget it.'

She swallowed her protest. More arguing would only make him more stubborn. He was a logical man. In time, he would realise the only safe course was for them to continue as they were.

As he emerged into the work-a-day world, Duncan stomped through his responsibilities, vaguely out of sorts. Reluctantly, he had let Jane go to the bakery and the alehouse alone while he met with the cook to make sure everything was ready for the beginning of the Lent term.

She had not been beyond the reach of his hand for nearly a

month and he ached for her. Beside her, he felt everything he had left the pele tower to find: grace, love, comfort. Coupled with her boldness and her courage, and an almost manly spirit, she had made his life beside her a continual surprise and delight.

How had he thought he could exile her from his sight?

Yet fear warred with need.

All he could see now when he looked at her was Jane. Her laugh, her smile, the way her eyes turned deeper blue when he touched her. God's bones! Anyone who saw the two of them look at each other would see everything at a glance.

The hubbub of the return and the beginning of the term would divert attention until they left for Westminster.

But waiting would not answer the question. What would come after? The situation seemed even more impossible in daylight.

He could offer her nothing now. Perhaps not for years. No woman would wait so long.

While he had never sought celibacy, he had never planned for marriage, either. It would be a decade, perhaps more, before he might leave the University and earn his living as a physician. He was bound by oath to teach for at least two years at Cambridge. To complete his medical education would take ten years of study, including a sojourn at a University on the continent.

As far away from the north country as possible.

Worse, marriage would mean exposing his whole life, his family, the life he came from. She had not told him all, but enough for him to know her upbringing had been more privileged than his. She was accustomed to fine things.

Things he had left the rough stone tower in the Eden Valley hoping to find. Things he was still searching for.

He could not give her a life disguised as a scholar in a hostel, that was certain. And he would not make her endure a life like the one he had growing up.

But his first concern must be his father's fate. All else must wait. When he returned, he could decide what to do about Jane.

Temptation told him to keep her close. But the longer they were together, the more likely his responsibilities would include a child as well as a wife.

He was a strong man, but no man could resist for ever.

He had taught her to be logical. In time, she would agree that they could not continue as they were.

Jane scooped up the onion pieces and dropped them into the simmering pot. The hostel was almost full again with hungry men to cook for. The flimsy linen around her breasts was damp with sweat, barely able to contain them. They had grown larger with freedom.

'Where's Duncan? Where's Little John?' Henry's voice boomed in the Common Room.

Little John's mask firmly in place, she darted in to give him a hug that would have been genuine if she hadn't dreaded Duncan's threatened announcement.

'You did not starve in the cook's absence,' Henry said.

Never one to look beyond his eyes, he seemed to have no suspicions.

Duncan came down the stairs, avoiding her eye, and replayed the greeting ritual with Henry, a mock fight, followed by a rough hug.

'Where's Geoffrey?' he asked.

'Visiting the parchment seller. He'll be back before supper if he doesn't forget his stomach altogether.' Henry turned back to her. 'I still don't understand why you didn't come home with me instead of staying with this big guff.'

Duncan laughed at the insult, easily, it seemed. She mumbled something about studying for her meeting with the Master of Glomery, without mentioning that she had barely spoken a word of Latin in a fortnight.

'I've something to talk to you both about when he returns,' Duncan said, glancing at her.

She pleaded silently, but his jaw was set.

But when the full darkness of a winter day fell, Geoffrey still hadn't returned.

The scholars lined the long tables for the evening soup and bread, but the reunion conversation was subdued. Everyone listened for a knock at the door.

After supper, she watched Duncan go into the street, looking from the tower of St Mary's back to Holy Trinity, as if he could summon Geoffrey with his glance. When he came inside, he put on his cloak. Henry and Jane grabbed their own and followed him back outside.

The evening was cold and sharp, the street quiet after the noisy reunions of the afternoon. Two beadles strolled by Holy Trinity, their breath trailing little clouds behind them in the air.

'He probably forgot the time,' Henry said.

Jane fought a shiver. She believed it no more than he. Geoffrey was a predictable man. If he said he would be back by supper, he would be.

If he had not returned, it was because he couldn't.

The beadles turned the corner and disappeared on to Bridge Street. Duncan motioned to Henry with a jerk of his head and started in the other direction. 'Stay here,' he whispered to her.

She ignored him and followed the two men. She knew how worried he was when he let her.

They passed under the shadow of St Mary's and turned on to High Street. A moonless sky did little to light the way, but the clear, crisp air magnified every murmur. Silent, they crept up High Street towards the parchment seller's shop, straining for a sound of something, anything that might be a clue.

A baby cried. A mother crooned. Laughter cascaded out of Physwick Hostel.

The shop door was shut tight, but a sliver of candlelight gleamed through a crack in the upper-storey shutters. Duncan pounded on the door until the shopkeeper opened them.

'Shop's closed. Go away.'

'I'm looking for someone. A scholar. Tall, narrow shoulders, thinning hair.'

'He left hours ago. No doubt home in his own bed as you should be.' The shutters rattled as he slammed them shut and turned the latch.

'We should separate,' she whispered. Cambridge had never seemed so large. He could be anywhere.

Duncan shook his head. 'A man alone is an easy target.'

As Geoffrey had been.

Henry flexed his hands, ready for a fight.

Duncan led them on in a methodical pattern, first circling the streets and alleys near the shop, then widening their search to the lanes between the colleges and the river.

In their search, she relived her last four months. Here was the stable she had slept in. Here, the corner where she and Hawys had talked for the first time. And there, the church where Duncan had left her that first day.

Then, she had been afraid of the unknown. Now, she knew exactly what to fear.

They came, finally, to the river. She stepped closer to Duncan. Henry closed in on her left side. The river could be less than welcoming in daylight.

Already they could hear the snores of a river man asleep on his boat. What was there to stay awake for but cold and dark? Trinity Hall loomed behind them, protected by fences and gates, feeble means to shut out whatever danger lurked by the water.

Then, she heard it. Something like a moan.

Duncan glanced at Henry, but put an arm around her shoulders, holding her closer. Hoping Henry could not see, she pressed her face against his side, taking comfort from the familiar rhythm of his heart.

She wished for last week and their safe, private world.

A groan again. Muffled.

She ran towards the noise, fighting her way through the grasses at the river's edge. 'Geoffrey?'

'Quiet!' Duncan called, but he and Henry were running, too.

She reached him first. He lay under a willow, eyes closed, cold mud smearing torn clothes. Duncan and Henry were right behind her, kneeling beside him in the wet mud.

Geoffrey's narrow chest rose and fell in shallow breaths. He could have been lying in the muck for hours.

She looked at Duncan, mute.

'We can carry him,' Henry said.

Duncan shook his head. 'Let me see what's broken.' His expert hands slid from Geoffrey's head to his pulse, then ran over arms and legs, feeling for broken bones.

Geoffrey's eyes opened and seemed to focus slowly. 'About time.' A smile wobbled on cracked, dry lips.

'You could have just asked us if we missed you,' Duncan said. She heard relief in his voice. No permanent damage, then.

'Don't tell Mary.' Geoffrey's words were weak.

'I'm going to tell her all about it,' she said, in Little John's teasing tone. 'Then *she'll* come and give you a real beating for causing us all this trouble.'

And as a woman, she prayed that Mary would never know how close she'd come to losing him.

'Who did it?' Henry's fists were ready.

Geoffrey grimaced as they helped him sit up. 'Townsmen in their cups.' The words came slowly. 'Spoiling for a fight. Guess I was handy, eh?'

'Can you walk?' Duncan asked.

He nodded, wincing. 'Just give me a hand.'

He needed more than a hand. He needed Duncan on one side and Henry on the other, half-carrying him back to the hostel. Then they had to tell the tale to the ones who were still up, and, before Duncan could stop them, two of the seniors were out the door and on the streets spoiling for revenge, not caring who they gave it to.

'Put him in my bed,' Duncan said, glancing at Jane as they paused at the bottom of the stairs.

She ran ahead, pulled back the covers, then built up the fire. Duncan and Henry carried Geoffrey the last few feet to the bed and laid him on top of the clean bedclothes, immediately smeared with mud.

Fetching a pot of water and clean cloths, she fended off questions from the rest of the men. No time for explanations.

When she opened the door of Duncan's chamber, a stifling wall of heat hit her, carrying the smell of dirt and blood. The water sloshed in the pot as she set it at the edge of the fire to warm. Trying not to look at the bed, she walked to the window.

A thread of crisp air slithered into the room. She closed her eyes and grasped it, wanting to be outdoors or downstairs in the Common Room or anywhere but here.

She looked over her shoulder. Duncan and Henry bent over the bed, blocking her view. All she could see was a spreading, purple bruise on Geoffrey's shoulder and blood-matted hair on his head.

She took a final whiff of fresh air, steadied and bent to pick up the muddy clothes strewn on the floor. Then, she dipped a clean cloth in the warmed water and wrung it out.

'Ja—John!' Duncan barked.

She glanced at Henry, too absorbed in a stream of conversation with the unresponsive Geoffrey to have noticed.

Her shoulder bumped Duncan's side, a silent signal. *I'm here.*

And though all his attention was on Geoffrey's battered body, he gave her a whisper of a smile as she handed him the damp cloth.

She was still breathing. She knew what she must do.

Hours later, they left Henry at the bedside and closed the bedroom door behind them.

Jane's shoulders ached from carrying water and wrapping

bandages, but Geoffrey slept. Though he was bruised and battered, none of the damage seemed irreparable.

Duncan's eyes were haggard and she slipped her hand into his and squeezed, wishing they still had the hostel to themselves. 'He'll be all right. You did as much as anyone could do,' she said.

He gave her a rueful smile. 'I'll call a physician tomorrow. I might have missed something.'

'Duncan!' A shout from downstairs. 'Andrew and Robert got in a fight with the St Benet boys. The beadles got Robert and Andrew's arm is hanging out of his shoulder.'

He sighed. 'I'll need your help on the shoulder.'

She nodded and followed him downstairs.

'I don't think Geoffrey needs to know a woman helped treat him,' she whispered.

Duncan nodded.

Nothing more was said of telling anyone about Jane.

Chapter Eighteen

A few days later, Duncan watched as Geoffrey limped down the stairs, leaning on Henry. His friend winced as he settled on the bench in front of the fire.

'How are you?' Was there something else he might have done for the healing?

'He's well enough,' Henry answered.

'Well enough that he's forcing me out of bed.' Fortunately, within a few days, Geoffrey had moved into his own room and was fit enough to start the term on time.

The two senior boys were not so lucky. Andrew's shoulder had needed a surgeon's help and Robert's cuts had suffered from a night in the gaol before Duncan could wash them with old wine and bandage them. Short on sympathy, he fined them both, though he did stifle a smile when he learned from St Benet's principal that the other hostel's students had fared even worse.

Jane came in from the kitchen and waved.

'I'm going to the bakery,' she said, not pausing. 'We'll need at least three days of bread for the road.'

'You won't set a foot outside this building unless you go with me.'

Geoffrey's attack had been a reminder. He had to find a safe place for her to live as a woman should. Every day she was here was a risk. He wondered at the wisdom of taking her to Westminster, but leaving her here alone seemed even more dangerous.

She stopped with a jerk and swivelled to face him. 'That doesn't make sense. During the past term, I've gone alone to the alehouse, the bakery, the parchment seller, the wood seller…'

Henry grinned. 'The lad's doing well in logic. That's a beginning worthy of a disputation.'

Duncan felt a flush creep into his cheeks. He'd set a bad precedent, it was true. There was a reason young scholars were not to be allowed out alone. 'That was before.'

'Before…?'

Before I knew you were a woman. 'I've got three injured men in this house. I won't have another.'

'I'm not going to start a fight in the bakery.'

'I'm more worried what someone else will do. You're no good with your fists, Little *John*.'

Now she was the one who turned ruddy, recognising the secret insult for what it was. 'Then teach me.'

'No.' He wanted to stop looking at her, but he couldn't.

'The lad's got a point,' Henry said. 'He should know how to defend himself.'

'We've trouble enough already.' It had taken two visits and a hefty fine to free Robert from the beadle's clutches. And the Chancellor said the next infraction would mean probation for Solar Hostel. 'I'll have no more.'

'Well, since Duncan's being stubborn, I'll teach you,' said Henry, rising.

'No!' Duncan grabbed his friend's arm. He could not abide the thought of Henry's hands showing her how to punch and wrestle.

All three of them stared at him. Waiting.

Jane grinned. 'Henry or you. You have a choice.'

He dropped Henry's arm. 'It'll be me.' No one else would be allowed near her.

He didn't want an audience, but it was too cold to go outside, and as they pushed the tables aside to clear the floor, the room filled with scholars, each one eager to give advice.

She raised her hands. Excitement touched her eyes. 'I'm ready.'

Watching her dainty fists wave in the air, he despaired. To his eyes, she was so clearly a woman, he was amazed that the gang of oblivious scholars couldn't see her as he did. Too mired in their heads to pay attention to the evidence of their eyes, he hoped.

'We'll start with your stance, then. Move your left foot a-front. That's the way, no, further.'

She tottered on her toes, her hips holding her back. 'Like this?'

He had no choice. He would have to touch her.

He moved behind her, nudging her left leg forwards with his, forcing himself to keep his eyes on her shoulders instead of the curve of her hips.

But his nose was too close to her hair and her scent took him right back to their narrow bed. Just a few inches more and he could take her in his arms again, she would nestle against him...

He coughed, hoping his stiff tarse was hidden. 'Point your toes to the right.' He looked down. 'Both feet. Keep your right heel up a little.'

She wobbled, then pitched back into his arms.

'Duncan's right,' Henry yelled. 'You fight like a she-goat!'

'Let it be,' Duncan whispered, close to her ear. Her hair caught on his lips. 'You're not meant for this.'

'No,' she whispered over her shoulder, as she regained her balance. 'It can be no harder than *De modo significandi*.'

He hoped not.

'Bring your hand up,' he snapped. 'Make a fist.' He wrapped his hand around hers to show her, ignoring the pulse throbbing in his palm.

Robert, his black eye blossoming, gave a catcall, which sparked a chorus of rude whistles.

Realising he'd kept her in his embrace too long, he let go and circled to face her. She looked ridiculous to his eye, wearing a man's clothes and a man's stance, as absurd as a sheep in a *cappa clausa*.

She held her fingers so loose they would crumple at the first blow. 'Tighter. Keep your thumb on top of your middle finger.'

She followed each instruction carefully, but it was tedious. He had known it all for so long, the stance, the balance. How could he explain it to a woman who had never had to fight and claw her way through life?

'Keep your shoulders down. Hold your elbows in.' He started circling and she followed his lead, her brow creased in concentration. 'That's right, keep moving. Keep me in reach, but be ready to dart away.'

How like a dance it seemed, circling opposite his lady.

'A round of Gascon red on Master Duncan,' someone yelled.

'I'll bet on Little John. He's light on his feet.'

Over her shoulder, he saw a clump of students perched on the tables, laying down wagers. He wondered who the odds favoured.

He forced his attention back to Jane. She *was* light on her feet, and kept smoothly opposite and out of reach.

It was time to try a punch. 'Now, shift back and throw your right forward.'

The hips that anchored her balance kept her punch from having the power that came from a man's strong back and shoulders. Her fist bounced harmlessly off his chest. If she fought this way on the street, she would be trampled flat.

The room booed.

'Shut up, ya heathens. Give the lad a chance.' He gritted his teeth to keep from whisking her away and locking her safely in his room.

But Jane had learned something in her time among them. Instead of discouraging her, the hazing sparked a determined frown.

'Harder,' he said. 'Don't be afraid. Hit me.'

She punched again, stiff-armed.

He flinched.

The onlookers hooted.

He rubbed his arm. His arm would be black and blue by tomorrow, but in a real fight, the blow would be no more than annoying. 'Keep a little flex in your elbow.'

'Here!' Henry jumped up. 'I'll show him.'

Before Duncan could protest, Henry was close behind 'John', touching 'his' waist, straightening 'his' shoulders.

She jumped.

Duncan's glance met hers.

This must end, he told her with his eyes. *Now. The risk is too great.*

He knew she understood. Time to give up and give him the victory.

'Let him go,' Duncan said to Henry, then turned to Jane. 'Try another swing.'

She moved closer and he watched her arm, ready to take the glancing blow before he returned it.

But the blow came from her knee, squarely hitting between his legs. He staggered, choking back a howl of pain, totally surprised when her fist hit his chin.

He crumpled to the floor.

The room broke into cheers and Henry raised 'John's' arms in victory.

She flashed a triumphant smile, but it lasted only an instant before she was on her knees beside him. 'Are you all right? Did I hurt you?'

He bit back a groan and waved her away. 'You win. Go to the bakery.'

He closed his eyes, wondering who had collected on the wagers.

Justin kissed Solay and the giggling babe as he tucked them into the cart. The trip to Westminster would take longer this way, but his wife was not yet ready to make a trip on horseback.

And he would not go without her.

Solay was recovered. His child healthy. He was a lucky man.

They had but one sorrow.

'When we get back,' she said, 'we can look again.'

He nodded. 'I'll go to Cambridge as soon as the Council meeting is over.'

He said it, but he knew what they were both thinking. The footman had talked to a student in a tavern who'd thought he had seen someone on the road on a pilgrimage months before.

If Jane was the pilgrim he had seen, she would be long gone.

Jane moved closer to Duncan as they walked Westminster's corridors. Being here, so close to royalty, brought it all back.

She was at last at the centre of the world, the locus of all power. The place she deserved to be. She wondered again why Solay and Justin had withdrawn from court.

The seat of government was huge and crowded. Her eyes hurt from staying open, trying to take it all in. The bustle, the clothes, the conversations, it was all a blur.

She had donned her best garb, but it was so simple and shabby that she drew the very eyes she had hoped to avoid. Fortunately, once they looked, they spared no more than a passing glance for a lowly lad at the heels of a Cambridge master. Yet as the men and women rushed by, she stifled her urge to shout *Don't you know who I am? Don't you know you are ignoring the child of a King?*

Duncan, grim-faced, wore his flowing academic garb like armour. Their conversations had been strained during the trip from Cambridge. How was she supposed to know he expected her to let him win their mock battle? She thought he'd be pleased that she could defend herself.

She tugged his sleeve. 'Look. The King.'

He followed her gaze. King Richard stood between two men, listening intently.

'Who is he with? Are they Council members?'

'The one on the left is. That's Mowbray, the Earl of Nottingham.'

She peered at him, surprised that a man so young could sit on the Council. He looked no older than Duncan. 'And the other one?' The man on the right was holding a parchment.

'One of Richard's clerks.'

She stared at the clerk important enough to write a declaration that would bear the King's name. Perhaps he was about to leave on an important mission to Bohemia or France.

Envy tweaked her. She remembered, as in a forgotten dream, the exciting feel of the Court. Important people gathered to do important things. Here, even *she* had been important.

She had missed that, in the years since. That was what she wanted, to matter. It could be like that for her and Duncan, if only—

The King, perhaps sensing he was watched, looked over.

She fell to her knees. Duncan, beside her, bowed. Jane held her breath as the King approached them.

'Well, here's the Master with his young Latin student.'

'Your Majesty.' Duncan's bow was brief. 'You suggested I come to make my case before the Council.'

A vacant look touched the King's blue eyes.

'For a quick invasion of Scotland. And for my father.'

'Ah, yes.' He looked at Jane instead. 'And how is your Latin coming, young man?'

'Very well, your Majesty. Master Duncan is an excellent teacher.'

'I'm sure that's true.' The King did look at Duncan when he said it. 'But there are even better masters at King's Hall. How would you like to study there?'

To attend King's Hall College, to be a 'King's Man', guaranteed a position serving his Majesty.

Beside her, Duncan stiffened. 'Your Majesty, the boy has yet to satisfy his Latin—'

The King waved Duncan into silence. 'Let the boy answer.'

She lost her speech. Everything she had wanted when she stumbled into Cambridge was within reach. All she had to do was say 'yes'.

Did she want it still?

She glanced at Duncan. His eyes were as unmoving as a stone. The choice would be hers.

Hidden by his black gown and proper accent, he was as disguised as she. Only she knew Duncan as he was: a funny, stubborn, sensitive, musical man of the north.

And only he knew who she was.

Not just that she was a woman, but that she loved Ovid and hated conjugations and burped after she finished her ale and could hold the last note of the drinking song for longer than he could and laughed when he made up funny verses and had a sensitive spot just above the inside of her elbow and a thousand other little things that made her feel as if she were alive and whole and perfectly content only when she was with him.

But the only thing he didn't know might be the most important: that the King who had issued the letters patent for King's Hall had been her father.

But if choosing the King meant losing Duncan, she was not ready to make that choice.

'Your Majesty is generous,' she began. She must turn down the King without angering him. 'And does me incredible honour. But I must be sure that I can be worthy of what you have bestowed on me. When Master Duncan feels I have advanced sufficiently to be a credit to you at King's Hall, I will be deeply honoured to attend.'

Her forehead nearly touched her knee.

She felt Duncan release a breath.

She raised her head, trying to assess the King's expression.

He was no longer looking at her, his attention taken by Nottingham and the clerk. 'Of course.' He waved a gesture of dismissal and left.

Duncan, without a word, walked away.

She caught up with him as he entered the Great Hall, where the King would formally receive visitors.

'I didn't really mean I would go to King's Hall,' she whispered, surprised how true it was. 'I just didn't want to make the King angry by rejecting his gracious offer.'

'Go ahead with ya. Makes no difference to me. I'm sure you'll find plenty of company there from Essex or Bedford or wherever yer from.' He refused to look at her.

She groaned softly. Here was the Duncan she hadn't seen in months. He had taken her words as a personal affront instead of a political necessity.

She wondered when she could lie naked in his arms again. There, as man and woman, all the rest would fade away.

Shielded behind Duncan's robes, she peeked at the men and women lining the hall. Amidst the crimson, blue and green of the courtiers, Duncan's robes labelled him as a man of learning, worthy of respect

She searched the faces lining the hall.

And then, she saw him.

On the other side of the hall, across a planked floor that seemed suddenly too small, stood her sister's husband.

She ducked behind Duncan's robes. She could fool most people, but Justin would know her immediately.

And if Solay was here—

She would be, of course, if she were able. The two of them were never apart. It was as if a limb was missing if one could not see or touch the other at will.

She understood that feeling now.

'There's the Lady Solay,' whispered a woman behind her. 'Motherhood agrees with her.'

She spotted her sister then, making her way through the crowd to Justin's side. Mother and babe both well, then. The gossip was right. Solay glowed.

Where was her nephew? And what would he look like now, at five months?

The whispers continued behind her. 'I'm surprised to see her. She and her husband are not often at Court.'

A wicked chuckle from another woman. 'If you had her mother, would you be?'

She bit her lip. Still. Always. She would be judged by her mother, not her father.

Solay had reached Justin. If she looked up, if she caught Jane's eye, or even saw her hair…

Not now. She must not be discovered now when so much lay unresolved.

She touched Duncan's sleeve. 'I need to leave.'

He searched her face, concern cracking his harsh expression. 'Are you unwell?'

'Just…just something disagrees with my stomach.' She hoped her voice sounded nauseous. 'I just need air.' She started for the door without giving him a chance to ask more.

But before she left the Hall, she turned, to get a final glimpse of her sister.

A mistake.

Solay's eye's widened in recognition.

Jane moved quickly through the crowd, out of the room, and started running.

She ran blindly, up stairs and down, following twists and turns of blessedly empty corridors.

Lost and alone, she rested, finally, beside a window high above the Thames, and watched the water moving cold and sluggish below.

Eyes burning with unmanly tears, she felt the sobs come.

She had run once more.

And every time she ran, her woman's body came along.

For ever, she had shouted at Duncan. How childish. She could not pretend to be a man for the rest of her life. Her breasts would grow. Her beard would not.

But every time she thought of living like a woman, like the rest of them, a tightness took her throat and pressed on her chest until she couldn't breathe. If she went to King's Hall, if she became a clerk to the King, if no one discovered her—

'Jane?'

She turned to face Solay.

Chapter Nineteen

First, they simply stared at each other. Then, Jane was in Solay's arms, crying on her sleeve, both of them murmuring *I'm so glad you're all right.*

'We feared you were lost to us,' Solay said at last, dabbing her eyes with a little white cloth and then handing it to Jane. 'I'm so glad you are safe and well.'

'And I, you!'

They laughed together.

'You are, aren't you? You and the babe?'

A smile banished the last of Solay's tears. 'William Edward is a healthy, howling, perpetually hungry young soul and Justin is a doting father.'

'I thought Mother would insist on Edward.' *For the King.*

A strange look came over Solay's face, then she shrugged. 'Perhaps next time.'

'And where is William?'

'He's here with his nurse. You must see him.'

Jane nodded and blew her nose.

Solay's eyes studied her, serious, taking in her chausses, short hair and her swagger. 'We always knew you were not happy, but Mother and I had hoped, when you grew, you would feel different.'

Jane pursed her lips. She did feel different, somehow, but it only made her more confused than ever. And she did not know how to explain it. Facing Solay took courage enough. She was not sure how she would ever meet her mother's eyes again.

'I've been at Cambridge,' she said, to speak of simpler things.

'So close! All this time! We were coming to look for you again, right after the Council meeting.'

'I tried to send word, so you would know I was safe without knowing where I was. I didn't want you to worry.' Jane's tongue tripped upon itself.

'Come,' Solay said, taking her hands and settling them on to the top step of the stair, away from the window's draught. 'Tell me all. How you got to Cambridge, what you've done, how you came to be here. Start at the beginning.'

The beginning. In that suffocating room where she had abandoned her sister.

'I know I should have helped you, but I was frightened.' She could still taste the fear—of not measuring up, of being trapped, of failing at all the things she was no good at. 'And I just ran. Can you ever forgive me?'

Solay sighed and smoothed back an unruly blonde curl. 'I know it has been difficult for you, womanhood.'

Her relief at being understood was belly-deep. Duncan knew her well, but this he could never comprehend.

'I went directly to Cambridge,' she began, saving Duncan for later. 'And I'm studying Latin. I'm to present to the Master of Glomery next month. If he approves, I can matriculate.'

At King's Hall, if I choose. She swallowed the boast. Her sister didn't need to know everything all at once.

'Where do you live?'

'In a hostel. I work in the kitchen to pay for my room and board.' And she explained the tricks she had used to stay hidden among men.

'And you've been safe?' She squeezed Jane's hands, frown

lines on her brow. Solay knew, would have known all along, what a risk she was taking. More than Jane had known.

'Yes,' she answered, without hesitation. She wanted to reassure her sister, not frighten her.

'And no one knows? That you are a woman?' Wonder touched her voice.

Jane smiled at her beautiful, beautiful sister who could never even imagine being anything other than a woman. 'Only two people know. One is a woman who's become a friend.' Strange word. She could not picture Solay and Hawys sharing confidences. 'It was her brother who came to visit you.'

'And the other?' Solay prompted, when Jane hesitated.

There was something in her sister's eyes, an expression that said she knew all and was just waiting for Jane to confess.

'He is here with me.'

She could see Solay survey the crowd in her mind. 'The master?'

She nodded.

'And you're happy.' It was not a question.

'I'm afraid,' she said, over the lump in her throat, 'that the madness you warned of has taken me.'

'So when you ran from womanhood the hardest, it found you at last.'

She nodded and swallowed the tears.

'You have lain together.' Her sister did not ask a question.

Was she so obvious to everyone or only to the sister who knew her so well? 'I want to be with him always.'

'And he?' Her expression was grave.

Jane nodded. 'He thought I was "John" at first. We were friends, then. Like brothers.' Her cheeks turned hot with memories. 'But now that he knows, he expects me to be like other women, to stop my studies, to wear a skirt, to live in a convent while he finishes his studies, but I can't!' Her words echoed down the hall. She slowed her breath. 'I can't. He will see reason, eventually. He must.'

Solay gave a great sigh. 'Will you?'

If, if, if, she had argued. But no 'ifs' could overcome God's dictates. She had been born a woman. And try as she had to be a man, she was neither fish nor fowl nor good red herring. She belonged nowhere.

But to admit it would mean to lose everything. 'As a boy, at least I can be close to him.'

'Does he not want to wed you?' She half-rose, as if ready to do battle with the man.

'Of course he does!' Had he ever used the word 'wed'? She could not remember. Dread seeped into her stomach. *No wallowing.* But he wouldn't treat her as he did those other women. Would he?

'Tell me all about this man,' Solay said. 'Start with his birth date.'

When she did, a smile nudged the corner of her sister's mouth. 'Ah, the sign of the lion. Not royal, but acts as if he is.'

'It's as if you know him!'

'No. But tell me so I will.'

So she did, proud to talk about the hostel he had founded, to boast about his study of medicine, to brag about his meetings with the King, even to confess that he was from the barbarous border country, relieved when Solay held her tongue when she discovered he was from the north.

'We are here so he can plead for the Council to pay his father's ransom,' she concluded, as her story ended. 'They *must* help us.'

Us. Such hopes and dreams captured in one word. Dreams she barely realised she had. Darkness had fallen, and she could no longer read her sister's eyes.

'It is difficult,' Solay said, finally, although speaking to a memory, 'when you must depend on the King.'

Yet hadn't the King just offered her her heart's desire? Surely he would do no less for Duncan.

'In a way, I envy you,' her sister continued. 'You feel free to grab for your love and your life without worrying about family. I didn't have that.'

'I have it because of you.' She recognized, in hindsight, how Solay and her mother had protected her. But she was responsible for herself now, as she had so wanted to be. And the choices and decisions were harder than she had expected.

But she didn't want to think about that now. 'Why are you and Justin here? I thought you no longer frequented the Court.'

Solay shrugged and wrinkled her nose. 'Mother was right. You can never escape the King.' Her expression became troubled. 'Justin left because he was unhappy with the Council's plans. Now, it seems, he is not alone. I think the King asked Justin to come to their meeting because he is one of the few who will tell his Majesty the truth.'

Solay grasped Jane's hand and stood. 'And his Majesty will not be pleased that I was absent from the audience. Come. We must find Justin and tell him you are safe.'

'No!' All the joy from the reunion drained from her. 'You mustn't.' Foolish request. Solay could no more keep a secret from Justin than she could stop her breath. 'I need time. To tell Duncan.'

'Tell him what?'

'He knows I'm a woman. Not that I'm…' She didn't know how to say it. 'Who I am.'

'You could tell him all else and not that?'

'He thinks I'm an orphan.'

Solay rolled her eyes. 'Jane, how is he to trust you after all the lies you've told?'

'But you don't understand!' Jane argued. 'I'm from the south, so he thought at first that I looked down on him, and I did, in a way. What will he think when he knows I have royal blood? You know what it's like. When they know whose daughter you are.'

Solay stood straighter. The harlot's daughter. That's what they had called her. 'But he has to know.'

'Not until the Council meeting is over. Then he can notify Pickering—'

The soft, understanding expression on Solay's face hardened. 'Sir James Pickering?'

'Yes.' A chill touched the back of her neck. Dread. 'Of Westmoreland. The Speaker of the Commons.'

'They are friends?'

She thought of the hours the men had spent, preparing for the Parliament meeting. Men called that time together friendship. 'Yes. Why?'

'It was Pickering who was executor of de Weston's will. He's the one who took our home away.'

Stunned, she stumbled back to sit on the stair. 'So even if Duncan can overlook all, Mother—'

'Mother could not.'

She propped her elbows on her knees, laced her fingers together and slumped, staring down at the stone stair. She had avoided any thought of facing her mother. Alys de Weston was not a forgiving woman. Begging her forgiveness for running away would be difficult. Getting her permission to wed the friend of a sworn enemy would be impossible.

He did intend that they wed. Didn't he?

She tried to remember Duncan's exact words. *Come let us love*, his song went. Not *Come let us wed*. But he wanted to be with her always. She was sure of it.

She looked up. 'Please. I need time. Don't tell Justin. Don't tell Mother. Anything.'

'*You'll* be the one to tell them. You're coming home with us.'

'No! Not yet. The Council meets tomorrow. Just give me until then. Please.'

Solay frowned. 'One day. No more.'

The next morning, Jane watched the sun make its shallow journey across the sky, and waited for Duncan to return from the Council.

He had left early and she stayed in the sleeping room they had shared with two knights and their squires, blessedly empty now. She dared not go out for fear of seeing Justin.

She did not doubt the outcome of the meeting. Duncan was an eloquent speaker and the King had all but promised that his father would be freed.

Duncan was still angry with her, she could tell. And the crowded room had given them no privacy to wrestle with either his misunderstanding or her secret. So in this quiet moment, she practised how she might calmly begin.

Duncan, I said I had no family, but I do. I'm the daughter of the late King Edward.

Perhaps when they were abed together, after they had made love and were curled in each other's arms. That would be a much better time.

Duncan, I told you my mother was a strong woman, but was not liked. She is Alys de Weston. And your friend Pickering deprived us of the last home and property left to us.

Bald statements she knew her tongue could never speak.

She recognised his step and rose to meet him. It was barely sext, the day just half-gone. A quick decision, then.

'Gather your things.' He tugged at his master's gown as if it were smothering him.

She helped him shrug it off. 'The King is to invade, then?'

'Oh, yes, the King will invade.' He paced as he collected his few things, fury fuelling his steps. 'When all is in readiness his men will tame the savage Scots. Teach them to respect the English. And lots of other blather, that sounds much more impressive in the Latin they used to write it down.'

This was not the story's end, she could tell, dreading it. 'When do they march?'

'Next spring. Next summer.' He punctuated each phrase by throwing a garment into his bag as if hurling a blow in a fight. 'After the Second Coming, perhaps. Whenever they choose.' He stopped pacing and looked at her, anger and frustration brimming in his eyes. 'But in the meantime, do you know what they've done?'

She shook her head, though he did not expect an answer.

'He's appointed new Wardens of the March *again*.' He was using his sarcastic tone. 'Both east and west.'

She tried to remember what she knew about the borders. Her concerns for war and peace had become small. Let the east be overrun with Scots. She cared about Duncan's home. 'Who is the new Warden in the West?'

'Oh, the West is too important for just one. We were honoured with three!' He rattled off the names.

Her knowledge of politics was hazy and the names meaningless. 'What does that mean?'

'That they'll spend more time fighting each other than they will the Scots! Mowbray's been given the east and he doesn't even hold any land in Northumberland!'

Mowbray. The intense Council member she had seen huddling with the King. 'I don't understand.' Weren't men supposed to be the rational ones? All this intrigue seemed far from the wise rule she had expected.

He looked up, eyes bleak. 'Let me explain. Richard has thrown us to the wolves for his own purposes, placing former enemies in positions of power like men on a chessboard.'

The realisation hit her like a bludgeon. She had thought, naïvely, all this time, that the King, at least, was free to rule wisely, as he liked. Even when he had disappointed Duncan before, she had thought there must be reason for it. But truth, it seemed, was far different. He had many powerful men he must placate.

And the poor folk of the north were not among them.

'It means,' he continued, 'there will be little money and fewer men to stretch along the border and that the King who promised to avenge us will be sitting in his southern palaces waiting for fair weather and a pleasant breeze before he lifts a finger.'

'And your father? His ransom? Was there any money for that?'

'Aye.' The word held no joy.

He pulled out a small bag. A few coins clinked inside, but it was so light, it swung easily at the end of his finger.

'It's not enough, is it?' she said.

He shook his head. 'Not half the sum. But a country bumpkin from Cliff's Tower is expected to be pleased with whatever his Majesty deigns to grant.'

'It is difficult when you must depend on the King,' she said, surprised to hear Solay's words come out of her mouth.

She had ignored that advice for so long, thinking it must not be so difficult for a man as for a woman. That a place near the King would mean a smooth path. But if Duncan had little influence, a clerk named 'John' would have none at all.

And her dreams of striding powerfully through the world of men shrivelled.

There was no easy power within reach of an outstretched hand. There was only hard work and small steps and hard-won victories difficult to explain to anyone else.

Even the woman who shared your bed.

She wrapped her arms around his waist, comforting him with closeness. 'You did everything you could and more than most.'

'Aye, but it wasn't enough.'

She leaned back to meet his eyes. 'Yes, it *was* enough.' She shook him with the word. 'God can move mountains and change the course of rivers and melt the hearts of kings. You cannot expect to do the same. You're not perfect, you know.'

He frowned and tried to pull away, but she would not let go. 'Well, thank you for reminding me of that. Here I thought I had won a great victory.'

'Do you think if you are perfect it will bring Peter back?'

The thrust of a sword could not have stopped him more completely. His lips parted and he stared blankly, as if seeing his brother's broken body again, reliving that moment and wishing more than life that he could take it back.

She cupped his cheeks in her palms and gradually his gaze cleared and he saw her again. 'You don't *have* to be perfect. I love your obstinate self just as you are.'

In answer, he put his hands on her cheeks and his lips, warm and true, on hers. She surrendered, feeling a wisp of something she did not recognise in his touch. Sadness, regret, the echo of a melancholy melody of home?

And when the kiss was through, he met her gaze, giving her only silence in answer to her heart's helpless questions.

Did I say too much? Do you want to wed me?

Will you if I tell the truth?

But the man who never lacked a ready word was mute.

Footsteps echoed in the corridor and they stepped apart. He ruffled her hair, as if she were Little John again. 'May his Majesty rot in purgatory for a thousand years. Then he might understand the life we mortals lead.'

How was she to tell him now that she shared Richard's blood?

'Come.' His mood had shifted again. 'If we leave within the hour we'll be back in Cambridge all the faster, and I have arrangements to make, quickly, before I leave.'

A cold shiver touched her neck. 'To go where?'

'North. I must take the ransom myself.'

'Why must *you* do it?' All her fear spilled into peevish words. She needed time to see Solay and Justin, to work out how to approach her mother, to work out what kind of life she might have with Duncan. She did not need a winter journey to the God-forsaken northland. 'It will take us weeks to get there and back. The Chancellor is unlikely to grant you such a long absence from teaching. And I've my presentation scheduled before the Master of Glomery.'

He looked at her then, and at his expression, everything in her stilled. What was in his eyes? Compassion? Pity? Sorrow? It was as if she could see the blow coming and could not dodge, but only stand and take it like a man.

'Well, that's the thing, honey. I'll be going alone. And I won't be coming back.'

Chapter Twenty

Duncan saw her stagger at his words and cursed himself anew.

He should have prepared her. Softened the blow. Made up a story as one would for a child.

But she had taught him to treat her as a man and it was hard to change that now.

'Why?' Fear and confusion mixed in her eyes.

A simple question, too difficult to answer.

'I will take what I have and meet with his captor and hope that it will be enough.' The King's coin mocked him. 'If not, I will tell them to let him go and keep me instead.'

There was no confusion in her eyes now. Only the terror of a child alone in the dark.

Or was it anger?

She gripped his arm. 'And what happens then, ya great guff? What if they decide to keep you both?'

The grim, dark irony brought no laugh. 'Well, then, I guess he and I will rot together.' A fitting end for him and the brutal bastard. Perhaps the only one that would ever end their war.

'And if they do let him go? Who will raise a ransom for you?'

His silence was answer enough.

'You have a brother. Why isn't he doing something?'

'Me brother's duty must be to his wife and child and the

tower and lands.' His brother fitted his station in life, unlike Duncan. 'My duty must be to bring me fadder home.'

She gazed at him like a hero then, though he knew she was only disguising her fear. 'And so you will. They'll take the King's gold and you'll both come home. And then you will come back. To Cambridge. To your oath.'

And there would be penance for breaking it, he knew. 'No. I'll stay and defend my home. How can I demand the King do it if I'm not willing?' She had asked him that the very first day, why he had left instead of fighting.

It wasn't because of fear. At least, not the physical kind.

He had tried to leave it, yet the barren, beautiful land lived inside him still, despite all his efforts to root it out. He had hidden it well, built a twilight life here, but one that succored only half his soul. And the two parts had brokered only a temporary truce, not a lasting peace.

I don't belong in either place, he had told her. The only place he seemed to belong was with her. And that was one place he could not be.

Her tears started, and if he had ever doubted her woman's heart, he could not do so now. 'You're a scholar, not a knight.'

Another of the many things she didn't know about him. They had not had time. Now, they never would.

'Do you think I grew up on the border without learning to fight? I'm a fair shot with the bow and arrow, I can swing a sword, or hurl a stone and if all else fails—' he held up his fists '—I've got these.'

She would have none of it. 'They slaughtered those men at Otterburn, the ones they could not ransom. Hundreds! You told me. Cut them down and just left them on the ground to die.'

He was sorry he had shared so much, back when he still thought she was a boy and needed to know.

He crossed his arms so he would not reach for her. When he looked at her he didn't want to fight. Didn't want to do anything but hold her in his arms for ever. 'I have nae choice. If the King will not save me home, I must.'

'Why you? Why always you? Why can't you let someone else bear the burden?'

'Have you learned nothing in your time among men?' A woman, still. She could not understand this thing. *Do you think it will bring him back?* Nothing would bring Peter back, but if he did not do enough, his fadder's loss would be on his soul as well.

'You're still breathin' so there's something else you must do. That's the answer, isn't it?'

Her words jolted him. And she spoke the challenge not with the sarcasm he expected, but with a deep sense of resignation, of acceptance of duty.

Yes, she had learned from living among them. 'Aye.'

'Then I will go with you.'

Now fear clutched him. Not fear of fighting or death, but of what she would find there.

'It's no place for a woman.' There were no soft edges to life there. Only what you could wrest from the earth and your enemy. And his hands were empty.

'I won't be a woman. I shall be John, your squire. We'll stay with the Scots or live in your tower and make rude remarks in Latin that no one else will understand.'

The stubborn fool. Ready to throw herself into danger with a boy's bravado. But she looked less like a boy every day. 'Ya can't, honey. Time has caught up with you. Your voice is too high, your hips too wide, your face too…' He cleared the catch from his throat and tried to focus on the practical, logical arguments. 'What will you do when, I mean, what will you do every month?'

'No one else will get close enough to see,' she said ferociously.

In that, she spoke true. Not as long as he was next to her.

He gentled his speech. 'It's too dangerous. I can't let you.'

'I can fight,' she said, blue eyes blazing. She raised her fists and tried to take her stance. 'You taught me.'

Here were all his good intentions come to bad effect. He should have sent her away the first moment he had seen Jane instead of John. But he had let her stay, hoping they could cobble together some kind of life. But he was a hybrid creature, like a centaur, lodged between two hostile worlds, fully part of neither.

And so was she.

'Jane, no.' He became calmer as she became more agitated. 'I am leaving alone.' She had no horse, no way to travel. Once he was mounted, he could leave her in the dust.

'If you do, I'll come after you. I'll find you. Now. Next week. Next year. I'll find you or die.'

Her words chilled him. He was no longer facing the Little John who had run away from home on a sunny August morning. More than her breasts had grown. She had melded female passion with male responsibility, honour and determination. And if he could no longer control her, he could not have loved her more.

She smiled, thinking he was beaten. 'You can't shake me. I can run faster than you.'

'No, you can't.' He looked at her, all their jumbled hopes and dreams churning inside him, and wished he could see the future with her foolish faith. 'I'm not gonna tell you again. I'm going to war. It's nae place for a woman.'

'But I won't be a woman!'

'Is it me you want or just the man's life you think I'll give you?'

She looked stunned as if he had slapped her. 'Can't *you* tell which part of me is John and which is Jane?'

'None of you is John. You're Jane. God's breath, you're a woman. Look at you!'

All the anguish he felt was on her face. 'But—'

He held up his hand. 'This disguising is over. You're going to your sister or you're going to the convent, but you're not going with me.'

Not where she'd see everything about himself he had hoped to forget.

'I'll run away!' Her pout was back and her lip quivered.

His throat ached with tears he wished he could shed. 'Ah, my Little Jane, ya canna run all your life.'

He forced himself to turn his back on her and throw things into his bag, not really seeing them.

Behind him, all was silence.

Then, she crept over, put her arms around his waist and pressed herself against him. 'Will I ever see you again?' Her voice was small, tired. Defeated.

He should say no, but he couldn't kill all her hopes. Or his. 'Maybe. Some day.' Yet he knew, as she did, there would be no some day if he left alone.

He could feel her shake and he wanted to cry with her, to howl at his loss. He could not look at her or he would take her in his arms and never let go.

'When will you go?'

'As soon as I can arrange affairs in Cambridge. Just a few days and then I'll ride north.'

Alone.

The tower would rise to greet him on the green slope of a wide valley, standing guard over the river crossing. If he lived, he'd wander the hills again when summer came and sing alone before winter's fire. And without this strange half-woman who saw inside his soul, there would ever, always, be a hole in his heart that nothing else would ever fill.

Sitting behind him on the horse, forehead resting against his back, she wept for all she could not have.

His eyes were straight ahead. He would not see.

Ya cannae run all your life.

Yet what else had she done? No wonder he did not want her with him. She was no better than a child, a burden, not a help.

Despite her promise to Solay, to herself, she had faced nothing. Resolved nothing.

Well, she had learned one thing, finally, in her time among men. Building a life was hard. A man must take responsibility for himself and his actions.

The time had come for her to do the same.

Until she did, she wasn't worthy of the royal blood she was so proud of. Her mother, too, had been strong, willing to do what she must, to fight for her daughters and her due. Solay had been the same.

But Jane? All she had done was to don chausses instead of a skirt and expect the world to open to her. And when it didn't, she waited for Duncan or the King to give it to her instead.

Solay would be looking for her this morning. When she discovered Jane was gone, they would come after her, just as soon as Justin could be free of his obligations at Westminster.

Then they would take her home, force her into a skirt and Duncan would ride north alone.

Perhaps to death.

Before they found her, she must make Duncan see that they belonged together, in Cliff's Tower or in Cambridge, but in a life that was different from others', even if she still did not know what that might mean. She was a woman. She was reconciled to that now, even delighting in it some days, though not a woman like the rest.

But even if he capitulated, if he agreed to take her with him, the lie still lay between them.

She would defy her mother if she must, but once Duncan discovered the truth, would he still want her?

Enough of searching for logical answers that did not exist. She *was* a woman. She had a way to bind him to her for ever, using the only weapon, in the end, that she possessed.

And use it she would.

Shamelessly.

Lifting her head, she let the wind dry her tears.

She would not let him leave alone.

Chapter Twenty-One

She crept into his room a few nights later and watched him, sprawled on his back in sleep, restless, as if he would wake any minute. She cherished the cool moonlight on his dark hair, the fan of his lashes on his face.

She had seen little of him since they had returned. He had to explain to the Chancellor how he would pay for breaking his oath, then brief Henry on how to take on his duties at the hostel until a new principal was chosen. He must have visited St Radegund's and spoken with the nuns, though she had refused to listen when he tried to explain where she would live.

Did he dream of her? Did he have regrets?

Quickly, she shed her tunic and unwrapped her breasts, able to breathe deeply again.

He would face her, she would face herself, as she was.

The January night was cold, and she wondered that he could sleep, chest bare and without a blanket. She touched his skin, her fingers nearly burned by its heat.

He grabbed her hand and his eyes flew open and locked with hers.

She rolled on top of him, taking warmth from his body, stopping his lips with a kiss before they could protest. She felt awkward, lying on him, her back chilled by the night air. Always before he had covered her and she'd been warmed by him above and the bed below.

His arms came around her. His tongue plundered her mouth. Below, he leapt to attention, immediately ready.

How astonishing, to be a man and ready to make love in a moment. And she knew, because she had roused him from sleep, his body would best his brain and he would not send her away until it was too late.

He tried to roll, to put her beneath him, but she dug her toes into the mattress, resisting in a wordless war.

She pulled away, leaning on her arms above him, and shook her head. 'Not this time,' she whispered. 'This time, you are mine.' She rose, poised on top of him. 'This time, you will fill me fully.'

She sheathed him in her softness, slowly. He moaned, unwilling, or unable, to protest. Her eyes widened as he entered her, even more deeply when she came to him from above. Surely, this way, his seed would find her womb.

From this unfamiliar perch, she discovered a new freedom. Her hips found their own pace. Her fingers found his hidden weak spots.

She revelled in her power. Her hips, her fingers, even her tongue spoke a language she did not know she knew. Not the language of love alone, though certainly the language of lovers. But also the language of seduction and strength and subversion.

Not the straightforward language of men, but the tongue that sheathed strength in weakness, that belonged to women alone.

Now, tonight, they would be truly one. Tonight, she would unleash that mysterious power that had terrified him so, to do the one thing only a woman could do.

Always, he had protected her, careful not to fill her with his seed. Tonight, she would be his master, wielding the elemental force of nature that at once separated and bound them.

She rocked him, the ecstasy on his face all she had hoped to see. But she had not realised that when he was below, his hands could roam at will. He put one on each side of her head and kissed her, hard, and then let his fingers slip to her breasts, more sensitive because of their long confinement. He stroked them softly, side to tip, giving her a shock that started in her breast and ended in the space between her legs where he swelled inside her.

He had turned the tables now, his nimble fingers touching and teasing the nubs of her breasts, then the one between her legs. Then, no longer gentle, he grabbed her arms as if he would hold her all night, and longer.

She was mindless then, rocking, twisting, wanting to consume him with her body. All the logic of seduction, the workings of her brain, disappeared until she was only a body, gloriously alive. A body that sang to his without words.

Skin was no longer a barrier, but a conduit for feelings that moved like waves, from one to the other and back. They merged into one being, neither man nor woman but whole, complete, creating something totally new.

Life.

An animal moan rose in her throat. She struggled to stop it before it became a scream of delight, of joy, of aliveness.

His hands were on her hips as she stroked, and she did not know which of them set the rhythm, higher, faster.

And she buried her teeth in his shoulder to stifle the cry that came so strongly that she knew the seed must have taken root.

Her body, still shaking, covered his and he pulled the abandoned blanket over her back, so she would not be cold.

She sighed, with a sense of peace, ready to enjoy the rest of the night. When tomorrow came, he would have to hear the truth.

He woke, realising he had dreamed of home.

Of the monks, cloistered in their yellow stone abbey. Of the peasants, barefoot and digging peat with the spades. In his dream, he joined them again, the earth firm against his feet, the wind wild at his back, the hills filling his eyes.

He had left, intending never to return to a home that held only emptiness.

His parents shared no bond that he could see, either with their children or with each other. They drifted through life like ice floating in the same river, bumping into each other, but never freezing solidly together.

Words were neither valued nor welcomed. Nothing he did elicited even a nod of approval.

So he escaped the tower to take the sheep to pasture and roam the hills or to work beside the men in the fields. The sheep were silent. Cowed and confused by the master's son, the serfs never spoke either, thinking him mad, he supposed, for playing peasant.

But he did it for the physical joy of feeling his muscles move. For the bliss of being close to the hills, the lakes, the land.

Out there, he sensed, and sometimes even grasped, the peace that was beaten out of him at home.

He had left, intending never to return, but duty, like a debt overdue, had found him.

Just after he had found the woman, the one woman, who seemed to understand. Who wanted to join her life to his.

He knew what she had done tonight. And why.

And it didn't matter.

It wouldn't have mattered, no matter what she had done.

He tried to picture it, introducing her to his parents: *This is me wife.*

His father would look at her clothes, scowl and insult her to her face. *What kind of a sow is that? Did ya get kaylied and get her with child? That's no reason for marryin'.*

And his mother would look at the dirt, silent, and he'd remember all the reasons he had left the place, looking for something else. Something *more*.

Too late, he had found it.

No, he could not take her to that barren place. She might learn to love the wild land as he did, but that wouldn't be enough.

When she met his family, she would curse him. She would see the chasm that separated her life from his, too wide for hands, even loving ones, to reach across.

And if there was a child to be raised in the hell he had suffered— No. That must never be. If there was a child, they would marry, but he would somehow find money to send, for the boy to be raised somewhere softer. Better.

Maybe, maybe, if he survived the Scots, he might find her again. But he couldn't see the pieces of that dream. Couldn't ask her to wait for it. Now, there was only duty.

As the rest of the night slipped into dawn, he held her to him, drained of words, of thought, of everything but knowing he must have her and knowing why he could not.

He loved her. And he would leave her. And as soon as she woke, he would tell her.

He felt her lips and heard the sweet babble of her voice before he even opened his eyes.

'It won't take me long to be ready, though I'd like to start us on the journey with clean clothes. If I wash them this morning, they should be dry by tomorrow. Is that soon enough?'

Soft lips brushed his nose and the mattress shifted as she rose from the bed, not waiting for an answer.

Thinking she already knew what the answer was.

He watched her poke the fire. A smile of perfect contentment lit her face. A woman. His woman. Carrying his seed, maybe even his child.

As if last night had changed everything instead of nothing.

Now. He must tell her now. 'Jane, come here. There are some things I must say.'

The fire flared, but instead of climbing under the covers with him, she walked to the shutters, blanket dragging behind her, and opened them a crack. 'No snow today. Fair weather for our journey.'

Cold air swirled into the room.

'Close the damn shutter and come over here. What I must say is about the journey.' He regretted his sharp tongue, but it was hard enough to speak at all.

The shutters rattled as she threw the latch and shut out both the wind and the weak sun. 'Before you start, I must say something myself. There's something you must know.'

The shiver that snaked up his spine was not from the chill air, but from her expression that had turned from contentment to foreboding.

'What, then?' he asked, afraid he did not really want the answer. 'Be quick about it.'

Chapter Twenty-Two

Jane watched his eyes, grey like a gathering storm, wondering what he was so impatient to tell her.

She knew she must not touch him. If she did, she would be lost in his body again and would hide the truth if that would ensure they could be together.

She pulled the edges of the blanket together. She had promised to face her life and make amends. She must lay the truth between them so that they could embark on their life together.

'I didn't tell you all,' she began, her voice shaking, 'about my family.'

'You didn't tell me you were a woman, either. What could be more astounding than that?' His brusque words dismissed her confession.

'If I tell you the truth, will you not be angry?'

Will you still love me? That was what she wanted to ask. But there might not be 'still'. He had never said the word at all.

'I won't be angry. What is it?'

Meaningless words, said in haste, when she longed for a lyric. 'Will you promise?'

'Ah, were you suckled on promises then, Little Jane?' His impatience had been replaced by something else. 'Those easily made are easily broken.'

Promise, she pleaded. But he had never promised her anything at all.

She would start slowly. So he might adjust to the idea. 'I told you I was orphaned.'

'You're not.'

She nodded.

'No more than I expected. Then who are your parents?'

'My father is dead.'

His face transformed then. 'I'm sorry, honey.' His brother's loss coloured the words.

She rushed on, because the death was not the truth she needed to tell. 'And he was the King.'

A sharp laugh washed over his concern. 'This is no time for a jape. And you're no princess.'

'No, I'm not a princess.' She took a large breath. 'I am the daughter of our late King Edward and Alys de Weston.'

His laugh crumbled. Stunned pain flickered over his face, then anger crushed it. 'So yer done playin' with me now. Is that what yer tellin' me?'

She felt the blood drain from her cheeks. 'No, that's not—'

'Well, ya needn't worry, honey. I won't be holding you to any "ever after" in the Godforsaken northland.'

Anger she had expected, but not this. 'What are you talking about?'

'Now that you've had your fun with the boys, you're ready to move up to a more powerful man. The King has already promised you King's Hall. That's a big step up from a hostel full of northern savages.'

'I told you I only said what I did so he would not be angry. This is about my family.'

But he had heard all he meant to hear.

'Did ya choose your next lover from the courtiers at Westminster while I was on my knees beggin' the Council for more than a farthing?'

'That's not true. Don't you know that's not true?'

'I was worthy of a grammar student, but you've earned your bachelors of the mattress, haven't you? When you're a master, do you bed royalty?'

'Stop it! Stop it!'

'I am honoured that I was your first. If I *was* your first. Or maybe you just wanted to know what a northern barbarian's tarse felt like. I may not have a royal *botellus*, but you didn't seem to mind when it was between your legs.'

She hurled her hand at his cheek and slapped him with all the force he had taught her to throw. 'I don't deserve that. And neither do you.'

He opened his mouth to deny it, but no words came from a face blank and uncomprehending.

She narrowed her eyes and stared at this stranger. Body, mind, heart—had she known him at all? Yet he'd assaulted her with words that said she was a stranger to him, too. Now that he knew who she was, everything he should have known about her was buried in his preconceptions.

You've heard the stories, have ya? One of the first things he had ever said to her. Well, he had heard the stories about Alys de Weston, too.

'You're ashamed, aren't you? That's why you won't take me home.' She laughed. There was even an edge of mirth in it. 'A woman who has lived among all those lusty young scholars— that's no woman you can present to your parents, is it?'

Everything shifted behind his eyes now, and then, she glimpsed Duncan again.

'That's not it,' he began. 'You don't know…what it's like there…about them.' The man who had swayed Parliament couldn't summon a simple sentence of defence. 'I can't take you, but not because of what you said. That's what I was going to tell you. Me fadder, me madder—'

She could barely sort out the excuses that tumbled from his

lips. 'Not another word about your mother or your father or your brothers or your Godforsaken hills and lakes.' She grabbed for her clothes, trying to put them on before she was blinded. 'You're known for your smooth tongue, Master Duncan, but you're a lousy liar.' His accent tasted like tears. 'If I was a shame to you, ya cudda just said so, honey. I would have understood.'

And she did now. No matter how far she ran, as long as she was the harlot's daughter, she would never be good enough to be anything else, man or woman.

'Not that. Never that.' There was something in his eyes she didn't understand, but it was too late to wonder at it. 'But you canna come with me. I'll take you home before I leave.'

'No. I don't want anything from you.'

'I'll ask Geoffrey and Henry to go with you, then. The roads are dangerous—'

'You will tell no one anything. About Jane or about my family.' She was responsible for herself now. And all her dreadful consequences. Just as she had always wanted. It was a cold and lonely feeling. 'I want nothing from you. From any of you.'

'But I must be sure you're taken care of. And if there's a babe—'

The word, a thunderbolt, stopped them both.

What would she do now, if a cruel God answered her prayer?

'If there's a babe,' he said, in a whisper, 'send word. We'll wed by proxy and I'll send you everything I have.'

Everything except himself.

She made the mistake of looking at him. 'You will not hear from me. You will not see me. You will not be burdened by me. Ever again.'

She paused at the door to swallow the choked feeling in her throat. 'Fare well.'

After she left, Duncan stared at the closed door, disbelieving. Boy. Woman. Child of a king. Daughter of a whore. Bent on sparing her from the miserable life that awaited him, his brain had scrambled at her announcement.

. At first, he thought she teased him, when he was in no mood to laugh.

Then, he decided she was rejecting him. If a dirt floor and a cold stone tower wasn't enough to offer Jane the orphan, how much less suitable would it be for Jane, the princess? No need to wait until she saw his family and his home before he felt her disdain. She scorned him already, just as he had expected.

And jumbled with that was his fear that all had been feigned, her innocence, her love, all of it. That she had merely amused herself before she moved on to the powerful men of Richard's Court.

He could dispute against the best masters, but when he tried to speak of his feelings to this woman, he babbled like a babe.

By the time he regretted his wayward tongue, it was too late. She was gone.

And why did he regret that? He had got what he wanted. She would not be coming with him.

But for all the wrong reasons.

You're ashamed of me. Her accusation, so ridiculous, now echoed in his ears. No shame in being born of a king and his mistress. He wouldn't have cared if she had been the laundress's daughter. He loved her anyway.

Could she possibly feel the same about him? Could she love him even after she met his parents, knew his life?

Fists pounded on his door and then it opened.

'Was that Little John?' Henry said. 'He looked like a she.'

'He *is* a she.' Geoffrey talked over Henry. 'I asked you, Duncan, and you lied to me! You've known all the time!'

Henry hadn't stopped. 'All this time, you've been swiving him, her, under my nose? Was she good?'

'Shut your mouth. Close the door.' He felt naked as a needle, and raised his fists, as if to protect her. 'And don't talk about her that way.'

Henry held up his hands in surrender. Geoffrey, on the other hand, couldn't stop talking. 'I asked you. You remember I asked you and you looked me straight in the eye and told me a lie bigger than St Mary's tower. What's her name? Who is she?'

The woman I love and just lost. He sagged, dropping on to the bed and holding his head in his hands. 'Her name is Jane and she's the daughter of King Edward and Alys de Weston.'

'Ha, ha.' Henry didn't even try to laugh. 'Now tell us the truth.'

'I am.'

They exchanged glances and sat, one on either side of him.

'I think,' said Geoffrey, 'you need to start at the beginning.'

Chapter Twenty-Three

She ran past Geoffrey and Henry and back to the boys' dormitory, lucky to find privacy to finish putting on her boy's costume again before she was discovered. Ducking under a blanket, she tugged her linen binding back into place, gasping for a breath as she forced it tight across her chest.

He did not want her. She had thought she knew so much about men, but in the end, she had been as foolish as any other virgin, giving herself to a man, all the while confusing love and lust.

Ya cannae run all your life.

It was time to go home, to make peace with her family. And with herself.

Geoffrey and Henry no doubt knew the truth by now. She could only hope it wouldn't spread before she could leave.

She gathered her things.

She glanced at herself in the mirror, one of the King's gifts to her mother. Until Jane had shared Duncan's bed, she hadn't understood the intimacy of the carving of the knight with his hand on the maiden's breast.

She understood that madness all too well now. And it was all she had ever feared.

The sack was as light as it had been on her first journey. Only her heart was heavier.

She would stop by the market for food for the road and by the alehouse to say goodbye to Hawys and thank her for being a friend. Strange that she had come here to live among men, yet it was a woman whose friendship would remain.

She crept down the stairs, past Duncan's closed door, and left Solar Hostel.

She would find a way to live. Not like other women, but as a woman all the same.

The thought put a swing in her hips. She saw Hawys under the vegetable seller's awning, and waved, eager to tell her.

'There! Get her!'

Rough, harsh hands grabbed her and dragged her off the street and in between two buildings.

Slammed against a wooden wall, she gasped for breath, taking in the smell of leather, then blinked, trying to clear her head.

Four ruffians circled her. She had seen them once or twice before when she was safely surrounded by Duncan and Geoffrey and Henry.

She had even been impolitic enough to correct their grammar.

The largest one was leering at her, wearing that face men did when they saw women a certain way.

And her joy in her womanhood vanished.

She tried to take her fighting stance, but two of them held her fast against the wall.

The leader, smelling of onions and ale, leaned closer. 'There's a trick! Smart ones at Solar. They dress you up like a boy so you can live there and service them all! We'd like some o' that.'

Steady. I must be John a little longer.

She shrugged against their hold, sticking out her chest and chin with her best man's bravado. 'You're blind if you can't tell a girl from a boy. Or maybe you're the kind who likes boys?'

One of them, taking her meaning, let go as if she had burned him.

'Don't let her fool you,' the leader said. 'She's no boy.'

'Yes, I am.' She kept her voice low and strong. 'So get your hands off me unless you want to be thought a sodomite.'

The others looked to the leader. A moment of doubt drifted into the big man's eyes. 'If you're a man,' he said, finally, 'prove it. Show us your tarse.'

Sweat escaped her scalp, drenching her hair under her cap. *Now everything she had learned must save her.*

She didn't look down at the sock rolled up and stuffed in her breeches, but she thrust her hips ever so slightly forwards, as if she had much to be proud of. 'It's bigger than yours, I'll wager, but I don't need to flaunt mine in the street. Or maybe you just want to show yours.'

'You first.' He reached for her, but she was quicker, flinging her foot into his crotch.

He yelped.

Then all four were on her, and she was on her back in the mud with one holding each arm, one on her feet and the leader sitting on top of her thighs.

'Now I'll show you mine.' He grinned, mouth full of missing teeth. 'Right between your legs.'

Fear surged in every vein. The risks had never seemed real when her men were beside her.

The leader's weight was crushing. 'Now let's see how much of a man you are.' And he pulled her chausses down.

The poor, crumpled linen unravelled, rolling off her hip and into the mud.

Without it, she was exposed. To everything.

She closed her eyes and prayed for forgiveness and mercy to a God who would have no reason to answer.

When she opened her eyes, she saw He had.

Duncan pulled the big man off her and pummelled his stomach. The other three jumped off her to circle him.

Duncan's eyes met hers, and all the love she would ever want to see was in them. 'Run, Jane.'

But instead, she pulled up her pants, cinched the tie and started swinging, trying to even the odds. She stayed out of reach, trying not to be taken again, hitting heads, backs, arms, anything she could reach.

In the blur at the edge of her eye, she saw Hawys and realised she must have run for help.

Duncan had told her he knew how to fight. Now she believed it. He fought like a man possessed. Beating, swinging, kicking— even the Scots would bow before such fury.

But he was still just one man.

And when one of them grabbed her arms behind her back, she was left kicking helplessly into the air. Three were free to wrestle Duncan to the ground.

Frantic, she looked for help, but Hawys had disappeared.

The leader, with a black eye and a bloody lip, clutched his stomach, nursing his wounds from her kick and Duncan's punch.

'So now we've bested the University man,' the leader snarled. He kicked Duncan in the ribs.

She searched the street. Where was Henry? Geoffrey? Was the entire hostel at lecture? Even a beadle would have been welcome.

'Hold his arm out,' he said, with a jerk of his head. 'He'll never throw a punch like that again.'

One of the men stretched his arm out and sat on it. Duncan struggled, but they beat his head and stomach until he was dazed. She kicked and screamed, her foot hitting the leader's leg this time. Backhanded, he slapped her head.

Her face throbbed and she sagged, dizzy.

Then, he turned back to Duncan, positioned his foot over the outstretched fingers and rolled his full weight over Duncan's right hand until she could hear the horrible crack of breaking bones.

'No!' Her scream, she realised.

They let him go, then, his hand bloody and crooked against the muddy street.

'You want her so much, take her. We would have shared.'

Duncan, gasping against the pain, raised his head, eyes full of fury that refused them the satisfaction of hearing him cry out. And he gathered the strength he needed to spit out one word. 'Never.'

The four took a step back, as if confronted by a spirit risen from the dead. The one behind her dropped her arms and she whirled, punching his jaw and then his gut. He dropped to his knees.

Rage drove her, stronger than logic or fear. They had hurt Duncan. They would pay if it took her life.

She flung her foot at the leader, missing his vulnerable spot, but he staggered. An elbow, a fist, a knee hurled at the others caught them off-guard.

Then, all three came towards her.

'Jane! Stop!' Geoffrey's voice.

She felt the strength of the group behind her and the ruffians ran, chased by Henry and a few others, halfway down the street.

The red haze of hate faded. Jane slumped against Geoffrey, the fear and anger that had propelled her both gone. He had called her Jane.

Her manhood lay trampled in the mud at her feet, no more than a soiled rag. She had no time to mourn her own loss. No time to process the violation of body and spirit.

It didn't matter now.

Only Duncan mattered now.

She fell to her knees and pressed her cheek against his sweat-soaked face.

'Ya threw a decent punch or two,' he said, sheer will forcing the words through a jaw clenched against the pain. 'Next time, go for the eyes.'

'Yer a stubborn fool, Duncan of Cliff's Tower,' she whispered, and gave his jaw a playful tap. She must not break down in useless sobs. If he could bury his pain and mask his fear, so could she.

She looked up. Hawys, who must have brought the reinforcements, stood at her shoulder.

Geoffrey, Henry and a couple of the other men formed a wall

around her and Duncan. Logic blessed her and she saw, with terrible clarity, what must be done.

She touched him carefully, arms, ribs, legs, trying to determine whether he had other injuries.

'The ribs may need wrapping,' he said, eyes closed, but with an ironic smile. 'And the hand.'

'Carry him home,' she said, praying the jostling would do no irreparable harm. Then she looked at his battered face and pasted a smile on her own. 'Yer a great lotta trouble, Master Duncan. It's a good thing you have mates to help you.'

He didn't hear her. He had finally let go.

Geoffrey scooped up his shoulders, Henry his feet. The right arm, with its mangled hand, dangled at his side. She took it, gently, crossed his arms over his chest and dropped back to follow the men.

Hawys walked beside her.

'I was leaving to go home,' she whispered. It was hard to remember what had happened now. It seemed years ago. 'Duncan didn't want me. He was ashamed…'

Pain stole her voice.

'Ashamed?' Hawys reared back, indignant. 'You're a woman and a half.'

She shook her head. No need to tell Hawys that half the woman was of royal blood.

Not allowed to enter, Hawys left her at the hostel door. 'I'll be praying for you,' she whispered.

Bereft, Jane watched her leave, then pulled the sodden cloak around her, hoping it would be disguise enough. 'Does everyone know?' she asked Geoffrey, before she crossed the threshold. No one would keep her out of Solar Hostel, woman or not.

'A few. They'll keep their silence.'

'See that they do.'

The Common Room fell silent as they carried Duncan, still limp, towards the stairs. No jests. No laughing insults. This was no ordinary brawl.

Once in his room, she closed the door on them. Explanations would come later.

Geoffrey and Henry laid him on the bed, then waited, as if she had the right to decide what to do. As if she would know, instinctively, how to nurture and heal.

'Henry, build up the fire, then bring me a pot of water and some rags. Geoffrey, get the surgeon,' she began.

He hesitated. 'Perhaps Matthew Gregory instead? He's a good physician.'

She shook her head, allowing herself the smallest laugh. Duncan had taught her that the prejudice against surgeons was misguided. 'Does this look like an imbalance of humours? He needs someone versed in bones.' Her words were a prayer. This would be beyond even the cleverest surgeon's experience.

Wood nursed into flame, Henry stood.

'And along with the surgeon, bring me the most potent wine you can find. For him,' she added, at the shock on their faces. 'And one more thing.'

They paused.

'Go to St Michael's and light a candle.'

Geoffrey hugged her, not the hug he would have given John, but one that tried to comfort without touching her as a woman. Henry wiped his hand on his shirt, then held it for her to shake.

She closed the door behind them, shutting out the waiting scholars. Let Geoffrey explain.

She rested her forehead on the rough wood. Fear lingered at her shoulder, smothering her breath. What if she failed him?

She tiptoed to the bed, forcing herself to look at his right hand.

Mangled beyond recognition, his hand—hard to call it that—lay on top of his chest. She stretched her fingers over it, wishing a caress would take away the pain instead of kindling it anew.

Blood had seeped into his clothes and the linens, flowing like the Nile ran red. She looked around the room, but there were no cloths to stop the flow. Then she felt the linen chafing the delicate skin of her breasts, and knew what she could do.

She slipped her arms out of her sleeves, unwrapped the cloth from her breasts, wrapped it into a ball and put her arms back into her sleeves.

Edging back to the bed, she unwrapped a length of the fabric and placed it loosely on top of his hand. But blood soaked the layers as quickly as she piled them on. She held her breath, trying to be careful, but her fingers shook and she touched him when she didn't mean to and felt his bones shift.

The familiar, helpless feeling washed over her. She stumbled away from him, backing up until her spine pressed against the bumpy wall.

Duncan lay helpless on the bed, unmoving.

She grasped at a sliver of air coming in the shutter. It did little to calm her queasy stomach.

This was all she had run from. The responsibility to care for another in a moment that could mean life or death.

I can't.

She was no good at this. Any minute Duncan might die while she stood by, useless. What should she do? Where should she start? What if her bungling made him worse?

Yet in this eternity while she prayed for the surgeon to come quickly, there was no one else.

No one to take care of her. No way to shirk her duty. No one to turn to in case she failed.

No one to depend on but herself.

She was still breathing. And so was he.

Sitting softly on the bed, she gripped his left hand in hers, as if to hold one would save the other.

Blessedly, he still slept, face and arms covered with cuts and bruises. She'd seen that in him from the first day: a man life had battered, but never beaten.

Jane would not let him be beaten now.

She might not be perfect, she might not even be good enough, but she was here and she loved him and she would not run.

She rolled up her sleeves to begin.

The wine arrived before the surgeon.

Geoffrey handed it to her and she poured a bracing sip for herself before she set the rest aside, hoping there would be enough to keep Duncan's pain at bay if he woke. She wished she'd paid attention when her mother and Solay had explained the recipe for dwale to dull the pain.

Henry had come with the water and rags and she had washed off the worst of Duncan's dirt and blood, gently. She had not touched his hand again.

A quick knock preceded the surgeon, who entered without waiting to be asked. With backward glances, Geoffrey and Henry left her with him.

The surgeon was a small man with a large nose and an expressionless face. She followed him to the bed, limp with relief, her tongue faltering as she explained what had happened.

'You're in my light,' he said, not looking at her. 'Step aside until I need you.'

Until.

She backed away, heart pounding. 'I'm not good at this.' She heard her voice rise. 'I don't know what to do…' Her hands waved in the air, like the flapping of a bird's wings.

She clasped them behind her back.

At least she *had* two working hands.

'I'll tell you when I need you.' He glanced up at her and around the room. 'Play a little for now,' he said, nodding toward the gittern, standing mockingly in the corner. 'It may soothe him.'

The instrument, mute, seemed to accuse her. 'I only know a few chords.'

'He won't criticise.'

She wasn't sure of that. Music had healing power. Her awkward notes might aggravate his pain instead of relieving it.

But she picked it up anyway, strummed idly for a few moments, then launched into the verse.

As brothers we wander
Eat, drink, love and squander,
As the Pope bade us do
Live as friends ever true.

The surgeon glanced across the bed at her with raised eyebrows. She shrugged. 'It's the only song I know.'

She could not tell whether it had comforted Duncan, but concentrating on the music calmed her. Watching her fingers, she couldn't watch the surgeon, or what he was doing to Duncan.

The surgeon interrupted the chorus. 'Are you his wife?'

She blinked. So obvious, of course, that she was a woman. She shook her head, hoping he would not report her for being in the hostel.

'A family member? He cannot speak for himself. Someone must make a decision.'

She thought of the pele tower far away. Of Henry and Geoffrey downstairs. None of them had more right than she.

None of them loved him as much.

'I will make it.'

'The bones are badly broken. I can leave the hand as it is, and he will lose all use of it. Or I can try to move the bones back into place. That will mean a chance that some will mend. I make no promises.' Compassion touched his eyes and he softened his voice. 'The pain will be severe and I suspect he will lose the use of it either way.'

And she knew, as if Duncan had spoken, what he would want her to do.

The world's no place for a cripple.

She leaned over to kiss his damp brow, then met the surgeon's gaze. 'Do anything you can to save it.'

And when Duncan began to scream, she started to sing. A different song this time. One she was not sure she knew.

To see you fills my eyes.
To touch you fills my hand.
To taste you fills my mouth.
To love you fills my heart.

Let us lay down together
Let me fill you forever
Let us love one another
As long as I've breath.

After the surgeon had left, she lost track of day and night. She followed his instructions, staunched the bleeding with fresh cloths, cooled Duncan's brow when the fever came. She had called for Matthew Gregory the physician after the surgeon left, always afraid that whatever she did, it would not be enough.

And she thought of nothing beyond these walls.

Finally, in a moment of peace, he dozed and there was nothing more to do and nothing left in the quiet room but pain.

She opened the shutters and blinked, surprised to see a day bathed in sunshine. Beyond this room, life flowed on. In the Common Room, the men gathered for a meal, murmuring their concern for Duncan, coupled with prayers of gratitude that they had been spared. Then they would go on, to classes, to church, to the alehouse, to their lives.

But Duncan's life would never be the same.

He would not go home to grip a sword or throw a rock, nor be able to mark a student's Latin letters. He would not coax a melody from the strings of the gittern again.

She turned her back on the world outside and watched him, hoping he would sleep in blissful ignorance awhile longer.

He did not open his eyes until the sun rose again.

She knew the minute it happened, for she had been watching him for hours.

His eyes, full of forgetfulness, met hers. Memory at bay, he smiled as he had so many times and started to rub the sleep from his eyes.

She tried to stop him, but the movement was so natural, it wasn't until he raised both arms that he saw it.

For a moment, he stared at the heavily wrapped, mangled paw at the end of his right arm as if he did not know what it was.

Then remembrance gripped his face.

She gathered both his hands in hers, hoping he would look at her instead of his wound. 'You are *alive*,' she said, the words urgent. 'I am with you. All will be well.'

He struggled against her, pulling his arms away, then tried to form a fist with his right hand, as if to pound his palm in frustration.

She reached for his flailing arms. 'You must stay still. You'll dislodge the bones and they may not heal.'

He met her gaze then, his own bleak and hard. 'They will not heal no matter what I do.'

'Perhaps. In time. If you are careful.' She had thought never to conceal the truth again, but she did so now.

'I am not a child to be fooled with a bedtime story. I have the training of a physician.' He held up the white, bandaged blob at the end of his arm. 'Even if the bones knit again, this hand will be good for nothing.'

'No, that's not true—'

He sat up then and shook the bloody bandaged hand in front of her face like a club. 'Will I be able to write with this hand? Will I?'

She pursed her lips and shook her head.

'Will I be able to hold a sword or a stone?'

She could not let him go on. 'I'm not sure, it's too soon—'

He rode over her feeble lies. 'Will these worthless fingers be able to touch you like ya like? To make you cry aloud in pleasure?'

'It doesn't matter. We'll find a way—'

He grasped her shoulder, awkward, with his left hand. 'Don't lie to me, woman.' His voice, a roar of anger and pain. He looked at the gittern beside the bed. 'Will I ever play again?'

She looked down at the instrument and then back at him, letting her eyes meet his. 'It will be difficult.'

He let go of her shoulder, practically pushing her away. 'Impossible, ya mean.'

It was better, that he died. That's what he had said of his brother.

'I will be with you. We will discover an answer together. You could still teach.'

His eyes no longer saw her. She faced a stranger. 'I had little to offer you before. I have nothing now. For you. For anyone.' He lay down and turned his back on her. 'Go. I don't want you here.'

Strengthened by those long hours alone with him, she rose. He had always helped others. He did not know how to be helped. It would take time for him to adjust.

She could wait.

She picked up the pitcher. 'I'm leaving, but only to get water and bandages. I'll be back.'

But when she returned, he had barred the door.

Chapter Twenty-Four

It was Justin's fifth tavern of the day and in each one, he'd bought the obligatory tankard of ale.

He sipped this one slowly, still out of sorts about his fight with Solay. They had agreed to tell the truth, always, but his wife had seen Jane at Westminster and kept it from him until it was too late.

By the time he had found out, the girl had disappeared again.

The little fool had done what they had all feared, run away dressed as a man and now the worst had happened.

Jane had told her some story about being in love and Solay was all sympathy. Soft-hearted, his wife. And soft-headed about this. He would have hauled Jane home instead of letting her go back to the clutches of a man who had obviously taken advantage of a poor, naïve girl.

A hostel, Solay remembered that much. But there were dozens. So here he was, haunting Cambridge's drinking houses, trying to pick up the trail. Scholars weren't supposed to be in taverns, of course. He was glad to see that rule was still honoured in the breach, just as it had been in his student days.

He set down the mug. He had lost his taste for student ale.

So he told the tale for the fifth time, the searcher, the story, the student. The master from the north country.

This time, the alewoman's eyes lit up. 'Ah, that'd be Duncan and Little John. They're here many nights with the rest, but not since the terrible brawl. It's been ten days, at least.'

'Where do they live?'

'Solar Hostel. Across from Holy Trinity.'

He thought of returning to the inn to tell Solay of his luck, but decided to wait until he had the girl in hand.

This time, she would not slip away.

Jane woke to see Geoffrey shaking her shoulder, a confused crease on his forehead. 'There's a man downstairs. Looking for John.'

She sat up and shook her head to clear the fog from her brain. 'How is Duncan?' When Duncan had locked her out, she had given Geoffrey and Henry instructions on how to care for him. They, in turn, had given her their room and she had slept deeply, for the first time in days. 'Did he let you in?'

He nodded. 'And the surgeon, too.'

She swung her legs over the side of the bed. 'Did he eat?'

'A little.'

Well, at least the stubborn man was not going to starve himself to death. 'What time is it?' Even the bells hadn't wakened her.

'After terce.'

She ran her fingers through her hair. She'd had on the same clothes for more than a week and wondered whether she could have a bath without anyone else discovering her sex.

'Geoffrey,' she began, 'you're probably wondering—'

'Duncan told us. Even before the fight.'

'Us?' It came back to her now. He had yelled her name in the street. 'You and Henry and who else?'

'Just us. I've made sure that the rest, if they suspect, will hold their tongues.'

Dear, sweet Geoffrey. 'Mary is a lucky woman.'

'What about the man who's waiting to see you?' Geoffrey asked.

She had forgotten him already. Probably a suspicious beadle

who wanted to fine them for fighting. 'Can you tell him you couldn't wake me?'

'He says he is the husband of your sister.'

'Justin? Here?' She should not have been surprised. 'Tell him I'm coming.'

She splashed cold water on her face, ran her fingers through her hair and tugged at the rumpled tunic, trying to make it look fresher. Her binding was long gone, so she put on a tabard, hoping the vest would hide the bumps on her chest.

Justin waited in the Common Room, not drumming his fingers or pacing, as Duncan would have, but sitting still. The normal verbal sparring that constituted disputation practice had stopped. Instead, the students looked down at open books, pretending to read.

When he saw her, Justin stood, before she had even reached the bottom of the stair. Relief flashed in his eyes. 'John, is it?' he asked, a twist in his voice.

'That's how I'm known, yes.'

'Where can we talk?'

She jerked her head up the stairs, towards the room she had just left. He followed her, shutting the door behind him, and sat beside her on the thin, straw mattress.

She had been able to cajole Solay, but Justin would be much less understanding. 'Let me explain,' she began.

'Please do.'

The words that had come so easily with Solay refused to form. How did one talk to a man if not 'man to man'? Well, she still had enough *virile animo* to do that.

She met his eyes. 'Solay must have told you all.' It was not a question. 'There cannot be much more for me to say.'

'I would never have forced you to marry.' Regret flashed across his face and she sensed perhaps some truth he had never told. 'Never.'

She heard it as an apology. One she did not deserve. 'I know that, because of what I have done, I will never be an acceptable bride. I didn't think of that when I ran.'

I didn't think at all.

How young and selfish that girl on the road with the wasp sting seemed, never imagining her adventure would come to an end and leave her an unmarriageable burden on Justin for all her days. 'I'm sorry.'

'Are you…has he…?' He struggled with the words.

How difficult it was, for men to speak of babes. 'No.' Somewhere in the blur of days in the sickroom, she had dealt with her blood as well as his.

'What of the man?'

He must have seen Duncan at the Council meeting. She wondered how Duncan looked to Justin's eyes. 'Things have changed.' How could she explain what she wasn't sure of?

Justin's eyes were cynical. 'It doesn't matter. Just come home.'

Home. The very word was temptation to return to that carefree little girl who played at being a boy. What choice did she have? She could not stay here.

And Duncan had locked her out.

Seeing her hesitation, Justin spoke again. 'Come, pack your things. I'll take you home and you can live as you like.'

The vision tugged at her. Cosy, safe.

But there, ultimately, she would be peripheral, her happiness borrowed from others, never her own.

She knew what she wanted. Knew it bone deep in a way she could not explain. Her life was with Duncan, whether he realised it yet or not. No matter how difficult the path or where it led.

'I mean to go with him. He is my home, now.' She stopped, not knowing what to say next.

'Has he asked you?'

She looked towards the window, searching for a hint of daylight. 'He has turned me out.'

Justin stood. 'If you still want him, I will speak to him. For what he did to you, he has a duty…'

She smiled, as yet another man rose to fight her battle. But the battle was hers. She touched his sleeve. 'It is not so simple. He has lost the use of his hand.'

Realisation flooded Justin's face. 'If he cannot provide for you, you have no obligation—'

'That doesn't matter to me. I want to be with him.'

'Child, you cannot force a man to wed you, no matter how foolish a reason you may think he has for resisting. I, more than most men, know that.'

'I am no longer a child, Justin. My love is that of a woman full grown.' She smiled. The difficulty, the responsibility, no longer seemed burdens.

'But I can't allow you to chase a man who doesn't want you and may not even be able to provide for you.'

'The choice is not yours,' she said, then smiled. 'Besides, royal blood is very stubborn.'

He frowned, opened his mouth, and then closed it before he finally spoke. 'At least come see little William.'

'He's here?'

'At the White Horse Inn with Solay and your mother.'

Her mother. She had promised to face her family. Now all her resolutions would be put to the test.

He coaxed with a smile. 'You betray no promises by coming to see them.'

She looked down at her smelly clothes. 'Like this?' Suddenly she wanted to be able to show them something for her months away. Something that would help them understand how proud they could be of what she had done.

He laughed. 'They will not even notice. Come.' He shepherded her towards the door and then paused. 'This man…?'

'Duncan.'

'I must speak with him.'

'Not yet. He is not ready. He needs time.'

And so did she. Time to persuade him to let her back into his life. She did not know how she would do it, but she must.

Because Justin was right.

She could not force him to let her stay.

'Leave us,' her mother said.

The laughter that had filled the inn's small, private sleeping room stilled. Jane's mother, spine straight in a small, wooden chair, made the room feel as formal as Westminster's Great Hall.

Jane handed William back to Solay, who had just finished pointing out every one of the baby's clever toes and fingers. Her sister threw her a sympathetic glance as she and Justin left the room.

Jane clasped her hands behind her back to straighten her shoulders, wishing again she had been able to bathe and change. Yet perhaps this way was better. Now, she carried all she had learned in the past five months on her back and in her bones.

In the room, a brisk fire crackled. Outside, through the half-opened shutter, she could hear students re-argue their disputations in the street. Their Latin phrases mingled with the squawk of waddling geese and the stink of horse droppings.

'You want an explanation,' Jane began.

The barest nod.

She struggled to bend her thoughts into something between a woman's emotional babble and a man's emotionless itemisation.

'I was once asked what my mother was like,' she began, 'and the first thing I said was that you were a strong woman. And then the man said to me, "Then you favour her".'

A hint of a smile touched her mother's lips.

'If I do, it is because I have learned how to be strong, even when I am not liked. Even when it is not easy.'

This next would be the hardest part. 'I ran because I was so afraid. Afraid I wasn't good enough, afraid I would hurt rather than help Solay. But I learned something from living among men. I learned to be afraid and do it anyway.'

'Tell me,' her mother said, in a voice kinder than Jane had expected, 'what else you have learned.'

'I wanted to be able to hold what was mine. So that it would not be taken away by a man, or a husband, or…' She stumbled. What could she call the King? 'Or when someone died or left. I thought, to do that, I must live as a man.'

'And what do you think now?'

'What cannot be taken away is within me.' It was a strange mixture of the unlikely woman she was and the things she had learned among men.

'Solay told me there is a man.'

So she sat on the floor at her mother's feet and spoke of Duncan, from their beginnings on the road until yesterday's barred door.

After she finished, the room darkened in silence.

Finally, her mother spoke. 'And for him, you will do things you never realised you could do.'

'Yes!' Relief at being understood washed through her like a stream set free of winter's ice. Had her mother loved so, once?

'Did you think I would withhold my blessing?'

'Will you?'

'Not if I am convinced of the rightness of it.'

But she did not say yes or no. 'Is there anyone else who must approve?'

'The King. But he is not likely to object. Things are much different now than when Solay was wed.'

'But the King will care? Because of my blood?'

Her mother nodded. 'What does that blood mean to you now?'

Today, it was a hindrance because of Duncan's reaction. But she did not want her mother to know that. 'I used to think that if I had manhood and royal blood, I would have all the world can offer. But I have seen the King. He is just a man, and not even as brave and honourable as the one I love.'

'There is something it is time that you know.'

She tilted her head, puzzled, trying to read her mother's eyes in the shadows. 'What?'

Her mother put her hands on Jane's shoulders. 'Your blood is no more royal than mine.'

'But why—?' And then, the larger question loomed. 'Who?'

'My husband was your father.'

William de Weston. A shadowy creature. Barely a part of her memory, unlike the ageing lion of a King who had held her on his lap. 'And Solay?'

'Both of you.'

'But why?' Her thoughts jumbled. She had never even seen this 'husband' until after the King had died.

'For the same reason you are now willing to give your life to a man others might shun. Because I loved a man very much. Enough to give him what he wanted most. The feeling that he was still a man.'

An ageing King feeling his greatness ebb. Yes, seeing proof of his manhood in his offspring would lift his life again.

And now Duncan, no longer sure he was a man, was unsure he could take care of a woman. 'I must do that for Duncan. How?'

'You must discover your own answer.'

She hoped she would. Soon. 'But why didn't you tell us after the King was dead?'

'I thought it would give you a reason to hold your head high.'

And it had. Until she had found her own strength. 'But you told Solay.'

'She only found out by accident when we were researching the lawsuit.'

The lawsuit. Pickering.

All the warm feelings of being understood trembled before a gale. 'Mother, there's something more I must tell you about Duncan. He is a friend of Sir James Pickering.'

Her mother sat quietly in the dark.

Jane continued. 'Solay feared you would forbid me to wed a man who was his friend.'

'She did, did she?' A chuckle whispered beneath her words. 'How could I hold a grudge against a good lawyer for doing his job? I had plenty of cunning legal advice myself over the years. But it wasn't Pickering's fault we lost the house. Or Justin's. It was mine.'

'Yours?'

'Because I kept the secret of your parentage. If I had told them you were William's children, there would have been no question that the house was yours.'

Not a man, then, who kept or lost what was theirs. A woman's decision all the time.

'Perhaps I should have told you,' her mother said. 'But I had so little to give you both.'

'I suppose it isn't important now.' Except to Duncan.

'Not important?' The old sharpness touched her mother's tongue. In it were the sacrifices of years.

'I'm sorry. I didn't mean—'

Her mother waved a hand. Lips pursed, eyes closed, she shook her head, then sighed. 'Strange, the agonies because of things you think are important. And in the end, they are no more than chaff.'

And no longer mattered except to her mother and a dead King.

The fire died. Through the open shutter, Jane saw the dark winter sky, cleaved with a sliver of moon, full of memories and old decisions.

Her mother's hands tightened on her shoulders. 'Edward would have been glad to call you his.'

Jane smiled.

'Bring to me, then, this man. If I find him worthy, I shall not stand between you. To have two daughters, both married to men they love and who love them, is a boon too precious to be ignored. With all the riches I once had, I was never so blessed as to have the love and the husband in the same man.'

Jane hugged her thanks, grateful.

But she still faced her greatest obstacle.

Duncan.

It had been too late to go back to the hostel, so she had stayed at the inn overnight and got her bath and her change of clothes and a cosseting because it was her birthday, which she had forgotten.

She told them she would have to return as John, but Solay was persuasive. Just see how it feels, she said, as she pulled out a blue dress, whisked the well-worn men's garb away, combed Jane's hair, pinched her cheeks, doused her in rose water and told her how pretty she looked.

And she did.

Yet Jane still felt as if she had simply donned another costume. The borrowed dress, even the smell, belonged to someone else. Neither woman nor man, she felt like one of those grotesque, hybrid creatures in the psalter, part-human, part-beast, capable of living in neither world, but only in some strange nether land.

Yet her heart ached as she held the babe and saw Justin smile at Solay when he thought no one was watching. His hand rested on his wife's shoulder and she pressed her cheek against it, quickly.

Would she and Duncan ever find such peace?

She knew who she was now, in a way she hadn't before, but she would never be the outward model of feminine virtues.

Even if Duncan relented, how were they to build a life? In those terrible moments after she had told him of her royal blood, he had tried to tell her of his family. So worried about her own, she hadn't thought of his since. What would they think of her?

He might be able to accept her as she was, but their world would always be larger than two.

How were they to make their way in it together?

By mid-morning, she insisted on returning to Duncan.

Justin relented, but only after a whispered conference with

Solay and a visit to the Chancellor and the hostel without her. He and Solay refused to return her men's clothes, which had conveniently disappeared into the laundresses' capable hands.

Justin's connection with the Court enabled her to receive special dispensation to visit the hostel. So she entered the Common Room wearing an unfamiliar, ill-fitting blue dress.

The men stared as if she were a stranger.

She was.

She hid in Henry and Geoffrey's room, quizzing them about the last day. 'Have you changed his bandages? Seen that he is eating and drinking?'

Geoffrey's eyes were kind. 'We've done everything you and the surgeon said. We can take care of him, too, eh?'

She regretted her unwitting insult. Forced into a dress, she had begun to cling to the things belonging to women, afraid to concede anything to a man lest she find herself empty-handed.

'Has he asked about me?'

Silent, Geoffrey shook his head.

No more than she expected. 'I must see him.'

'He doesn't want to see you.' Blunt Henry. Refusing to soften the blow.

Geoffrey shook his head. 'Give him time.'

'He's *had* time. Don't you see?' They cared for her. Their intentions were the best. But they had no idea what havoc good intentions could create. '*I* don't have time! What did Justin tell you when he was here?'

They exchanged glances. So, as she suspected. Man to man. Conspiring to take care of her.

If they wouldn't tell her, she would tell them. 'You are to humour me and he'll be back before curfew.' The surprise on their faces proved her point. 'Don't you understand? He's going to take me away and, next time, I won't be able to come back.'

Her mother might not stand in the way, but that would not be necessary. The expectations of the world would do it for her.

Now that she had been discovered, she would not be allowed in Solar Hostel again. Her family would take her home and tell her that when Duncan wanted to see her, of course he could.

Meanwhile, Duncan would be certain that her disappearance simply proved that she did not want to spend her life with a cripple. Even to ask where she had gone would feel like grovelling.

And that was something Duncan would never do.

'Is the door still barred?'

'No. He's letting us come and go.'

'Then step aside and let me pass.'

She walked down the stairs, the unfamiliar dress letting a draught swirl between her legs. As she approached the door, she heard soft chords from the gittern.

She closed her eyes to stop the tears.

He was trying. At least he was trying.

She swallowed and blinked. She must not cry in front of him.

The notes jangled, full of pain and frustration, as if he had ceased to try to create music and simply wanted to batter the instrument.

She lifted her head, knocked sharply, as a man would do, and opened the door.

He sat upright in bed, head back, eyes closed, the gittern a dead weight on his lap. His right hand was now a large ball of linen, only the tips of his fingers exposed.

He sniffed, catching a whiff of the unfamiliar rose water, and opened his eyes. They reflected surprise. 'Go away.' Words more weary than angry.

'No,' she answered, the tone not negotiable. Had he given up? She would rather he hate her than seem so indifferent. She walked to the fire, fiddling with it, careful not to get ashes on Solay's dress.

She would not tell him what she had discovered about her father. He would never believe the reversal. That would have to come later, from her mother.

But first, he would have to agree to meet her mother.

'You look different,' he said, finally.

'I feel strange as hell,' she said bluntly.

'You're going to get us all in a bloody mess of trouble, being here, lookin' like a woman.'

'D'ya think I've learned nothing?' she said, taking on his accent again like a familiar cloak. 'I've dispensation, at least for today.'

'Well,' he said, his voice softer than she could ever recall, 'it's good to see ya, no matter how you look.'

She sat gingerly on the edge of the bed, reaching to brush the hair on his forehead.

He jerked away from her fingers. 'Yer goin' home with them, I hear.'

'Who told you that nonsense?'

'Well, look at you. And Geoffrey told me you left.'

'Only after you locked me out.' She had much to explain. 'When we were at Westminster, I saw my sister—'

'And you didn't tell me?' There was a flash of the old anger.

'I was going to and then…' *And then the world changed.* 'She and her husband followed me here.'

'It's for the best.' So quickly, the anger had drained and left only weariness. 'If you've family that visits the Court, you've more than I can ever give ya.'

'What makes you think so?'

'I was trying to tell you when I tangled the words.' He sat straighter and spoke clearly. 'My father, he's not a lettered man. My mother never says a word. My brother knows swords and sheep and nothing else. I'm not sure how they'll take you.'

Be afraid and do it anyway. 'Well, we can give them a chance to decide. That's what I did with my mother. And she wants to meet you.'

But he was hearing none of it. 'And if I stay in the north? What then?'

She swallowed. 'Then I'll stay, too.'

'Don't decide until you see the place. I told you the land was beautiful and it is. But there are no books, no music except what I make, naught that's soft or beautiful. There's nothing but wrestling a living away from the ground or the Scots. It's a cold and dreary life.' He touched her face then, with the fingers of his left hand, the gesture awkward. 'With nothing for a beautiful woman like you. Nothing.'

'Nothing but the man I love.' This life, should they choose it, would take all the courage she could muster. There would be no mince and curtsy, no Latin recitations. But there would be an empty page where she could write the words. 'And that's everything.'

Bitter sadness touched his face. He waved the mangled, bandaged hand at her, taunting them both. 'That's nothing. I can offer you nothing without this!'

'Do you think I loved only that hand?' She bit her lip. The question mocked her. She *had* loved that hand. The way it stroked her, the way his fingers felt in her hair or touching her mouth or teasing the space between her legs.

She had loved his fingers, the pads at the tips slightly larger, the way they held a book or drummed the table or moved over the strings—

She pressed her lips together. The gittern in his lap blurred.

'The man you loved is dead. Now get out of here. Go home. Find a real man. I won't have you spending your life fetching for a cripple.'

'*You* won't? You're a pigheaded oaf, Duncan of Cliff's Tower. My life's not yours to arrange. Once you found out I was a woman, you thought you could make all the decisions.'

'The ones you made weren't so wise.'

'Some of them were. Besides, you're acting as if you are the only person on this earth who can get through life without help from anyone else!'

She saw the struggle on his face. To be a man was to help others. Without that, he was no longer a man.

Well, as most people used the term, she wasn't a woman, either.

'I wanted to care for you, to provide for you,' he said. 'I can't do that now. I can't do anything.'

'Are ya still breathin'?'

He stopped breathing, as if her words had pulled the air out of the room.

'Yea, I'm breathin'.' He turned his face away. 'I'll be taking in air I haven't earned for the rest of my life. No good to man, nor beast.'

'So there's more you can do.' She said the words as harshly as she could.

'Not with one hand!' He flung the gittern into the wall where it splintered, clattering to the floor, a broken string jangling, as off-key as his rage.

'I have two hands,' she said, taking his left in hers. 'One of them can be yours.'

His face crumpled. He grabbed her left hand with both of his. She completed the circle with her right, then pressed her lips against the top of his head as he bent over their joined hands.

And she felt a tear slide between her fingers.

'You're a stubborn woman, Little Jane. And I love you with all I am,' he said, the words muffled as his lips pressed against her knuckles.

Then, he raised his head, not blinking against the tears. 'So tell me,' he said, in his broadest accent, 'how many relatives besides me Majesty must I petition before I can receive your hand in marriage?'

Chapter Twenty-Five

Duncan's decision gave him new energy.

Jane argued, but he insisted on rising, bathing, dressing and walking to the inn to meet her family before the afternoon ended.

She held his left arm as they walked, not sure whether she was trying to give strength to him or to herself. With her other hand, she clutched the unfamiliar skirt, struggling to keep it out of the filth on the street. Impractical garment. How did women cope? Yet she was beginning to enjoy the swish of it.

The inn's Common Room was empty except for her family, gathered around the fire. When they entered, Justin stood, surprise on his face as he recognised the man he'd seen in the Westminster Council chambers.

Jane and Solay exchanged glances as Duncan and Justin took each other's measure.

Justin, taller, dressed simply, but with an edge of sophistication remaining from his days at Court. His expression, always severe, except when he smiled at Solay, remained so as he looked at Duncan.

Duncan was poised between earth and poetry. He loved to laugh, loved the life of the body, and yet had a mind so quick his tongue could barely keep up with it.

And she loved him absolutely.

Duncan did not pause long, but dropped to one knee before her mother.

She'd never seen him bow so deeply except to plead for his father before the King. He managed it alone, more easily than she had expected, though he touched the floor with his left hand to steady himself.

'Lady Alys.' He raised his eyes. 'Lord Justin. Lady Solay. I wish to wed Jane and crave your permission.'

Jane held her tongue. Even Justin waited, silent, for Alys to speak.

Her mother met his gaze for a long quiet moment and then swept a glance from head to sole. 'I understand you are a stubborn man, Master Duncan.'

'I've been called so, milady,' he answered, shooting Jane a glance.

Jane clamped down a smile.

'It will take a stubborn man to handle my younger daughter.'

Now he was the one who smiled. 'Then we will suit.'

Jane squirmed.

'She tells me,' Alys continued, 'that she loves you.'

'She tells me that, too,' he said. His eyes softened, dappled, and he leaned his right arm on his knee and reached for her hand with his left. 'Though she's more than I deserve.'

'I doubt that.'

Jane frowned at her mother, whose smile was a wry one.

'But I hope she knows,' he said, now looking at her, 'that I will love her until I take my last breath.'

And with those words, he took hers.

'I suspect,' her mother said, 'that your life together will be singular. You have my blessing. Now rise.'

As Duncan rose, Justin reached out his left hand. Duncan clasped it in greeting and rose with its help.

'We must wed within the week and leave for the north,' Duncan said, sounding like himself again.

'But, dear,' Solay began, looking at Jane, 'we have only just got you back. And the King must agree to this marriage. He may even choose to attend. All of this will take time.'

'We don't have time,' Duncan said.

'What's the need for hurry?' Justin asked, frowning.

Solay looked at Jane's belly.

Jane shook her head.

'My father still rots in a Scottish castle. I carry the ransom money authorised by the Council for his release.' He squared his shoulders and looked at Jane. 'And if it is not enough, I will stay in his place.'

She cherished the return of pride to his voice. To offer his body in exchange for his father's freedom. That, he could still do.

'But Jane?'

'If he must do this, I will stay with him,' she answered, looking at her mother.

Alys remained silent.

Solay did not. 'But what about your parents? You cannot bring home a bride they do not know.'

Unspoken was the fear—what if they reject her?

'I can bring home no other. It will not matter to me what they say.'

'But it might,' her mother said sharply, 'matter to Jane.'

She took his hand. She would be a challenge to any man's family, even if she were not Alys de Weston's daughter. 'If Duncan wishes to wait for his parents' consent, I will travel beside him as his betrothed instead of his bride.'

'Impossible!' Justin exploded.

'Because it will compromise me?' Now Jane was the one who laughed. 'Certainly no more than six months in a hostel.'

'I do not want to wait,' Duncan answered. 'I cannot make promises for another man's actions. I can only promise to protect and provide for her as best I can, all of my life.'

'I promise him the same,' she said.

'This promise will bind me no matter what my parents say about her background.' He smiled. 'Or about her chausses.'

She shared his smile, though she could think of times now that she might like to don a skirt.

'But what happens after that? Where will you live?' Solay said. 'When will we see Jane again?'

'I have no answers now,' Duncan said. 'I just know Jane and I will ask the questions together.'

'Well,' Alys said, 'a stubborn man indeed. I suppose we should be honoured they consulted us at all. Justin, ask the innkeeper if he has a drinkable Gascon wine hidden away. We had better celebrate quickly. And we may need to hurry his Majesty's consent or these two will do without that, as well!'

Jane couldn't stop smiling. She was going to a land she'd never seen, far away from all she knew, to take care of a man who was likely to be crippled for life.

She was happier than she had ever been.

In the end, Jane had to persuade Duncan to wait a few days longer.

They moved to the White Horse Inn while Justin rode to plead their case to the King. Jane discovered the womanly joys of playing daughter, sister and aunt. And, reluctantly, Alys told Duncan in private about Jane's father.

'Well, honey,' he told her afterwards, shaking his head, 'I suppose you are no more royal than I am.'

'Do you care?' She studied the set of his mouth, wondering whether it would make a difference to him.

He hugged her. 'Not unless you do.'

And she didn't.

Justin returned from his meeting with the King with the news that the Scots had not waited until the summer to invade again. They had plundered the borderlands once more, invading Gisland this time, and the new Wardens of the March were planning their retaliation.

Duncan, uncertain of his father's fate in light of the new hostilities, was eager to start north.

'I think the story of the two of you gave the King a welcome laugh,' Justin told them. 'He gave his approval and he said that he understood that young John would not be attending King's Hall.'

'Thanks to the Virgin,' Jane said. 'I was afraid he might be angry that we fooled him.'

Duncan had been packed for days, and his horse was ready to go. 'Then we'll beg the priest to marry us tomorrow and start north the next day.'

'The King sent more than his good wishes,' Justin said. He pulled out a pouch of clanking coins and handed it to Duncan.

His hand sagged under the weight.

He untied the bag, poured them out on to the table and laughed.

'What is it?' she said, looking over his shoulder.

Duncan looked up, tears topping off the laughter. 'Had I known, Little Jane, that wedding you would have persuaded the King to pay my father's full ransom, I would have asked you long ago.'

Jane, sitting up front on the sturdy black pony, held her cloak against the March wind whipping down the valley. Yet Duncan had pointed out the first few yellow affodyles of spring.

'We're almost home.' Duncan's whisper was warm and eager in her ear. 'There,' he said, pointing. 'You can see the tower.'

It stood, squat and square as he had described, next to a yellow stone church.

'And there are the fells.' He let go of his hold on her waist and stretched his arms wide.

She turned her eyes to the snow-covered mountains that beckoned in the distance. 'I'm going to need bigger boots before we hike those hills.'

He squeezed her tightly again.

She felt the call, the wild *differentness* of the land, but as the tower loomed larger, that was laced with a wobble in her stomach.

What would Duncan's family think of her?

The ground was hard-packed at the tower's base. The building rose before her, forbidding and windowless.

The horse stopped, as if knowing he would find shelter there.

Duncan dismounted first, unsteady without his right hand, then helped her down. Even short of a hand, his arms still felt strong and sure about her.

Two men emerged from the tower. One had Duncan's build, though a face less used to laughter. The other looked as Duncan might look years from now. Still compact and sturdy, but with hair grey enough to match his eyes.

Duncan's father.

Beside her, Duncan stumbled. She moved to his side and they walked closer.

Two women waited inside at the tower door, as if afraid to emerge without permission. Was that a woman's lot, here?

'Fadder?'

Duncan did not trust his eyes, or his voice. The old man's eyes, always hard, had turned the colour of Alston Moor lead.

Each took a step forwards.

'When were ya freed?' He did not know whether to laugh or weep.

'Not a month.'

'But how?' The gold, like so much lead in his pocket.

'I sold the flocks,' Michael said. 'Cattle, goats, all of it.'

Duncan looked around the empty yard. No bleating ewes, heavy with soon-to-be born lambs. No smell of damp, unsheared wool in the tower.

They had given all they had, then. And now, so had he. 'I came back t'save ya.'

'But yer a master,' said his father, a quizzical expression on his face. 'Y've important work.'

'None more important than me family.'

'Do ya mean to stay then?' Was there a hint of hope in his father's voice?

Duncan looked at Jane. Her eyes were brave and steady, but he would make no promises without knowing how she would fare here.

Or how he would.

'Until my child is born.'

In the silence, the men had studied Jane, now registering that he was a she. 'This is me wife. Jane,' he said.

And waited.

One word against her and he would pummel either man with the good hand he had left. And then he would leave and never come back.

His mother and Michael's wife came into the yard, out of the tower's shelter.

The wind whistled around the tower's corner and lifted her cloak as Jane walked over to Duncan's father. Tall, blonde, slender, she held out her hand. 'I'm honoured to meet you.'

His father tilted his head, puzzled. 'What have ya brought me, son? A man or a woman?'

Duncan moved up behind her, putting his good hand on her shoulders. 'She's a woman and a half, fadder. She was willing to have me as I am now.' He raised his right hand. No further words were needed. 'And willing to come with me when I thought I would have to trade myself for you with the Scots. And I'll be proud to have her beside me for all my days.'

His father looked down at his hands, gnarled and empty. 'We've not much t'offer.'

He knew the shame in that look. He'd felt it. 'But we've something to offer you.' He pulled the money from his bag. 'This was to be your ransom. Instead, turn it into sheep, goats, horses, grain. Whatever you need.'

His fadder's eyes met his. There would be a time later for questions, for answers. There would be a time to prove himself still a man, even as he was now.

But he saw there the respect he'd waited for all his life.

And even a touch of love.

'A woman and a half, eh?' He stuck out his hand and clasped Jane's. The women ran over, children at their skirts, and swept him into a hug, then embraced Jane with giggles.

Duncan's eyes met his father's. And then he was enfolded. 'Then she'll be a match for you, son.'

It was time to start over.

November 1389

He started to run when he heard Jane scream.

Dropped his staff in the pasture, left the sheep and ran, chasing the screams up the road, into the tower and up the stairs. They cascaded, one after the other, as if the baby were clawing its way out of her belly.

Out of breath, he paused at the door of the birthing room with his bag of herbs, shears and thread, for he had been planning for this for a long time.

His mother blocked the door. 'Birthing is women's work.'

He frowned. 'I have a wife who lived among scholars and studied Latin. And she has a husband who can help deliver his own child.'

She raised her eyebrows and shook her head, but moved aside. They had learned, finally, not to argue with Duncan and his hoyden bride.

Jane smiled to see him and he grasped her hand and tried to squeeze with the wounded fingers that still would not bend. 'I'm here, honey, meself and me one good hand.'

He looked down at her sweat-soaked hair on the pillow. She was between contractions and her blue eyes locked on to his, warm and steady. 'Birthing is woman's work, you know.'

He laughed, joy wiping out his fear for a moment. 'How can that be, when makin' the babe takes two?'

She had grown heavy with child all summer, and as autumn had ripened, even walking was an effort and the midwife had muttered she'd never seen a single babe so large.

Her pains came again.

And he squeezed her hand to help her push until his son slipped out of her womb, squalling, to greet the world.

Followed by his daughter.

She nursed one at each breast the next day as he strummed the made-over gittern at her bedside. The instrument was battered, but still useful, much as he was. He could no longer pick the strings, but he could still coax chords from them, songs that she recognised and sang along to.

Let us lay down together
Let me fill you forever
Let us love one another
As long as I've breath.

'They answered,' he said, in the silence that followed. 'The College in Paris.'

She looked at him, eyes wide with hope. The renowned surgical College de St Come allowed married masters, unlike all the others. 'And?'

The smile cracked open. 'They said yes.'

She reached to hug him, but the babes prevented her and he stood to hold them all in his arms for a moment.

So they talked of how they would travel to Paris in the spring and how she would help him in his work and how they would return, in time, to bring the knowledge back to the country she, too, had learned to love.

The Scots had signed a truce at long last. Geoffrey had come north to wed his Mary.

Some day, they would come home again. But first, they would see the world.

'Here,' Jane said, shifting the black-haired babes. 'Take the girl. She's finished.'

He took the tiny bundle in his arms.

'I'd like to call her Alys,' she said, thoughtful. 'But what shall we call the boy?'

'There's only one name for my son,' he said, loving the rightness of the sound, the weight of his daughter in his arms, and the sight of his wife who was as much a part of him as his breath. 'His name must be John.'

Author's Note

This is a work of fiction, but certain events—the invasion of the north-west, the Battle of Otterburn, the Council meetings and Cambridge Parliament, and the ransom of Hotspur—are documented historical fact.

For those true students of history, I am aware that the city was not called 'Cambridge'—nor the river called the 'Cam'—until after this period, but chose the familiar names as more accessible to the reader.

Jane was inspired by a real person, the younger daughter of the notorious Alice Perrers, mistress to Edward III.

Even less is known of her than of her older sister, whom I call Solay and who was the heroine of *The Harlot's Daughter*. Such is the confusion—both are called 'Joan' in some records—that it is not always clear which was the older and which the younger.

In my initial research on Jane, I could find no birth date, and no death date. There was only the report that she married Richard Northland. As Chris Given-Wilson and Alice Curteis report in *The Royal Bastards of Medieval England*, both girls 'rapidly sank into obscurity'.

For those curious about how a bastard son would be treated, Alice had one of those, too, whom I have ignored for the sake of the story. He was John de Southeray and he received the kind of acclaim that Jane had envisioned. Knighted beside Richard, the King of this story, he also married the sister of Henry, Lord Percy, the Hotspur whose ransom was enough to build a castle. He went on to a military career and is thought to have died about four years before this book is set.

There is evidence Jane was ultimately recognised as the legitimate daughter of William Windsor—whom I called William de Weston. This gave her some claim to the property they had lost, which she subsequently sold for a life rent of twenty-six pounds.

Records are muddled, however, and this reversion of rights and sale has been reported to both the older and the younger daughter. More recent scholarship identifies both Richard Northland and Robert Skerne—a lawyer and my inspiration for Justin, Solay's husband—as husbands of the older daughter, who remarried after being widowed. According to this line of research, the younger girl married a man named Despaigne and was widowed by 1406.

I prefer to believe Jane and her Richard from the 'northland' found their 'happily ever after' in the obscurity of Westmoreland's wild fells.